Another Life,
Another Love

Eileen Stafford

This first world edition published in Great Britain 2003 by
SEVERN HOUSE PUBLISHERS LTD of
9–15 High Street, Sutton, Surrey SM1 1DF.
This first world edition published in the USA 2003 by
SEVERN HOUSE PUBLISHERS INC of
595 Madison Avenue, New York, N.Y. 10022.

British Library Cataloguing in Publication Data

Stafford, Eileen
    Another life, another love
    1.   Becket, Thomas, Saint, 1118? - 1170 - Fiction
    2.   Women biographers - Fiction
    I.   Title
    823.9'14 [F]

    ISBN 0-7278-6001-1

Typeset by Palimpsest Book Production Ltd.,
Polmont, Stirlingshire, Scotland.
Printed and bound in Great Britain by
MPG Books Ltd., Bodmin, Cornwall.

ANOTHER LIFE, ANOTHER LOVE

Recent Titles by Eileen Stafford

BOUNDARIES
A BOUQUET OF BRIARS
DANGEROUS DREAMS
DARK SECRETS
RAINBOW IN THE MORNING
WHIRLWIND *

* available from Severn House

Acknowledgements

I have received help and advice from many sources during the writing of this book. Thank you first to Dorothy, my agent, for her patience, and to all my friends in the writing group who have listened, criticised and praised, probably in equal parts. I should also like to thank the staff of Canterbury Cathedral for their advice, and the ladies who answered my frequent telephone calls to Pevensey Castle. I must also mention the gentleman who sent me emails describing the delights of hawking, and the priest who gave me insights into training for the priesthood.

Lastly, and perhaps most important of all, I should like to record my gratitude to my late husband for his encouragement, and for the positive faith in this book which he always maintained during the long months of his illness.

That which hath been is now; and that which
is to be hath already been
Ecclesiastes 3:15

Voices under sleep, waking a dead world
Murder in the Cathedral, T.S. Eliot

One

Kate Kimberley shouldered her rucksack, tucked her mobile away in an inside pocket and fixed her headphones firmly to her head. She swung out of the school gates for the last time. 'Life, here I come,' she said to no one in particular as the pulsating beat of the latest single reverberated through her brain.

Her friend caught her up. 'Doing anything special in the hols?' she mouthed.

Kate shook her head. 'Just Devon as usual. Dartmoor, the wilds.'

'Poor you. We're going to Greece.'

'Too hot for Phoebe.' Kate pulled the headphones down around her neck. 'Have a great time. Text me.'

'OK. Don't want to make you jealous though.'

'You won't. I like Devon. See you!'

The two girls parted and Kate replaced her headphones. The throb of the music competed with the racket of the London street. She bounced along the pavement in time with the pounding beat in her head, and she grinned to herself and thought of Dominic, although why this particular piece should remind her of Dommy she couldn't think. He would absolutely hate it. Phoebe wasn't very partial to rock music either. That was what came of living with your grandmother, Kate thought. But it was something you got used to. Kate had never known anything else so it wasn't a big deal either way. From what she'd heard, parents were often much more of a problem. Phee was young for her age, pretty cool really considering all she'd gone through. Kate often marvelled at her grandmother's energy levels. Throughout all the traumas of bringing her up, with no help at all, she'd written the books that fed and clothed the two of them. She had cooked and cleaned and generally coped with the hassle of being a single mum while she was of course no such thing.

Kate sang a few words aloud as she swung along the road. Must make the most of the short journey home, for as soon as she reached the flat she'd be bombarded by Radio Three. Phee would have it blaring out from the kitchen. Of course, Dommy preferred Radio Three too. No surprise there. Weeks ago Kate had decided that she must mug up on some classical stuff, and even Gregorian chant, for goodness sake. Dominic professed himself a great devotee of this weird gloomy music. As he was intent on becoming a priest, perhaps that was understandable. Kate frowned. She hated to think of her cheerful, handsome Dommy entering the Church. It was one of the problems she preferred to ignore at the moment. Dominic sometimes brought her complete delight and at other times total despair. Her mood changed suddenly in sympathy with her thoughts, elation giving way to melancholy, a blanket of gloom that no amount of mind-bending music could do anything to lift.

While Kate was enduring her last day at school, Phoebe was sitting on the edge of her chair in the office of Dudley Pascoe, her literary agent. She listened in disbelief and horror as he outlined his suggestion for her next book.

'I have a major coup for you, Phoebe,' he said. 'Thomas à Becket.'

'You're not serious?'

Dudley gave her a pained look. 'A biography has been commissioned. It's yours. I know you can do it.'

'A twelfth-century saint isn't quite my line of country,' she said weakly when he had finished outlining his plans for her next masterpiece. 'Can't you find me someone more amusing, more attractive, and preferably alive?'

Dudley stretched his long legs beneath his desk and regarded her with some amusement. 'My dear girl, he was one of the most handsome and charismatic men you could hope to meet.'

'But I shall not be able to meet him, shall I, Dudley! He has been dead for centuries. I have no wish to write a biography of someone who is dead. People are usually more fun when they are alive.' She stared at him in dismay. Her previous clients had mostly been media or sporting personalities, and usually pleasant and agreeable. This latest one was something quite different, a subject right out of her experience, and for that matter, her interest.

'You will manage it brilliantly, Phoebe dear.' Dudley's voice and manner were totally confident. He refilled her glass and his own with the champagne he had ordered especially for this afternoon. He had obviously expected some resistance to his idea. 'Here's to your certain success,' he said. 'To Phoebe Kimberley, prospective author of a brilliant new biography of Thomas à Becket, chancellor of England, Archbishop of Canterbury and saint. This book will hit the headlines and you will become famous.' He held his glass aloft and then drank copiously.

Phoebe ignored his optimism. 'Why, at this particular time, do you want me to write a biography of a long-dead saint?'

'Firstly,' he replied, 'the commission is from an eminent publisher. That should be a good enough reason, but secondly there is renewed interest in all things religious and super-natural. There seems to be a general feeling going around that life is much more than just the physical and earthy. And thirdly, with so many uncertainties in life these days there's a nostalgic yearning for some golden age, a turning back to the past. Haven't you noticed the media concentration on history? Perhaps we want to know if our ancestors did it better than we did.'

Phoebe laughed. 'You sound very serious, Dudley. Not your usual line at all. And why choose me? You have other, more capable, authors.'

Dudley shook his head. 'None better than you, my dear. Believe me. Your other biographies have been brilliant.'

'Thanks. I'm flattered, and I very much hope that you're right about the success of this new one. That is, *if* I agree to do it. I can't begin to imagine what my granddaughter will say.'

'The charming Kate will be intrigued and delighted. I think you told me that she hopes to be a historian or an archaeologist. What could be more fitting?'

Phoebe greatly doubted Kate's enthusiasm for this latest project. 'She was hoping my next character would be some hunky celebrity,' she said dryly.

1130

Gilbert Becket is very proud of his stout manor house in Cheapside. Unlike most London homes it is made of stone rather than wood. There are rushes and herbs strewn on the floor and the smell of smoke hangs in the air, combined with the odour of animals and crushed mint and rosemary. It is a big house, a well-to-do merchant's house with a great courtyard, a spacious hall on the ground floor and steps leading to the solar above.

On this winter day in the reign of good King Henry, son of William the Conqueror and nicknamed the Lion of Justice, England is peaceful, and for many men, Gilbert amongst them, there is prosperity. Thomas, Gilbert's son and heir, is with his mother. He has just come home from Merton for the school holidays. He is full of excitement. 'My father has promised that I may go the horse fair tomorrow,' he tells her. 'I am to have a mount of my own.'

Roesa smiles at him indulgently. He is her only son, her favourite child. She remembers the words given to her when she was at prayer. 'This child shall be great in the eyes of God.' She is filled with pride and with fear too, a blackness of mind that sometimes clouds her thoughts. At those times she turns to Mary, her eldest daughter, for comfort.

Mary is a quiet child, fourteen years old and determined to become a nun, and so make her parents proud. She studies Latin with Catherine, their neighbour's daughter.

Catherine! When Roesa thinks about Catherine the blackness deepens. Catherine is a shining star, a bright and beautiful child, and Roesa knows that even at ten years old she possesses that bewitching quality that could be the downfall of her cherished and brilliant son. Already they are close friends, as much as any boy and girl could be, and if Thomas is to be a great scholar and have a brilliant career in the Church, as the visions tell her, then no such entanglements must be

4

allowed. Roesa dreams of Catherine often, and the beautiful, agreeable child is transformed in her dreams into a sinister creature full of witchcraft and darkness.

Thomas breaks into her gloomy thoughts. 'Father says he will choose a big fierce mount for me now that I am twelve.' His face is flushed and his eyes sparkle in anticipation of tomorrow's outing.

'Your father will see that you get the right horse,' Roesa says. 'Not a fierce one as you say!'

He laughs. 'Do you want me to have a little palfrey then, Mother? A palfrey so that my friends think I am a girl?'

She shakes her head. 'Something in between.'

He goes to the window of the solar. 'Where are my sisters? And where is Catherine?'

As soon as Phoebe reached the comparative peace of her apartment she flopped down on to her typing chair and turned her computer on. Vibrant colours flashed across the screen and she watched them absently. Was a strange, rather dour priest going to occupy the next year of her life? Could she bear it?

Then, suddenly, she remembered that one of his murderers had come from Bovey Tracey . . . William de Tracey, that was it. He'd given his name to the place. She thought of the little town with renewed interest. Soon she would be down there in Devon for three glorious weeks. Perhaps she could find out some riveting new facts.

She was tapping out a few random ideas when her grand-daughter erupted through the front door.

'Hi, Nonna. What's new?' Kate said as she clattered into the kitchen. She still used her affectionate childhood name for Phee from time to time. She dropped her psychedelic rucksack on to the floor and opened the refrigerator.

Phoebe, in her tiny study off the kitchen, swivelled round on her chair. 'New?' she asked. 'What do you mean, new?'

Kate, seriously into health foods, poured herself a large glass of freshly squeezed orange juice and perched on one of the bar stools. 'You were seeing your dishy agent chap today, weren't you? What gorgeous hunk does he want you to write about next?'

5

Phoebe grinned. Kate's choice of words was always apt. 'Gorgeous hunk' perfectly described the young footballer whose life story she had recently finished. Not Beckham it was true, but a good second best. 'A dead one actually,' she replied, savouring with delight the reaction this would surely produce. She was not disappointed.

'Dead?' Kate spluttered into her drink. 'You can't be serious. Who, for goodness sake? How could you want to write about someone who is dead? It sounds perfectly gross. For you anyway. You aren't into that kind of stuff.'

'Just what I tried to tell Dudley, but he was quite determined. And of course it's not *gross*.' She stressed the word and wondered exactly what it meant in this context. 'Hundreds of authors write life stories of characters who are dead. Biography is very popular.' She was beginning to feel slightly more positive about Thomas à Becket. She had discovered from her computer's encyclopaedia that he had lived in Cheapside as a child. So there were two connections she had already. London and Devon. He was beginning to feel a little less remote.

Kate finished the juice, took two peaches from the bowl on the worktop and proceeded to scrub them violently at the sink. 'Who then? You haven't told me who. Who is this dead person?'

Phoebe glanced at her computer screen and saved the few notes she had made. 'Dudley wants me to write a biography of Thomas à Becket,' she said as casually as she could manage.

Kate, peach juice running down her chin, stared at Phoebe in horror. 'What? *Murder in the Cathedral* and all that? Oh Nonna, you can't. It won't sell. You won't make a penny.'

'Dudley thinks it will. It fits in with the latest craving for all things historical, spiritual and paranormal apparently.'

'Paranormal?'

'The healings and miracles that happened after his death. They went on for hundreds of years.'

Kate took the peach stone from her mouth. 'I still think he's boring. It was mostly Church and State, wars and politics. I did him last year in school.'

'Then you'll be able to help me, won't you? How can you possibly call him boring? I thought you liked history.'

'Liking history and spending absolutely ages writing about a dead saint are two completely different things.'

'I could jazz him up a bit, give him a love life.'

'Love life?' Kate's horror levels increased dramatically. 'You aren't serious? He was a celibate priest, an archbishop, a highly regarded saint. It's well known that he had no interest in women.'

'Are you so sure?'

Kate started on her second peach, shook her head and frowned. 'Well, come to think, perhaps I'm not really all that sure,' she said, suddenly serious. 'I've always accepted the fact of his blameless life like everyone else.'

'And that's why you think him dull? It's got to be sex with everything now has it, if it's going to grab any attention at all?'

'Probably,' Kate said. 'Pity, but there you are. You can't mess about with the life of someone like Thomas à Becket though. You absolutely can't. It's just not on.'

Phoebe regarded her granddaughter with surprise, but perhaps she should have expected a reaction like this. At eighteen Kate was slightly more earnest than was always comfortable. And her friendship with Dominic was worrying. But Phoebe supposed that she must be grateful the rebellious difficult years hadn't happened, and probably wouldn't now. University loomed in the autumn. 'Sorry, love,' she said placatingly. 'No, I was only teasing. I shall write a sober and scholarly biography of a very great man. I don't like debunking our heroes, as you know, or saints either for that matter.'

'Well that's a relief. It's not your line of country though is it, an ancient saint for goodness sake! Where are you going to start?'

'Devon. I've discovered that Thomas had lots of connections with Devon so I shall be able to do that bit while we're on holiday.'

'Really? I thought the south-west was cut off and a bit wild back then.'

'Not too bad from what I've read, and one of his murderers came from Bovey Tracey.'

'William de Tracey! Of course,' Kate said. 'De Tracey of the quick temper and pious wife!'

'Just so, and thereby hangs an interesting tale. I'm looking forward to sussing it out. Litford will be just the place.'

Kate sighed. She liked the wildness of Dartmoor, but three whole weeks in the ancient farmhouse all alone with her grandmother could be a bit dire. Of course there was her aunt's family in their big house just along the track, and if cousin Janice was home then it might be more bearable. Then again, Dominic might come down, and in that case she wouldn't want anyone else at all! 'Dommy's bound to like it,' she said casually.

'Dominic?' Alarm bells rang in Phoebe's head.

'I thought he might come for part of the time. He wouldn't be a nuisance. He'd bring his tent and camp in the garden. Would you mind, Nonna?'

Phoebe felt a chill of misgiving. He was a nice young man of course, but a trainee priest for goodness sake. Kate was bound to get hurt. *Stop being so fussy and interfering*, she told herself firmly. Then she fixed a determined smile on her face. 'I suppose I don't mind,' she said. 'If he wants to come.'

'You don't sound very enthusiastic.' Kate frowned. 'It'll only be for a few days I should think. He has holiday schedules to get through apparently. He's interested in history and things. Actually I told him about Litford and he looked it up on the Internet. It's named in the Domesday Book apparently.'

'Yes, I know that. So you've asked him already?'

'I mentioned it, yes.'

'OK then. And he probably won't need to bring the tent. Talitha told me that Garth and an army of builders have made a good job of the recent modernization. There's an extra bedroom and a decent bathroom this year.'

'I hope they haven't ruined it.'

'Of course not. Garth employed a specialist firm. Litford is a listed building so there are numerous rules and regulations. You can trust Garth to do everything just so, no expense spared.' Phoebe thought of the efficient and capable man her sister had married. Talitha had always been the lucky one, always choosing correctly, always right. Garth was a country vet, up to date and successful, and he had bought the old tumbledown farmhouse which stood on a piece of wild, heather-clad moorland adjoining his house and practice.

'It'll be interesting to see how he's managed it,' Kate said. She slid from the stool, dropped the peach stones into the pedal bin, washed her hands and face at the sink, and looked seriously at Phoebe. 'I know you don't really want Dommy to come down. Yet you've always liked him.'

Phoebe tried to be honest. She could feel problems ahead with Dominic. 'Of course I like him. It's his overenthusiastic devotion to his God that I'm not very keen on.'

'Nonna, that's shocking.'

'Perhaps it is.' She cast her eyes to the ceiling. 'Sorry, God.'

Kate laughed and retrieved her rucksack from the floor. 'I need a bath,' she said. 'We're going out tonight. He's got tickets for the Festival Hall to celebrate the end of term and all that. Glinka, Sibelius and Prokofiev.' She sighed dramatically.

'Great,' said Phoebe a trifle faintly. She had still not quite come to terms with Kate's recent interest in classical music. It was because of Dominic of course. One of his plus points! 'Are you eating out?' she managed to ask.

'Sure. Dommy's discovered a fab veggie restaurant.'

Another plus point. No smelly vegetarian meal to foul up the kitchen. Phoebe loathed fried onions and garlic, the principal ingredients, it seemed, of all her granddaughter's meals. She turned again to her computer. Just time to fax Dudley and tell him she would definitely accept the Becket contract.

1132

Catherine stands at the solar window and stares, unseeing, at the winter scene below. The dream came again last night and she cannot expel it easily from her mind. Who is this person with the form of a girl and the clothes of a man? Kate, Kate, why are you haunting my dreams?

The smell of horses and dogs wafts upwards and the groom is busy with brush and leather. Her senses register

9

the familiar comforting things but her mind is busy else-where.

She makes another attempt to banish the memories of the night and thinks of Thomas instead. Sometimes he brings her exquisite pleasure and at other times pain and doubt. Sometimes she is sure that she can divert him from his destiny, keep him to herself, persuade him to some less exalted path. But more frequently self-doubt crowds her thoughts, depression sweeps over her like some great all-encompassing mist, like the fog that she has been told comes in from the sea. Catherine has never seen the sea but it strangely excites her.

She and Thomas have been friends since they were small children, for their parents are close. She thinks fondly for a moment of his clever sister, Mary, lately gone as a novice to a convent. She misses her greatly. Both Mary and Thomas have far too great a devotion to their God, she thinks wickedly.

Soon Thomas will be gone too. His school days are over and Catherine knows that he is looking forward to spending time with Lord Richer at Pevensey Castle. He has told her that he expects to ride the great warhorses that are kept at the castle, to wear the shield and lance and to take part in the practice tourneys where he will learn to unhorse his opponent. Catherine has seen his eyes sparkle in anticipation of the delights that await him at Pevensey. But his heart is still set on entering the Church and later he is to go to the college at Notre Dame in Paris.

When she thinks of all this she experiences the familiar deadening of her spirit, for although he professes love for her, she knows that she is only a very small part of his life. Yet he has promised to write whenever there is a courier coming to London with mail.

The tapestry on which she has been working has been flung carelessly on to a chair and she now looks at it with distaste. Her mother insists that it must be finished before spring. The cold stone walls of the solar are covered with admirable pieces fashioned by the women in her family for generations, but she has never been able to summon any interest in this necessary feminine accomplishment. She craves the freedom of her brother and of Thomas, but there is no freedom for a girl. Only in her dreams is she free, and this liberty vanishes as soon as she awakes.

Her dog, a great hound, bounds up the stairs and shakes himself all over her, but she welcomes the diversion gladly. She sometimes thinks that Calder is the only friend she will have in the coming empty months. He flops down on the hearth, as near as he can be to the fire burning smokily in the great fireplace. Catherine rubs his wet coat with a rug, hugs him to her and then holds her hands out to the warmth of the meagre flames.

The smoke makes her eyes sore so she closes them for a moment and flops on to the deerskin which covers a pallet. And then the strange figure that frightens and intrigues her comes once more as it often does when she is about to fall asleep. She knows that this girl is only a figment of her imagination, part of a dream, but so real that she longs to reach out and touch her. Catherine is sure that it is a girl who haunts and fascinates her so, but the clothes she wears are extraordinary. Catherine knows instinctively that her name is Kate but she has no idea why she knows this.

Kate lay in the bath and listened to Radio Three. Dommy mustn't think her too crass and ignorant. She wished she'd gone to concerts with Phoebe all those times when her grandmother had tried to persuade her. But at least Dominic was in favour with Phoebe for his musical tastes. It was only his religious ambitions that caused problems. 'For me too,' Kate said aloud. 'Never mind though. I'll probably be able to persuade him out of all of that when . . .' She grinned confidently to herself and breathed deeply of the ylang-ylang oil which she had swirled lavishly into the water. It was supposed to be erotic. She wished she could put some into Dominic's bath. An idea perhaps, when they were at Litford. She thought of lovely Devonshire and the ancient house with sudden and unexpected delight. What a contrast to this apartment in the middle of London where she had grown up. She lay back in the water and gave herself up to Mendelssohn.

Her thoughts were still restless though, and she began to consider her grandmother and the two men in her life: Dudley, her literary agent, and Hugo, her lover. Good old-fashioned word, lover. Well it suited Hugo. He was quite a charmer for his age, rather ancient of course, sixty-ish at least, but nice. They never stayed the night together in the flat but occasionally Phoebe would come home remarkably late from an evening date. Kate laughed in sudden amusement. What was it like having sex when you were old? All those wrinkles. How gross. Not that Phoebe had many wrinkles yet – hardly any in fact. Slim too. Kate turned the hot tap on again with her toes, put more drops of oil in the water and closed her eyes sensuously in the blissful perfumed heat.

She stood up eventually, wiped steam from the long mirror that Phoebe, in an excess of slimming zeal, had one day fixed in the bathroom, and stared at herself critically. Too thin, but that was preferable to being fat. Hair that would never do what she wanted, good complexion. Like her mother, so Phoebe said. Her thoughts turned to Laurel and her father, Phoebe's son, the parents she had never known. It must have been absolutely dire for Phoebe when they and grandfather Gerald were killed in France. How absolutely fearful to lose all your loved ones in one fell swoop and end up with a snivelling brat, herself, aged ten months. If it hadn't been for her wonderful grandmother she might have been brought up in some children's home or a foster family. Yes, there was no doubt about it. Nonna had been great, absolutely great. She towelled herself dry and in a sudden rush of affection she actually cleaned the bath.

When Kate left for her concert Phoebe switched on her computer and worked all evening, and at midnight went to bed. No good worrying about Kate's whereabouts. She reminded herself forcefully that her granddaughter was eighteen and perfectly at liberty to come and go as she pleased, and to decide the course of her life.

She lay sleepless in bed and wondered how it would be when Kate went to university. It would be strange to have the flat to herself. Hugo was always suggesting that they might live together or even marry, but at the moment neither option was in her scheme of things. Friendship was great, total commitment definitely not at present. 'I like my freedom too much, Hugo dear,' she had said.

Her thoughts turned to her work, the writing on which she and Kate depended. She wished she could write fiction, but since the accident in which she had lost her entire family apart from Kate – then a baby – she had preferred writing about other people's lives. It needed no originality, no inventiveness, and simple biographies about media personalities were usually fun to do. She had told Dudley that she would only attempt light-hearted biography, nothing to do with illness or death.

And now he had asked her to write about a murdered saint! She turned restlessly in bed, drank some water, contemplated making a cup of tea, and wondered how she was going to find a way into this new project. Far below, the London traffic hummed and sometimes roared. Phoebe loved this flat set high above the noise and fumes of the street. It was right in the centre of things, a situation that suited her very well indeed. All of life was here.

The harsh street lighting crept around the edges of the thick curtains, and now and then a police or fire siren wailed in the distance. Phoebe lay flat on her back and her eyes followed the moving shadows on the ceiling. Thomas à Becket would have no understanding of a London such as this, yet he was a Londoner. How was she to create his London? How could she have any perception or understanding of this place as it had been more than eight hundred years ago?

Without switching on her bedside lamp she impatiently threw back the overpowering duvet, only 4.5 tog, summer weight, and still too hot for tonight. She pushed her feet into slippers and padded across to the window. As soon as she had swished the thick curtains aside the room became flooded with garish orange light so that it became one with the street scene below. She stared down at the youths who were swaying unsteadily and noisily past and she was glad of the security of her eyrie ten floors high in the sky. In Devon there would be darkness and owls and the screech of small hunted creatures. Perhaps that would be more compatible with Thomas's life than this turbulent modern city. He had lived without electricity, gas, microwaves, running water, cars, aeroplanes and computers. How could anyone alive now, after having lived through the last years of the horrifying and wondrous twentieth century, possibly begin to conjure up that other London, that impossible life?

She opened the door quietly and went into the kitchen, stared for a moment at its streamlined, expensive units trying to see them with twelfth-century eyes and totally failing. She filled the new kettle she had bought just yesterday because it boiled with greater speed than the old one. Was time then so precious? Before she could find the teapot, the mug, the milk, it had bubbled victoriously and switched itself off.

She carried her tea back to bed and put her radio on. Later, with the tea finished and the curtains and duvet pulled back into place again, sleep still eluded Phoebe. Thank God for radio continuing all night. World Service, jazz! Oh no. Try something else. Five Live, no better, a phone-in on asylum seekers. Radio Three might do. Gregorian chant! An omen? Of course. Thomas à Becket's sort of stuff. It was probably the only music he heard. *Vide, Domine, Post sanctus, Vere sanctus, Vere benedictus.* She tried to relax, tried to think herself into the twelfth century. She slept at last and dreamed not of her granddaughter but of a strange unknown girl, a girl wearing a kirtle, long hair held back with a silver circlet.

Catherine? Catherine? Who are you and who is the boy standing so protectively by your side? Her hand is on the collar of a great dog. Phoebe has never seen so large a beast. 'Calder,' the girl says, 'Calder be quiet.' There is the scent of herbs – rosemary or lavender, Phoebe cannot tell which. And in the distance the sublime Laudate Dominum, quoniam bonus est psalmus.

She hovers into wakefulness as the music comes to an end. She reaches out and switches the radio off. The chanting has ceased, the dreams are receding. A police siren wails along the road below. The twelfth century fades, the twenty-first returns.

Two

H ugo Green sat alone in his fairly opulent Wimbledon house and thought about Phoebe. Curse the woman, she dominated his mind by day and filled his nights with desire, devilishly uncomfortable at his age. He'd like to marry her, but she wasn't too keen, said she preferred her freedom.

He frowned at the television from whence came the grunts and groans of a couple in bed, elegant legs and beautiful bodies entwined. Always young, of course. Sex didn't seem to equate with age these days, although of course he knew that it did. It was just less attractive to the morons who watched TV, he decided crustily. He picked up the remote control and changed channels, going through everything available to him. Nothing, absolutely nothing he wanted to watch. Perhaps he should give in to media pressure and go digital. Plenty of choice there he was led to believe.

There were three guidebooks lying on the table. One about Devon, another about Canterbury, and an English Heritage leaflet setting out the charms of Pevensey. He'd found them in the library after Phoebe's startling announcement on the telephone that morning that her next book was to be about Thomas à Becket. A twelfth-century saint of all people! Quite a change for Phoebe. She'd said a lot about the Devon connections. Bovey Tracey figured quite prominently in the research she wanted to do, apparently. He remembered it from their holiday last year. Nice little place. It all sounded interesting, and for a few nights away with Phee he'd put up with any amount of prowling around ancient cloisters and ruins. He began to feel slightly more cheerful. Phoebe and Kate were going to Devon soon and he was determined to join them later.

'So you are going to Pevensey today?' Catherine says. For Thomas and herself the years have passed. They are no longer children and life is more difficult. They are standing in her father's courtyard and Thomas is watching critically as one of the grooms brushes down the bay mare that he has just ridden.

He turns to her and smiles affectionately so that that some of Catherine's hurt melts a little.

'Lord Richer has a new hawk he wants to show me,' he says, as if this were reason enough.

Catherine sighs and realizes that she will never hold a man like Thomas Becket to her side with reproaches. He must always be free and occupied, must be for ever sampling new activities, making new conquests. She forces an answering smile, flashes her eyes at him and tosses her head.

'Is it true that the king is to come to Pevensey this summer?'

'Possibly. He will pass nearby on his way from Winchester to Normandy.'

'I should like to see him and his court.'

Thomas laughs at her and had they still been children he would have pulled her hair and challenged her to a race. Now their relationship has changed. He knows her feelings for him and loosely returns them, but his future is not yet clear. His brilliant mind, his splendid physique, and his popularity with everyone all lead him to think that there might be some dazzling career ahead. He can accept no ties.

Although he has recently been tonsured, a sign of commitment to God, he is not entirely sure just what that vow will entail. And for now anyway, life is full and agreeable. There is little room for specific plans, or for Catherine. He lives for the delights of the moment.

'You wouldn't like Pevensey,' he says, hoping to mollify her.

'Pevensey is the first place I want to visit,' Phoebe said,

surprised that Hugo should take such an interest in her next project. 'I hope to fit it in before we go to Devon.'

'Thomas was the archbishop wasn't he? Canterbury has to be pretty central to your story,' Hugo said.

'Not at the beginning though. We'll keep it for later. I have a gut feeling that Devon is going to prove very central indeed. William de Tracey lived there, in Bovey Tracey, the place where we went to do our shopping last summer. Quite a coincidence really.'

'Right,' Hugo said. 'Pevensey first, Devon for August, and Canterbury later. Are those the plans?'

'Pevensey is where the miracle happened.'

They were sitting at their favourite table in a corner of their favourite pub and Phoebe was possessed with a great sense of well-being. She was now deeply into the research for this book and was looking forward to writing it, in spite of her earlier misgivings. The more she studied her new subject, the more enthusiastic she became. 'Do you know,' she said, 'I have never been to Pevensey. Frightful really. Thomas visited the castle frequently when he was young. Parts of it are reasonably well preserved. In fact, the leaflet I picked up in the library said that it was used in the war.'

'What war?' Hugo looked up from the menu he had been studying.

'The Second World War of course. When France fell it was strategically placed.'

'Good heavens. What a quaint idea.'

'Why quaint? Its walls are still thick and strong apparently. A good defence against invasion.'

'Right then,' Hugo said. 'We shall go to Pevensey. Want me to drive you? We could do it in a day, or perhaps stay a night,' he added hopefully.

'A day will be enough,' Phoebe said. 'I have to pack for Devon.'

Thomas rides to Pevensey with just one groom, for the roads are comparatively safe. The king keeps a strict and upright regime. There are harsh punishments for robbery, rape and murder, but law-abiding citizens can travel with a fair assurance of safety. Henry I has given England a time of peace and prosperity.

In spite of this, however, Thomas's mind is not completely tranquil. He wonders how Lord Richer will react to his tonsure. He frequently raises his hand to the shaved crown of his head and sometimes he is tempted to wish he had not been so hasty in allowing it to be done. The bishop had arrived at Merton during the last school term and persuaded the boys to submit to the rite that dedicated them to the religious life. Thomas knows that vows of poverty, obedience and chastity will be hard to bear if he is forced to keep them faithfully, but surely they are not yet binding upon him? As he rides through the pleasant Sussex countryside he thinks often of Catherine and of her reaction to his tonsured head. 'But your father does not intend that you should become a priest,' she had said. 'You assured me that the office of cleric would be more suitable.'

'But even that would entail entering the lower orders of the Church,' he had hedged. 'Don't worry though, Catherine. It's not an inevitable step. I'm not as dedicated as I once was. Nothing about my life is set in stone. Perhaps I shall study law, or find a job working for a great lord. Some of them can scarcely read and most cannot write, so they are often in need of a Latin scholar such as myself. My hair will soon grow again if I wish it.'

He was well aware that she had not been reassured, and he still vividly and painfully remembers the pallor of her face and the beating of her heart against his as he held her briefly in his arms. However, sombre thoughts never possess Thomas for long, and as he nears Pevensey Castle they are gradually replaced by a glow of excitement. Tonight the wind is strong and he can smell and hear the sea as it roars on to the beaches around the isthmus on which the fortress was built years ago by Roman invaders. There are lonely calls from curlew and oystercatcher as well as the eerie drumming of snipe, sounds that set his heat racing with a strange unrest, an almost magical awakening. It is a feeling totally removed from both the worries and bustle of London and the constant labour and high expectations of Merton.

The outer bailey is peaceful just now with the evening quiet, horses stabled, men at rest. The Roman walls still stand protecting the newer battlements of the great Norman keep. There is a sturdy wooden gate to the inner bailey but it is opened for him and he rides through, passing easily from introspection and quietness to life and laughter. He has friends here whom he sees every summer and he is hailed with delight. There is extra excitement this year because of the expectation of the king's visit. A new grandson has been born in France to Matilda, Henry's daughter, and the king is anxious to visit this tiny heir, another Henry. Pevensey lies on the route he will take between Winchester and Anjou.

Hugo drove the car into the castle car park. 'Castles shouldn't have car parks,' Phoebe said. 'It's totally out of character.'

Hugo laughed. 'It's the twenty-first century or had you overlooked the fact?'

'I sometimes think I have,' Phoebe said. 'Ever since I started thinking about this book the past becomes more real than the present now and then.'

Hugo drove round three times. 'Jolly full,' he remarked unnecessarily.

'There,' Phoebe said suddenly, pointing. 'Someone just coming out.'

Carefully Hugo edged the car into the cramped space and they managed to squeeze out of it with difficulty. 'School holidays are not the time for any kind of sightseeing,' he grumbled as he rummaged in the boot for camera and panama hat. 'Bet it wasn't so crowded when your Thomas arrived here.'

'Different kind of crowds,' Phoebe said. *Abruptly she was aware of them, men in strange, motley clothes, horses neighing, snuffling into hay-bags, the smoke of fires, and it was evening.* It was only a momentary thing, a fleeting glimpse, but frightening, and she walked beside Hugo in something of a trance.

When they reached the ticket kiosk Phoebe felt quite detached, as if she didn't belong. She watched Hugo hand over his money and she forced herself back to normality. 'I need a guidebook,' she said. Hugo bought two and handed one to her.

'We can have an audio tour,' he said.

She stared at him in dismay. 'You take the audio tour, Hugo. I don't really think I want to.'

'OK, if you're sure,' he said. 'It might be good for your research though.'

She shook her head. 'You can tell me what it's like afterwards.'

In the shimmering heat of that summer day the great walls of the Norman keep seemed to have some living quality, repositories of a million stories from the lives of people who had lived and died here over the centuries.

Hugo opened his guidebook and read bits aloud. 'The outer parts were built by the Romans. Repaired and extended by the Normans, defended by the brave Lady Joan Pelham in the fifteenth century and, would you believe, finally refortified in 1940 for the Home Guard.'

Phoebe didn't want to know about the Home Guard. 'Do you mind if I go off on my own now, Hugo, while you sort out your audio tour?'

'Fine,' Hugo said. 'I'll meet you in the tea room in an hour from now.'

'Tea room?'

'Yes my dear Phee, tea room,' he said patiently. 'You know, the place where we can get scones and cakes and a cuppa. Have you got that?'

Phoebe glanced at her watch. 'Yes. Yes, Hugo. Half past three.' Then suddenly she was aware of a wave of fear enveloping her, a coldness that had nothing to do with the hot afternoon, with Hugo's wish for tea, with anything tangible at all. The ruins appeared tranquil enough. Why then this strange unease? The crowds, children with dripping ice creams, harassed parents, earnest students, all seemed to fade and she was filled with a deep disquiet.

Unaware of this, Hugo found an empty bench and flopped upon it. 'Off you go then. Get on with your research and daydreaming. I shall stay here for a bit and watch the world go by and then do the audio thing.'

Phoebe looked at him with affection and tried to banish her out-of-life feelings. She took her camera from its case

20

and took his photograph. He laughed at her and blew her a kiss, and then she walked away towards the inner bailey. The heaviness persisted. Thomas had been happy here, hadn't he? She had read that he was a favourite of Lord Richer, that he hoped for advancement and privilege. So why did she feel this oppressiveness, this presentiment of something not quite right?

She tried to concentrate on her photography for this would be useful when she came to write the Pevensey chapter. She took photographs of the Roman walls, of the keep, and even, where she could, of the camouflaged pillboxes of World War Two. On her little tape recorder she captured the calling of the gulls, and when she was, for a short time, alone in the inner sanctum of the castle, she spoke some of her own thoughts and fears quietly so that no one should hear. Then she sat down on some stones, part of a ruined wall, and without trying, easily recalled another time, another age. 'Where are all times past?' she whispered. 'Tell me where all times past are.'

Thomas is riding with Lord Richer. He has been chosen before the other boys and he is excited and full of confidence. He has a fine young peregrine hooded on his wrist and one of the great destriers between his legs, a warhorse such as he has never ridden before. True enough it is an old beast, for he cannot be trusted yet with any of the more valuable younger mounts, but this sturdy animal beneath him is a whole world away from the gentle little mare that his mother usually insists he should ride. His wish for a large and bolder mount of his own has not yet been granted. He has been spending most of his spare time at Pevensey with the hawks, and under the careful eye of Lord Richer's chief falconer. Hawking has fascinated him since he was a little boy, and now he is skilful and the birds know and trust him, come to his call and respond to his every movement. Lord Richer is riding beside him, very close, the dog bounding ahead, and then very gradually Thomas's elation begins to change to a certain uneasiness. There is an intentness in Richer's eyes that he has seen before but has dismissed. He cannot dismiss it now that they are out in the forest alone together.

21

Thomas knows that some men are different. They like to keep boys almost as pets, as lapdogs. He also knows that there is more to it than that and sometimes at Merton in the enclosed masculine company of the monastery school he has felt these uncomfortable stirrings himself. But every time he has returned to London he has looked upon Catherine's beauty, and the unwanted fancies have disappeared. His studies of the Bible have told him that the feeling of man for man is unnatural. He'll have none of it. Yet now Lord Richer is staring at him so intensely that all logical thought is driven from him and his unease is beginning to affect the young hawk on his wrist. She flutters her wings restlessly.

Suddenly they come to a reedy place near the river and the dog flushes out some duck which rise into the air in terrified flight. Quickly, without thinking, Thomas removes the peregrine's hood and casts her off. Bells tinkling she flies swiftly to a point far above her prey and then falls through the air and takes one duck, but misses a full grip and the wounded bird flutters to the ground.

Dogs and horses race along the river bank for they must find the bird before the peregrine flies off in search of other quarry and be lost. Thomas, his misgivings temporarily put aside, plunges through the undergrowth but the soft earth has been further softened by Lord Richer's great horse and suddenly Thomas's mount, older and not so sure-footed now, slips into the river just where the water gathers speed before it reaches the great paddles of the nearby mill wheel. The horse regains his footing and scrambles out, but Thomas is caught by the current, is swept towards the murdering roaring paddles. Water is thundering in his ears and filling his lungs. He thrashes out with flailing hands but he has never learned to swim, and even if he was able, the current is too swift.

Lord Richer turns and sees what has happened and gallops down to the mill, hooves and mud flying. He screams to the miller to stop the wheel, but nothing can be heard above the crashing of the turning stones and the rushing water. Yet at that very moment the wheels do stop turning. The miller, hearing nothing, knowing nothing of the youth about to be swept to his

*death in the thrashing blades, has stopped the wheel. Thomas
is safe. It is a miracle.*

*He is pulled to the river bank, the water pressed from his
lungs, and then he looks up and sees Lord Richer staring
down at him, and suddenly, through his fear and confusion,
Thomas knows that he cannot stay any longer at Pevensey. He
cannot live here under the patronage and at the direction of
this man. He turns to the miller's wife who has come bustling
from the house carrying towels and blankets. And then he sees
Lord Richer turn, mount and ride away, and he understands
in a moment of suddenly revealed truth, that the great baron
has painfully recognized his protégé's revulsion. Lord Richer
will have no more to do with him. The fun, the good life, the
privileges of Pevensey, are over. Yet Thomas perceives also
that in the miracle, in the saving of his life, he has discovered
a greater destiny.*

*The hawk has not returned. She has flown away to reclaim
her freedom. So must he.*

Phoebe had read about the miracle, the mill wheel that stopped
by the hand of God, and she thought about it as she sat
and allowed the spirit of the castle to envelop her. The
blackness she had felt earlier had passed. She remembered
now that Thomas had been disturbed and troubled here, but
his deliverance from death in the mill race had freed him, had
shown him a greater future.

She stared at a small rowan tree that was growing beside the
vast ageless walls. It still had some berries, blood-red against
the ancient stone. An omen? The birds had not yet stripped it
bare. A magical tree. Did Thomas believe in the magic of a
tree or were his thoughts more pious?

Of course the miracle was merely a wonderful coincidence,
but coincidences can influence the whole course of a life and, if
you believe that there is a divine plan behind the wonder, then
the effect is all the more astounding. A seeming coincidence
is often no such thing.

Phoebe smiled to herself. Mothers are perhaps more gullible
than others and it was Thomas's mother who, according to the
books she had studied, had been convinced that this miracle

was a further sign that her son was special, a chosen one. She stood up and brushed bits of grass from her trousers. How was she to write of such things in this sceptical modern age? Yet Dudley had told her that scepticism was out now and signs and wonders were in.

She took some more photographs and eventually found her way, at the appointed time, to the tea room and to Hugo.

He was waiting for her and had managed to find and keep an empty corner table. 'Seen any ghosts or ghouls?' he asked as he rose and pulled out a chair for her.

She winced. Her oneness with the past couldn't be trivialized. 'No,' she said. 'No ghosts, just presences.'

'Same thing,' he said. 'Perhaps they'll show up in your photographs. Now that really would be something.'

She sat down and looked around at the pretty room, at the mouth-watering display of home-made cakes and scones, and at the feasting holiday-makers. It was all so far removed from the world she was trying to recreate, from the pictures in her head. She thought about Hugo's remark and smiled at him, trying to be generous. 'There's a castle in Devon where the ghosts are photogenic,' she said. 'They're even known to break cameras now and then. Some people believe such things anyway.'

He laughed and she told him about Thomas's miracle.

'We still believe in weird and wonderful things,' he said, confirming Dudley's convictions. 'Think of all the programmes on the telly about strange phenomena. If it happened today you can be sure some producer would jump at the story. God might not get the credit for stopping the mill wheel though. It would probably be some water goddess or other such weirdo.'

Phoebe tried to imagine Thomas and his mother telling their story on television and could not. 'Let's order tea and some of those yummy cakes,' she said. 'I'm starving. Next week it'll be Devonshire scones and clotted cream.'

'Dominic doesn't think he'll be able to come to Devon for more than a week,' Kate announced almost as soon as Phoebe entered the front door. Her face was a picture of misery. 'He's found a job for the hols. He needs to make some money.'

Phoebe, secretly pleased, made sympathetic noises. 'Well you'll have more time to ride won't you? Janice has a new mare if you remember.'

Kate gave her grandmother a dismissive look. 'You're glad of course. You'd rather he didn't come at all!'

'I don't want to see you hurt, darling,' Phoebe said. 'You were so miserable the other night. As you said yourself, he's going to be a priest, celibate and all that. Ever read *The Thorn Birds*?'

Kate shook her head. 'I'm hoping he'll change his mind, or perhaps the Church will. Maybe they'll have married priests soon.'

'And what if neither of those things happen?'

'I don't want to think about it. I suppose we'll just live together. Lots do.'

'Not very satisfactory,' Phoebe said. 'Not with someone of Dominic's high principles. You'd have to keep it all very secret.'

'Did you enjoy Pevensey?' Kate said, in an effort to change the subject.

'So-so,' Phoebe stalled, then she thought suddenly of Thomas's supposed miracle, the event that had set him apart so spectacularly. Celibacy: blessing or curse? *Thomas Becket, called by God or called by his own soaring ambition?* Dominic, called by God, and therefore destined to break Kate's heart? Or . . . not?

Three

H igh Mead was an impressive farmhouse set in an enviable
position on the slopes of Dartmoor. Talitha and Garth,
Phoebe's sister and brother-in-law, had bought it some years
ago along with the local veterinary practice. It was solidly built
of granite and never failed to give Phoebe an intense wave of
pleasure every time she drove down the winding Devon lane
leading to it and to Litford, the more ancient longhouse in
which they were to stay for their holiday. There had always
been a sense of otherness, as though in arriving here she entered
a different dimension in time, another world that had nothing to
do with the hectic quality of her London life. She always tried
to ignore the satellite dish that stood out so vulgarly from the
sturdy walls of High Mead. It was so incongruous that when
she had first seen it she had stared in disbelief.

Talitha had laughed. 'We're not complete yokels down here
you know,' she had said. 'And Garth likes the sport.'

That had been some time ago, and now she and Kate were
here again, this time to stay at Litford rather than in her
sister's home. Talitha had been jubilant when Garth had
bought the older neighbouring house as an investment, and
since its refurbishment she let it to special people wanting a
retreat or a unique holiday.

Phoebe drove slowly round to the back of High Mead and
pulled the car to a halt avoiding various hens and a strutting
cockerel. 'Well, here we are,' she said unnecessarily.

Kate unclipped her safety belt. 'Thank goodness,' she said
with feeling. 'You've been driving very fast. Frightened me
out of my life once or twice.'

'Did I really?' Phoebe was considerably flattered. It was
better than being told you were driving like an ancient. She

26

opened the car door and stepped out gingerly. You never knew what you might be treading in at Talitha's.

'Hi,' her sister called, emerging from the back door at the sound of the vehicle. Her face was red, an apron was tied around her waist, and her hair was untameable as usual. Thick and curly, this was an inheritance from their mother that Phoebe had always envied. Her own was fine and straight and must always be sprayed into submission if she was to keep it in any kind of order.

Phoebe threw her arms around Talitha's ample body in an affectionate hug and then stood back and they looked at each other critically.

'You look great,' Phoebe said.

'Too great. I've embarked on a diet once again.' Then Talitha turned her attention to Kate. 'How's things?'

'Mega, thanks, Aunt Tally.' Kate kissed her aunt on both cheeks. 'Glad to be here in one piece after Nonna's driving.'

'Thanks a bundle,' Phoebe said.

Talitha grinned. 'A sign of age, fast driving!'

'Well that's just great to know. I thought it was the opposite. I shall crawl along at thirty miles an hour in future.'

'Well, you're here safe and sound. Come inside and we'll have a cuppa to celebrate and then I'll take you over to Litford and show you where everything is. You'll like all the alterations.' Talitha pushed an assortment of dogs out of the way and ushered them into her large comfortable kitchen. She filled the kettle and put mugs and a plate of scones on the table. 'I made them especially. Very noble since they're not on my diet . . . Well, what's new? I want all the gossip.'

Phoebe looked around in total satisfaction, and for a moment she visualized her own tiny modern flat, comparing it with this vast stone flagged room. This was the right place to get into the thoughts and mind of someone eight hundred years away in time. 'I told you about Thomas à Becket when I telephoned didn't I?' she said.

Talitha produced milk and cream from the refrigerator and a pot of home-made jam. 'Yes you did. Gave me the shock of my life. Not really you is it sister dear?'

'That's what everyone says, and what I thought myself at

27

first, but I'm getting quite excited about the idea lately. I even go back to the twelfth century in my dreams now and then.'

'I keep telling her to be careful or she might find herself staying there,' Kate said. She put a large helping of cream on her scone and piled jam on top. 'Not a very comfortable time to live.'

Talitha took an apple from the sideboard and put it on her plate. She filled the teapot, carried it to the table and flopped down. 'I remember you always used to have these strange flights of fancy when we were children, something to do with Dr Who or H.G. Wells probably. Time travel and all that. I was always very impressed, but honestly Phee, the twelfth century or whenever is a long time ago and a dead saint isn't exactly a rave is he?'

'Dudley seems to think it'll be a winner, make lots of money.'

'Well he should know. Good on you then if you're set on it.'

'She's bought a new computer,' Kate announced. 'In Thomas's honour. A laptop. I'm green with envy.'

'I suppose we shan't see much of you then. You'll be beavering away all day.'

'I'm going to take a day or two off now and then. This is supposed to be a holiday.' Phoebe spread a scone with the thick yellow cream and bit into it with intense pleasure. 'These scones are superb, Tal,' she said. 'How you can sit there and watch us eat them beats me.'

'Beats me too,' Talitha replied. 'But I've lost a stone and have another to go to my target. How come we're sisters and you're as slim as a stick while I'm . . .'

'No idea,' Phoebe said, licking her jammy fingers. 'And "stick" is hardly flattering.'

'I'd change any day.'

'She's just lucky,' Kate volunteered.

'Apart from my awful hair,' Phoebe said. 'You've got the curls and they're coming back into fashion now.'

Talitha ran her hand through her hair, finished her apple and got to her feet. 'My will power is running out. Let's go and have a look at Litford. I'm dying to know what you think

28

of the new additions.' She took a large key from a hook on the dresser and held it up for inspection. 'The modernization hasn't extended as far as the front door yet. In fact it's still rather ramshackle on the outside, but we have to obey all the rules for ancient listed buildings. Rather tiresome sometimes. All mod cons are artfully concealed. We'd better take the car as you've so much luggage.'

'I'll walk,' Kate said.

'Right. See you there.' Talitha heaved herself into the front passenger seat of Phoebe's car. 'Hope the ghosts aren't there to greet us.'

'Ghosts?' Phoebe started the engine and drove gingerly round to the front of the house. 'You didn't warn me about ghosts.'

'Only joking. Just thinking about your time travelling and all that. Parts of the building go back to medieval times.'

They bumped up the lane that led to the open moorland and passed Kate on the way. The house stood at the end of the lane as though guarding the old track, challenging anyone to go any further, to set foot on the narrow path that led through heather and gorse to the granite outcrop of rock crowning the hill behind the ancient walls. The roof was newly thatched and the ground rose gently behind so that the house appeared to sink into the land, becoming part of its surroundings as though it had been there for ever.

'Really cool,' Kate announced as she caught them up. She stood quite still and stared at the low-slung building, its granite walls mellow now in the afternoon sun. 'The new thatch is really fab.'

'Cost a bomb,' Talitha said. 'But we had no choice. You have to do what you're told with an ancient house, even if you own it.'

Phoebe climbed out of the car. 'Did you say it was fourteenth century?'

'Probably, but the foundations and some ruins at the side date from the twelfth, I'm reliably told.'

'Thomas's time! Quite remarkable,' Phoebe said. 'I didn't think too much about history and things like that when we came down last year. Now it seems more important.'

'He had some Devon connections of course,' Talitha added. 'Bovey Tracey church is named for him.'

Phoebe nodded. 'There are lots of legends and stories, and some recorded facts too.'

'Let's go in,' Kate said. 'I'm dying to see what you've done inside.' She opened the boot and heaved a suitcase out. 'Lead on, Aunt Talitha.'

The kitchen had been sensitively modernized except for a garish fluorescent strip light which disfigured one of the oak beams. 'That's horrible,' Kate said, staring at it with disgust. 'But it'll frighten away any ghost I should think.'

'Garth insisted on it,' Talitha said. 'We had a row about it actually, but he won. He said we needed it in a place with such a lot of crannies and hidden corners.'

Phoebe switched it on and blinked as it flashed a couple of times before its light flooded the kitchen.

'Tom, where are you? Thomas don't leave me!' Phoebe heard the voice clearly in her head. It was young, distraught. She put her hand to her eyes for a second and the kitchen faded, the objectionable light changed, was replaced by a totally inadequate flickering glow and she shivered in spite of the hot August afternoon.

'Phoebe!' It was Talitha's voice she heard now. 'Whatever's the matter? You look as white as a sheet.'

'I just felt cold suddenly,' Phoebe said. 'Did the lights fail for a second or two?' She tried to regain some control and a degree of normality. 'I hope you don't get power cuts down here. They're not good for computers.'

Talitha laughed. 'Not usually, and no, the lights didn't fail. Are you sure you're all right?'

'Yes, yes, I'm OK. Honest. Everything went black for a moment. I expect I'm just tired. The traffic was pretty horrendous. I'll have a nap before I come over to you for dinner tonight.'

'Good idea,' Talitha said. 'Now let's get your stuff in and Kate can unpack.'

Like the rest of the house the bedrooms had been charmingly restored. The floors were wooden, well scrubbed and treated and covered with hand-woven rugs, and the small windows were curtained with light floral cotton. Phoebe flopped down on the bed and found it soft and absolutely to her liking. 'Perfect,' she said.

Half an hour later, with their things stowed away, her computer placed strategically on the little desk beneath the window, and Kate and Talitha walking back together to her sister's house, Phoebe lay quietly on top of the patchwork covered duvet. Kate had not wanted to leave her, but she had insisted. 'I need a sleep, and with you clattering about it's the last thing I shall get,' she had said.

The peace and quiet of this lovely old house was just what she needed. A silence like this was strange, almost bewitching, an experience not often enjoyed in London. Certain places, and especially old houses, were often imbued with the happiness, the pains, the traumas of other years, even other centuries, she thought. Perhaps all you had to do was tune in to those vibes? Was that what had happened at Pevensey, and occasionally at other times and places during her life? Was she especially susceptible? Psychic perhaps? Kate had jokingly remarked that she must have a sort of time machine in her head. The idea troubled Phoebe a little. Could one really go back in time? Was it possible to see into the mind of someone who had lived hundreds of years ago, perhaps even *be* that person? Some people claimed to be able to do so. Others believed in reincarnation. Phoebe had no liking for that strand of belief. She had no wish to actually become someone else, or even worse, to come back as another being in some frightening future age.

She closed her eyes and thought about Thomas à Becket's world. Was her mind really taking her to a past century? She grimaced a little at the unlikelihood of such a thing. It was bizarre, but if there was any reality in it at all then she must be in total control, must only go back in her imagination when she wished to do so. This, however, had not proved easy so far. There must have been triggers, she thought, things that had catapulted her back without warning. What were these triggers then? She must find out, for only then would she be in charge. Was it a place, or something she had recently read, or even eaten? And who was Catherine?

Why that name? Had she seen it somewhere during her research and stored it away in her subconscious? Probably, she thought. How strong was the Devon connection? What had this Catherine to do with the serious biography she was attempting to write? Had her flippant remarks about giving Thomas a lover caused her imagination to conjure this girl out of the ether? Phoebe regretted now that she had ever considered such an outrageous idea.

She tossed the questions around in her head and wished that she could put them all aside and sleep. She closed her eyes and felt the longed for drowsiness sweep over her at last.

'I am going away,' the girl says. There is anguish in her words, anguish carefully concealed. But she has not been able to prevent the tears, just a few, which she hopes he has not noticed.

'Why, Catherine? Tell me why? And why so far?' He is holding her in his arms, looking down intently at her face, brushing the tears away with part of his cloak which he wears slung carelessly over one shoulder and held in place with a silver buckle.

'I am to be married,' she lies. 'My father has arranged a very suitable match. He tells me the man is young and handsome and very rich.' She pulls away from him. 'I am learning to be happy about it. There has never been room for me in your life, Thomas, and there will be less in the future.'

He stands and stares at her, but he is not seeing her. He sees the marshes at Pevensey and the miracle at the mill. All the amazing details flash through his mind. He has been set apart by God. He must never let anything interfere with the greatness that awaits him. Even this girl whom he loves must not hinder the will of God. 'And you are content?' He is seeking reassurance for the separation which he knows must come. He even feels slight relief that the initiative has come from her, that he needs to make no difficult choices.

She nods. 'I believe my father has chosen well. I shall want for nothing. I am to be allowed to take Calder with me, and when I get used to being so far from all else that I know I shall be perfectly content.'

Catherine is determined to be brave for the sake of this young man whom she loves. Indeed, because she loves him so much she will sacrifice her whole life to him. If this entails never seeing him again, never telling her secret, so be it. She will live a life of service and goodness and will do her best to be happy whether she is called to celibacy in a convent, or to eventual marriage. Her father will make all the decisions for her. The fabrication of an immediate marriage is forced upon her by her family in order to keep their good name and to atone for her sin. Devonshire, a place she has never before heard of, will be a safe haven, and so far away that she will be able to keep her secret. What will become of her child she does not yet know, but her father has promised that it will be cared for and brought up in a manner worthy of his grandchild, even though it will never be acknowledged. With this she must be content. She places her hands across her slim stomach. She can hardly believe a new life is growing there, a curse and a punishment. But she will not be afraid. For Thomas's sake, and for the sake of the babe whom he will never know, she will be courageous and resolute.

She pulls herself out of Thomas's arms and runs from the room. A great dog follows her, a hound, Calder. There is another scent now, that of crushed herbs, rosemary surely. The spiky leaves are bruised beneath the girl's small leather-clad feet and her trailing robe brushes through them, making the evocative perfume even stronger.

Thomas makes no move to follow her. He stands quite still and watches her go. He is cold, his emotions in turmoil.

Phoebe awoke slowly, luxuriously, wondering at first where she was, why it was so quiet. Then gradually the dream came to her and she sat up in bed, startled, the peace receding rapidly. 'Kate!' she called. 'Kate, where are you?'

There was no reply and she remembered that Kate had gone with Talitha to help prepare the evening meal for all of them, and to see the new mare. Phoebe jumped from the bed and stared at the white painted walls, the prettily curtained windows, the central heating radiator.

It had happened yet again, that inexplicable feeling of

oneness with the past. Yet it had not been like the other times. This was definitely a dream. She pushed her feet into slippers and went to the window, and as she stared at the moor rising wild and beautiful to the summit, more of her dream filled her mind. Catherine, definitely Catherine again.

She mentally shook herself and wondered if she would put any of this into the book. Certainly the ideas were coming thick and fast thanks to her dreams and her imagination. Could a biography contain fiction? Yes, of course it could, if properly acknowledged. 'Were you a real person, Catherine?' she said. 'Could you have had any connection with this old house? Highly improbable, but perhaps your story, fiction or not, will be transferred from my dreams on to my computer. No one will ever know the truth. You were pregnant in my dream, weren't you? How did I know that? Who was the father?'

Then realization dawned. Dear God, pregnant. Is this just a dream or are my subconscious worries for Kate projecting themselves back eight hundred years?

Phoebe gathered up the splendidly romantic robe that Hugo had bought for her last birthday and went into the bathroom. Talitha had put towels on the rail and scented soap on the basin, and yes, it was modern, quite luxurious. She turned on the bath taps, the hot one as far as it would go. She swirled bath oil into the water and stepped into the scented luxury of the twenty-first century.

After her bath Phoebe dressed slowly and with care. Gradually the bizarre quality of her dream left her and she was almost able to laugh at herself. The quietness of the lovely old house wrapped her around with a sense of tranquillity. If anything bad had happened in this place it must have been more than covered by happiness for she could feel no coldness, no misery. She was not at all afraid of being left alone here. Litford, in spite of all the things its old walls must have witnessed over the centuries, appeared to be a remarkably serene house, perfectly at ease with itself.

When she was ready to leave for her sister's home she looked at herself critically in the long mirror on the back of the old wardrobe door. She had dressed completely out of character tonight. The long sturdy skirt she had chosen was eminently suitable for a walk down the rough track and for the attention of numerous dogs and cats, and the silk blouse added a little glamour. She threw a shawl woven from the wool of Jacob sheep around her shoulders, and grinned at the picture she presented. It was so far removed from her usual London garb of either smart suits or jeans and trainers that both Dudley and Hugo would hardly recognize her. But these clothes suited her mood. She knew that Talitha would be making a special effort with this first meal of the holiday, always something of a celebration, and she must dress to match.

The evening was still and warm. Phoebe locked the great studded door, put the hefty key in her bag and, delighting in the country smells and sounds, strolled down the track to High Mead.

'My goodness, you look rather way out,' Talitha said. 'Not like you at all, Phee. I like the effect though.' She was stirring something on one of the Aga's hotplates and she glanced up briefly as Phoebe came into the kitchen. 'Fetch yourself a drink. Everything's ready.'

'Can I help?' Phoebe said.

'No. Sit yourself down and talk to Garth. He's opening the wine. You're on holiday.'

'If you're sure?'

'Of course I'm sure. Off you go.' Talitha shooed her away with a wooden spoon.

In the dining room Kate was putting the finishing touches to the table. 'Hi, Nonna,' she said. 'You look fab. Where did you get all that gear? Oxfam shop?'

'The skirt, yes,' Phoebe admitted. 'Rather fun isn't it?'

'Why haven't I seen it before?'

'I hid it.'

Kate laughed. 'Sensible. I'd have pinched it.'

Garth was sampling the wine. He looked at Phoebe appreciatively. 'Well, how are you Phee?' he said. 'You get younger every year.'

'Flatterer.'

'Not at all. I hear you're writing a weighty biography? How come?'

Garth was a large, attractive man. Certain veterinary programmes that Phoebe had watched lately on television had
given her a better idea of the likely things he might do each day,
and she looked at him now with respect and not a little awe. She
could well imagine him pushing a recalcitrant bull around, or
hauling a calf from the unforgiving innards of some poor cow,
but performing a delicate operation on a hamster? Yes, she was
sure he would be competent at that too. She grinned at him and
wondered for a betraying moment how her sister had managed
to keep him faithfully at her side for so many years.

'A commission,' she replied. 'Life of Thomas à Becket no
less. I'm getting quite keen actually. It's a complete change
and a challenge.'

Later, with the first course served, Garth turned to Phoebe
again. 'Didn't Becket have a secret love in these parts?' He
eyed her mischievously. 'Wife of William de Tracey if I
remember rightly.'

'It's possible. Vigorously denied by the Church and the
early biographers of course. He was merely giving her spiritual
guidance.'

'Well now, there's a change.' Garth laughed heartily. 'Spiritual guidance covers a multitude of sins.'

'Very romantic if it's true,' Janice said. Janice, Talitha and
Garth's daughter, had always been intrigued by her aunt's
various literary works. 'Do you think it might be factual?'

'The spiritual guidance or the sex?' Garth asked.

'Garth!' Talitha reprimanded him sharply. 'Phee is writing
a serious biography.'

'Every book needs a bit of . . .' Garth paused and looked
around at his family with amusement. 'Malarkey,' he added.

'Dad!' It was Janice's turn to chide now. 'If you mean sex,
say it. Malarkey! What kind of word is that?'

'A good old-fashioned one,' Phoebe replied. 'But anyway,
Thomas's love life or complete lack of it is all rumour and
legend.'

'So how will you liven the book up, Aunt Phee?'

'You think it will need livening up?'

'Certainly. Nothing sells now apparently if it's not full of
sex and violence.' Janice sounded very earnest.

'There was plenty of violence in the twelfth century,' Phoebe said. 'But, if the records are to believed, not a lot of sex in Thomas's life. Difficult to believe of such a charismatic character.'

'Then you'd better give him some.' Garth winked at her.

'Enough of this,' Talitha said. 'I shall change the subject.' She turned to her husband. 'Garth, you've forgotten to light the candles.'

He leaned across the table and took the box of matches that were set beside a bowl of pretty floating candles. He struck a match and carefully lit all five, and then the three tall ones which graced a silver candelabra in the centre of the table.

They all stared at the flickering points of flame that seemed to transform the whole room. The haunting smell was as much a part of the magic. Phoebe recognized it at once. Lavender. She remembered that Tally had said something about scented candles.

Catherine! The name slides effortlessly into Phoebe's mind. The bedroom is cold, stone-walled with a tapestry fixed upon it. A girl is sitting up in the bed and there is fear in her eyes. She clutches the blanket about her. She speaks to someone else in the room. The words sound strange to Phoebe's ears but somehow she can understand.

'They came again,' the girl says. 'They look at me and sometimes they talk together. Their features are familiar. When I look at the girl it's like looking at myself.'

The woman comes close to the bed. She is carrying a candle and she shades it with her hand so that the wind creeping around the window frame should not blow out its feeble light. She sets it on a low table and sits on her young charge's bed. 'Just a dream, child,' she says. 'There is nothing and no one to harm you in this house. Your dog would protect you with his life if there was danger.'

Catherine relaxes a little, puts her hand down to stroke the eager head of the great hound who has slept silently on a deerskin rug beside her bed. He is sitting up now, alert, looking from one to the other, not understanding their anxiety, yet not quite sure whether he should trust this woman into whose home they have so recently come.

'They're strange,' Catherine says. 'They dress rather like men yet they have the form of women. There are two of them, one young and the other is older.'

Eluned holds her hand out cautiously to the dog, but he pays her scant attention. 'See,' she says. 'Calder knows and accepts me, but if there had been strangers in the room he would have awakened at the first sound.'

'Then who are they? Why do they come to me so often? Although I cannot understand much of the things they say I know their names. The girl, if she is a girl, is called Kate and the other one is Phoebe. I don't know anyone with such a name as that.'

'They are just dreams,' Eluned says firmly. She has had enough of these bizarre fancies. Every night for the past week Catherine has called out in terror. Eluned longs to return to the warmth of her own bed, to the comfort of her husband's sturdy snoring bulk, and wonders if she has taken on more than she had bargained for when she agreed to look after this girl until her baby was born. 'I expect it was my little Dinah you were dreaming of,' she says dismissively. 'You spend a lot of time with her during the day so it's quite likely that you'll dream about her at night.'

Catherine shakes her head and her eyes fill with tears. 'No, Eluned, it's not your little girl in my dreams, if they are dreams as you say. It is definitely Kate that I hear inside my head and she speaks to the older woman. And although I cannot understand the words, I know quite clearly what they are saying. I'm quite sure of it, and it makes me so frightened.'

'Why be frightened of such dreams? They sound pleasant enough to me.' Eluned tries to appear reassuring, but she is perplexed and wonders privately where these curious fancies come from. 'I shall bring you a soothing drink,' she says gently, 'and then you'll sleep soundly without your spectres.' She takes the candle and lights another from it, leaving one comfortingly in a sconce in the old stone wall. 'I'll be very quick. Calder will look after you.' She goes down to the room below where she keeps her dried herbs and remedies, and a little later returns *with a brew of camomile, hops, valerian and a small measure of precious honey. She is being paid well to look after this pregnant child and is anxious that no malady of mind or body should befall her.*

Catherine drinks it slowly, gratefully. She has benefited from her mother's knowledge of the ancient cures all her life and she recognizes the scents of this comforting infusion. When she has finished she hands the vessel to Eluned who tucks the blanket around her and bends to kiss her fondly. Catherine is grateful. Eluned is full of a gruff kindness, a homely warmth.

'Remember, I can hear if you call, and Calder is by your side always. Your dreams are only dreams, child, nothing more.' Eluned tiptoes out, puts a deerskin rug at the door so that it shall not close, and returns to her own bed. She fails to see the girl in jeans and denim shirt standing beside the window. Catherine, comforted by the tranquillizing herbs and the simple loving kiss is slowly drifting into a blessed dreamless sleep.

Kate moves silently across the room. Her trainers make no sound on the wooden floor. She looks down at the sleeping girl and frowns. It is like looking at herself, a strange copy, but herself nevertheless. The dog registers no emotion, makes no response. She walks across the room to him, hesitates, then bends to stroke him. As her hand runs from his head down his shaggy curled-up back, his great tail swishes slowly from side to side and eventually he looks sleepily up at her, crosses his paws, puts his head on to them and closes his eyes. She is familiar to him. She poses no threat.

Kate quietly withdraws, stepping silently over the rug in the doorway. The wooden stairs, which creak so alarmingly when Catherine walks cumbersomely down them, make no noise for Kate.

Phoebe ran her hand over her eyes and stared at the candles and at Kate sitting opposite her. They are so alike, this girl from her dreams and her granddaughter. Kate was looking at her and so was Talitha. Phoebe saw the concern on their faces.

'Are you all right, Phee?' Talitha's voice broke through the mystifying images of her imagination.

'Yes. Shouldn't I be?'

'You had that gone-away look about you again.'

Phoebe was frightened but tried to laugh at the fear she felt. 'Sorry everyone,' she said. 'Author's licence or something of the sort. I suppose the candles wafted me a few centuries back for a moment.' Her light tones belied her dismay. Once again she had not been in control. This episode could hardly be called a dream either. It reminded her of what had happened to her at Pevensey Castle. She thought briefly of Canterbury Cathedral, which she knew she must visit. What might happen there?

'Nonna has her own time machine,' Kate said. 'It's in her head.'

They all looked at her, laughed a little. Garth, still busy with his huge meal, announced between mouthfuls, 'Scientists say it might be feasible one day.' He sounded surprisingly serious. 'We shall all go zooming off to our favourite century.'

'And what about the future?' Janice asked. 'Shall we be able to go forward a few hundred years to some strange time that hasn't happened yet? That would be great. I've frequently regretted not knowing what the world will be like when I'm dead.'

'Too horrible to contemplate,' Talitha said.

'It might be better than going backwards if you are a woman,' Kate contributed. 'It was pretty awful for women in any past century. Women have been oppressed by men for ever, and still are in many benighted parts of the world.'

Garth grinned at her. 'Didn't know you were a feminist, Katy dear.'

'Of course I'm a feminist,' Kate said. 'How could I be anything else?'

Now what did that mean, Phoebe wondered, and then realized that she was seeing another girl in another age who looked just like Kate, and who was indeed oppressed. Reincarnation? The thought came to her again. Her alarm grew. What was this book doing to her mind? Was it sending her crazy? Perhaps she should give up the whole idea, do something modern and flippant. 'Maybe I shouldn't write about Thomas à Becket after all,' she said. 'We are all becoming too introspective and serious.'

'Nonna!' Kate made the word a sort of wail. 'Of course you'll do it. You have to write the truth. I was a bit gutted at the idea at first, but it's grown on me.'

Phoebe looked at her, startled again. 'What do you mean, write the truth?'

Kate looked vague. 'Did I say that? I don't know what I meant.'

'How can I ever discover the truth?' Phoebe said. 'And if I do, and if I write it down, perhaps I shall be excommunicated.'

'Excommunicated? From what? Whatever are you talking about, Phee?' Talitha had started to clear some of the dishes from the table. She stopped on her way to the kitchen hatch, casserole and gravy jug precariously balanced.

'From the Church of course,' Phoebe answered with no hesitation, surprising herself.

'That's a bit odd seeing you never go!'

'Just a joke,' Phoebe said. 'Just proving I'm identifying with my characters.' Her tone was deliberately light, but her heart was beating furiously. What could she have meant? Where had that extraordinary idea come from?

Garth hovered with the wine bottle. 'Drink up, Phee,' he said. 'This is a good South African red. Bet they didn't have anything as splendid as this back in the twelfth century.'

He winked at her and suddenly normality returned. She drained her glass and pushed it towards him for a refill. 'Thanks, Garth,' she said breathlessly. 'Certainly not from South Africa anyway.'

Four

B oth Phoebe and Kate found sleep difficult that first night. The eerie cry of owls, wind in trees, birds in thatch, all the small country noises contrasted strangely with the customary racket and din of the London streets. The close proximity of environment rather than humanity was strangely disturbing, a tranquillity that needed more than merely a few hours' adjustment.

Eventually Phoebe slipped from bed, threw her shawl around her shoulders and went to the window. The moon was bright and she could see the moors rising stark and beautiful against the sky. Close by were the stones of an earlier building. The site had been cleared recently and the outline of some ancient walls discovered. She stared at the ruins for a long time. The whole scene looked quite ethereal, mysterious in the moonlight. Then abruptly she drew the curtains across the window and put the bright central light on. The room was immediately flooded with a garish brilliance.

She looked at her computer, wondering if she should switch that on too. Mercifully the keyboard was almost silent in use. If sleep refused to come, then perhaps the words would flow instead. She pressed the switch and watched as the machine sprang into life. It was a magic box of hidden miracles from which this next book with all its complex characters would emerge. She pulled her shawl more comfortably around her shoulders and began to write. Her fingers flew over the keyboard and she was unaware now of the glaring light. The room smelt vaguely of things out of place, wood smoke, animals, herbs again.

An hour later she stared at the screen and then saved her work to the hard drive and floppy disk rather than print it out.

The printer was noisy. She would wait until morning for that. She switched everything off and slid back into bed, and this time she slept.

Kate in the next room had been awake for what seemed like the whole night. At the first glimmer of daylight she too pushed back the duvet and padded softly in her bare feet over to the window with its view of the great sweep of moorland. She longed to be out there on the path that led to the top of the hill, wanted to stand in the very centre of the ancient hut circle that lay just below the tumble of rocks. If Dominic were here they would go together. She wrapped her arms around her body and longed for him. The longing was worse than she had expected. First love was supposed to be all-consuming, a passion that devoured one to bits. Well, she must be experiencing it for real. The magic of early morning in a place like this pandered to a broken heart!

Silently she pulled on jeans and sweatshirt, pushed her feet into trainers and creaked her way down the uneven stairs. The great iron bolt slid easily back, and the large key turned silently in its well-oiled keyhole. Once outside she stood transfixed, overcome by an unexplained rush of singular emotion. The sun had just risen and the sky was a brilliant dappled crimson. She walked quickly up the footpath that led to the open moorland, pushing through the tall bracken that threatened to obliterate the track here and there.

Eventually she came out on to the open space at the top where heather and gorse bloomed together at this time of year, the yellow and purple making a great fiery vista of colour that almost matched the sky. Every blade of grass touched with early morning dew appeared to be quivering and alive, while every note of birdsong echoed in her head with strange intensity.

A granite outcrop crowned the summit. Kate found the ancient hut circle just below it and stood for a moment quite still in its centre. Then she sat down feeling the sun's first rays warming her back. 'Dominic, where are you? Why aren't you here with me in this magical place?' She spoke the words aloud, but she knew that he never really would be with her.

His vocation, his calling to become a priest would always be an impenetrable barrier between them. The occasional nights they had spent together had always been totally chaste. 'Why not the Church of England?' she had said. 'They have married priests.' He had merely shaken his head and hugged her close, which made it all so much worse.

And now Phoebe was writing about Thomas à Becket! And suggesting that he might have had a lover! Suddenly she was overcome by a strange trembling feeling of enhanced sensation, uncanny feelings of immeasurable grief and loss, a despair that seemed not to be of this time or even of her own life, and definitely of this place.

She hugged her knees and gave herself up to these mysterious perceptions. She looked around expecting to see someone, but there was nothing, just empty moorland and a pony munching the sparse grass. Making an effort to gather her thoughts she jumped to her feet, aware now of the cold wetness of the dewy ground seeping through her jeans and trainers. Quickly she retraced her steps down the track. Aunt Tally had suggested last night that she might like to come round for a cooked breakfast every morning and suddenly it seemed like a wonderful idea. Phee would only be having her customary muesli and fruit.

Running down the track, jumping over stones and patches of tufty grass, she came again to Litford. Phoebe was up, just pouring a bowl of cereal. 'Hi, Nonna,' Kate said. 'I couldn't sleep either. I heard you working in the night.'

There were some sheets of paper lying on the breakfast table. 'I hope I didn't wake you,' Phoebe said. 'I wrote a surprising amount actually. It just flowed.'

'May I see?'

Phoebe put her bowl down and picked up the papers. 'Yes, I suppose so. I've just printed it out.'

Kate read silently, totally engrossed. Eventually she looked up. 'It's amazing. Where did you get it all from?'

Phoebe shrugged. 'I've no idea really. Out of my head I suppose, but it was a bit of a surprise, even to me.'

Kate very carefully and precisely put the papers down on the table again, straightening the pages. 'Are you being taken over, Nonna?' she said with an effort at flippancy. 'You know, like people who write music and stuff and say that Mozart or Shakespeare is using them to recreate themselves.'

'Don't be silly,' Phoebe said sharply. 'I'm an author. I'm supposed to have a vivid imagination.'

'Well, it's exciting.' Kate brushed grass from her jeans and washed her hands at the sink. 'I'm going over to Aunt Tally's for breakfast. She offered me a fry-up. Garth likes the whole works.'

'Fine,' Phoebe said. 'And after that? Any plans?'

Kate shook her head. 'Not as far as I know. I think Janice wants to show me her new mare. We might ride a bit. Do you want to be left in peace?'

Phoebe nodded. 'That's OK by me. See you when I see you.'

It was midday before Kate bounced into the house again. 'Still at it?' she asked. 'It's a lovely day, Nonna. You should be outside instead of stuck in front of that computer.'

Phoebe had brought her laptop into the kitchen where it now sat in the centre of the table surrounded by papers and books. She grinned at Kate. 'Just what I was thinking. And another thing I was wondering about is whether I should go to France soon?'

'France? Whatever for? We've only just arrived here.'

'Thomas spent a lot of time there. He went back and forth as though it was the easiest thing in the world. I thought I might go from here just for three days or so. Would you mind?'

Kate looked at her in amazement. 'And leave me all alone in this creepy house? I'd be terrified.'

Phoebe shook her head. 'It was an idea I had while I was working this morning. I could go with Talitha. She needs a break. You could stay over at High Mead.'

Kate considered. 'In that case I suppose I wouldn't mind. You're right about Aunt Tally. Have you asked her yet?'

'No. I wanted to see what you thought about the idea first.'

Kate opened the refrigerator and poured a glass of orange juice. 'Want one?' she asked, carton poised.

'No thanks. I need a coffee. Caffeine keeps my brain cells

working.' Phoebe got up, stretched her aching back, did a few shoulder exercises and put water in the kettle.

'How will you get to France from here? Wouldn't it be easier from London?'

'Plymouth to Roscoff. It's just Normandy I need to visit for now.'

Kate flopped down on one of the kitchen chairs. 'Who's going to do all the cooking for greedy Uncle Garth? Janice and me I suppose?'

'That was the rough idea.'

'We're both vegetarians,' Kate said.

'Then convert him.'

'You must be joking, but OK you're on. It might be fun. If Janice and Aunt Tally like the idea I'll go along with it.'

Talitha was enthusiastic, and with the plans swiftly made they were across the Channel and heading for Avranches, their first point of call. On the evening of that first day, after checking in at their hotel, they strolled into the grounds of an old friary, now a public park. Phoebe looked around her with pleasure. 'Thanks, Tal,' she said, 'for arranging everything, and for driving. The hotel seems great too.'

'Just a lucky dip,' Talitha said. 'I hope the Bayeux one is as good.'

But Phoebe didn't hear this last remark. She stopped, suddenly transfixed, staring at a paving stone at her feet. Slowly she read aloud, 'Here King Henry II knelt to make amends in public for the murder of Thomas à Becket!'

Talitha stared at it, fumbled for her guidebook and opened it at the page she had already marked. In the failing light she too read aloud, 'On the site of the destroyed cathedral, the spot is marked where Henry knelt to do penance for the murder in 1170 of Thomas à Becket in Canterbury Cathedral.' She paused for a moment and looked at her sister. 'You're not going funny again are you?' she asked.

'What do you mean, going funny?'

'Like you did at home when Garth lit the candles?'

Phoebe paled a little, but then she laughed. 'No, I won't

46

go back eight hundred years just yet,' she said. 'What else does it say?'

'That there's a memorial here to General Patton too, the Normandy landings and all that. A bit more up to date. A mere fifty-odd years ago.'

Across the water sea birds called eerily in the rapidly falling dusk, adding to the poignancy of the quiet garden. 'Such a lot of ghosts,' Phoebe said.

1172

There is no garden, but a great cathedral in Avranches. Henry II, holding the Holy Gospels in his hands and with his young son beside him, swears that he had not desired the killing of the Archbishop of Canterbury, and that he bitterly repents the words he spoke angrily and in haste which sent his impetuous and foolhardy knights speeding from France to England on their bloody errand.

The sounds of plainsong blend with the calling of gulls and Henry weeps for his folly. He kneels in humility before the papal legates and vows to carry out all their commands. He must provide, at his own expense, two hundred knights to fight the Crusades in the Holy Land for a whole year. This will be under the command of the Knights Templar. He promises to return all the possessions that have been confiscated from Thomas to the Church of Canterbury, and he is to fight the Moors in Spain if the Pope so wishes. He acknowledges that Thomas, his one time friend and latterly his enemy, is a martyr and will possibly be canonized as a saint. He shudders at the enormity of his crime and bends again to kiss the cathedral floor. His tears run down and darken the stones like Thomas's blood darkened the stones of that other cathedral far away across the breadth of France and England.

In the small French hotel that night Phoebe partly awakens from sleep and cannot tell where she is. She lies awake and yet not awake, seeing clearly the ravaged face of a man, a king. She is not familiar with kings. This king weeps. The great cathedral in which she appears to be was destroyed in the French revolution. The guidebook told her so. She remembers seeing the stone marking the place of the king's remorse in the garden yesterday.

Slowly she becomes fully awake. She can hear the rhythmic breathing of her sister in the other bed and gradually she remembers that she is on holiday in Avranches, and that she is in the twenty-first century, not the twelfth. She wishes that French hotels had tea-making equipment. She longs for a cup of tea. She will say nothing of this strange dream. She lies still for a time and convinces herself that it really is only a dream, nothing more dramatic.

They reached Bayeux in the afternoon of the next day, found the hotel that Talitha had booked and to Phoebe's delight managed to find a shop offering real English tea. 'How did Thomas manage without a cuppa?' Phoebe said flippantly.

'It seems more important to you than the cathedral you've come to see!' Talitha said.

'Almost.' Phoebe poured herself a second cup and stared out of the window at the great, soaring walls of the ancient building that she was just able to glimpse. 'I can't wait to see the tapestry though. That's the most vital bit of research.'

'Tomorrow,' Talitha said. 'We'll get there early. I believe there are usually long queues.'

That evening they went for a walk through the town's narrow medieval streets, tantalizingly past the closed gates of the museum now housing the tapestry, the *Centre Guillaume le Conquerant*, past antique shops and tourist shops until they came to the cathedral itself. The great walls were floodlit and Phoebe stared at the ancient stones in awe. 'They give off vibes,' she said, touching them. 'Just think, Thomas probably came here to see the tapestry.'

'In the cathedral?'

Phoebe nodded. 'I've been reading up on it. It was hung in the nave and was dedicated in 1077, even before Thomas's time, so presumably it was there during his endless visits to France. It was only moved to its special building in comparatively modern times.'

'And we'll see it tomorrow,' Talitha said. 'You're even making me feel excited.'

The crowds were almost impossible, but Phoebe was determined that nothing should spoil this visit. First she and Talitha shuffled a trifle impatiently past the series of obligatory displays explaining the background and history. Clutching their audio guide that told the whole story as they reached each section, they moved along with the throng. All nations seemed to be here, each person magically listening to the commentary in their own language. Phoebe hardly heard the clipped English words. Her eyes were on the still vibrant length of embroidery behind its protective glass, and she was completely enthralled.

'It's all here, Tally,' she whispered. 'This is how it was. All of life is here just as Thomas would have known it. Look at the animals, the food, everything.' She clasped her hands together, closed her eyes for a fleeting second, opened them and saw not the twentieth century display, probably a replica, she had been dismayed to learn, but the same pictures, the same elaborately worked portrayals of twelfth-century life, hung not here, but around the ancient nave of the cathedral.

The precious masterpiece is unprotected and the light is dim. Candles flicker in the draught from a window or door. Phoebe puts out her hand and touches the cloth, feels the unevenness of the embroidery and her heart fills with a sense of loss that she cannot understand. And there is the same fragrance of herbs that she is so often aware of. Then perspiration, the clinging stench of unwashed bodies. Always the two together.

1138

Thomas is walking around the nave, examining the pictures that have been hanging here for more than seventy years. He thinks of Bishop Odo, Bishop of Bayeux and Count of Kent, who had commissioned the work. It tells of the Norman conquest of England in 1066, sixty years before his birth. His heart swells with self-importance for he is proud of his Norman ancestry, but nevertheless he looks with pity at the portrayal of the Saxon

*King Harold with the arrow in his eye. He walks around the
dimly lit display and touches the threadwork on the surface of
the linen. He thinks of Catherine and the embroidery which
she hates. Then his heart thumps betrayingly and he wonders
how she is faring in the far south-west of England where her
parents have sent her to be married. He thinks of her unknown
husband with a stab of hatred, an emotion so strong that it
surprises him mightily.*

*But his thoughts do not remain with Catherine for long.
He is here with his friends, fellow students at the college
of Notre Dame in Paris. They have ridden down to Bayeux
specifically to see this tapestry and to glory in their Norman
inheritance, but also to enjoy themselves. Bayeux is a town of
many pleasures and Thomas thinks, a trifle reluctantly, of his
vow of chastity. He is determined to keep this rather uncomfortable pledge whatever the temptations to do otherwise. His
future career probably depends on it. The Pope disapproves
passionately of married clergy, and even clerics in the Church
are outwardly chaste. His deep and early love for Catherine
helps. If he cannot have her then he will have no one.*

Phoebe blinks and puts her hand out to touch the tapestry
again but she cannot. It is well protected. Yet she can still
feel the fabric, the stitches beneath her fingers. A dream, a
vision again. She is not in the cathedral of course, but in the
new museum built to house this ancient treasure. Talitha is
beside her and there is a great crush of tourists.

They came out into the sunlight and Phoebe felt bemused, a
little frightened. Her strange visions were happening again and
without her consent. But this latest time had been so beautiful.
Perhaps she should accept what appeared to be happening to
her. Maybe it was some priceless gift.

Back in Devon Kate and Janice were in Talitha's splendid
kitchen preparing the evening meal. 'Dad will only eat proper
things,' Janice said, raising her eyes to the ceiling. 'By
proper he means meat, lots of it, roast potatoes and three
vegetables.'

'Disgusting. I don't know how your mother puts up with

50

him.' Kate put water on to boil for the runner beans that Janice was laboriously slicing.

'Easy. She likes the same things on the whole. She's never worked so she has plenty of time.'

'What do you mean, never worked? It looks like hard labour for life to me.'

Janice shrugged. 'I suppose so. Wouldn't do for me. I've no intention of getting married. Might shack up with a guy one day as long as he's veggie and prepared to do all the cooking.'

'Dommy's old-fashioned,' Kate said. 'Not a new man at all.'

'You're not really serious about him are you?' Janice scooped the beans into a pan.

'I wish I wasn't.' Kate looked dreamily out of the window. 'I adore him to bits. What am I going to do?'

Janice flopped down on one of the kitchen chairs, cupped her face in her hands and stared at Kate. 'As far as I can see you've got three choices.'

'Oh? And what are they then?'

'The first one's obvious. Give him the push. The second is to persuade him to move into the twenty-first century. As far as I can see he's living in a sort of time warp. The third choice, if he really goes on with this idea of being a priest, is to live with him secretly. You'd be his mistress and slave for the rest of your life. Pretty dire if you want my opinion.'

Kate poured boiling water on the beans, set them on the Aga and sat down opposite her cousin. 'Saint Augustine had a lover,' she said. 'And even a wife I believe, but he was more keen on the salvation of his immortal soul than supporting the mother of his son.'

'Typical,' Janice said. 'Where do you get all this fascinating information?'

'Phoebe's research. Hugo dug it up for her from the library I believe.'

'Interesting. Do you think Thomas à Becket really had a mistress down here in Devon?'

Kate shrugged. 'Who knows? Phee said that according to the records of the time he led a blameless life. In that department anyway.'

'Impossible, unless he was gay.'

'No one knows about that either. It's all conjecture.'

Janice laughed. 'Let's have a drink.' She fetched a bottle of red wine from the rack and struggled to open it. Eventually succeeding she poured two glasses and slumped down again. 'Excellent,' she said. 'I'm glad my dad appreciates good wine. It's one of his better points.'

'I keep dreaming about a girl of the period,' Kate said. 'Her name is always Catherine and she's a friend of Thomas. It's very odd. Of course Phee is constantly talking about her book and I suppose it sticks in my mind. The dreams have been more frequent since we came here.'

'D'you mean you get into the time travelling thing as well then?'

Kate shook her head. 'No, just dreams. I should be scared if I had some of the experiences that Phee has.'

'Do you think she really does go back?'

'No, of course not. At least, I keep telling myself that she can't. It's not possible is it?' There was alarm in her voice now.

'I don't know. You hear all sorts of odd things lately.'

Kate shivered in spite of the heat of the kitchen. 'Let's talk about Dommy. He'll be here in a day or two.'

Janice got up and removed the beans from the hottest plate of the Aga to the cooler one. 'Are you going to sleep with him?'

Kate shook her head. 'No, we never have. We've been strictly platonic, like we're brother and sister. It's horrible.'

'Seduce him then.'

Kate looked up, startled. 'D'you think I should?'

'Why not? I know I would. Try, and see what happens!'

Dominic looked up from the book he had been reading all the way from Paddington. He stared out of the window amazed at the closeness of the sea. This was the first time he had been to Devon.

'Lovely view.'

He nodded agreement. The girl sitting opposite him had been a great annoyance for most the journey with her frequent telephone calls and inane conversations with faceless cronies whom he could only imagine were as witless as she appeared to be. He looked at her and at the offending mobile which she was now, thankfully, putting into its case. Perhaps at last he was to have some peace.

'Dawlish,' she said. 'Sometimes the train doesn't stop here. If it's rough and the sea's over the wall you can't get off.' She hauled her rucksack from between the seats. 'You going much further?'

'Newton Abbot,' he said.

'Only about ten minutes. Pity we didn't get talking before. You were so into that book I didn't dare interrupt. Visiting the girlfriend?'

Speechless, he nodded.

She grinned at him and winked. 'Have a great time and don't be good. Wish it was me. Cheers then.' She shouldered her rucksack and staggered down the carriage.

On the platform he watched her search the windows and when she saw him she waved and blew a kiss. He waved back, slightly embarrassed and thanked providence that she hadn't pressed him to talk during those long hours. Perhaps even the intrusion of a mobile phone was better than that. He closed his book, put it into his bag and stared at the sea which was so close to the track now that it seemed the carriages would at any moment plunge into the waves. He watched children paddling and a multitude of people enjoying themselves on the beach.

He thought of Kate. Why was he coming all this way to see her? He knew that their relationship might come to nothing eventually and she probably knew that too. So could they go on seeing each other like this? Could a man and a woman have a lasting and entirely platonic friendship? He doubted it. If he couldn't force his appetites and desires into submission perhaps he had no right to enter the Church. He had agonized for weeks and was no nearer a solution. Yet he was sure he had been called by God to this vocation and must submit to this calling however hard it proved to be.

Thomas watches at his mother's bedside and his eyes fill with tears as he sees her weakness. He has spent two years studying in Paris and had hoped for much longer. Learning delights him and he takes pride in his quick mind and powerful intellect. But a messenger came lately from London with the news of his mother's illness. His father needs him and now he has come. The journey has been difficult, for England's roads are not safe for the traveller as they had been in the reign of good King Henry I. The new king is weak-willed and does not enforce law and order.

The house is quiet and Roesa lies in the solar on a fur-covered pallet, for although it is high summer she is cold. Her daughters are with her: Agnes, young and full of misery; Roheise, named in likeness of her mother, married now and expecting her first child; and Mary who has come from Barking Abbey. Thomas looks at his sisters and especially at Mary and he remembers Catherine. The girls had been friends. He can see them in his mind as they were when they were all children. They had played together and Mary and Catherine had studied with the same tutor. Catherine had wanted to be a scholar, impossible for a woman unless in the confines of a convent, a vocation that Mary has chosen.

A great well of misery, of emptiness, fills his heart and this is not for his mother alone. Now that he is back in London the full measure of what he has lost overwhelms him. In Paris he could comfort himself with thoughts of his work and his great ambitions, but here he can see Catherine in every corner, can hear her merry laugh, can remember the way she looked at him during those last days, and most poignant of all, can remember the day she lay in his arms for that one time of sinful, forbidden loving.

And now she lies nightly in another man's arms. His hands clench into fists and his face flushes red with anger and resentment, anger made more terrible because he knows that it is of his own making. Had he insisted, he knows that their parents would have given in to his wishes eventually. Catherine would have been given to him for a wife, and he is sure that is what she wanted too.

Roesa dies at Lammastide when the sun is bright and would have been streaming into the solar had not Roheise hung a tapestry over the window so that its light should be muted. Thomas remembers other Lammas days when his mother had baked special loaves from the first ripe corn so that they could be consecrated in the church in thankfulness to God for the harvest. He brushes tears from his eyes surreptitiously. They are tears for his mother and his lost love and the two are inextricably bound.

He has given up the girl he loves, partly because of his mother's intense desire to see him fulfil a great vocation in the Church, and now she will not be here to see that fulfilment, and Catherine is not here either. He is doubly bereft.

He kneels and takes the cold hand in his and vows silently that her hopes for him will come to pass. There is nothing left to him now but the will to succeed. Nothing shall stand in his way. Perhaps his mother is already in the heaven in which she so firmly believed. And if so she will surely know that her son will strive with all his might to be worthy of her. Perhaps one day Catherine too will know that the sacrifice they have both made is for a worthwhile end.

After the ceremonies are performed and Roesa is buried in the hard sun-baked earth, Thomas and his sister Mary sit alone in the solar. Their married sister has returned home.

'What will you do, Thomas?' Mary enquires. 'Will you return to Paris?'

'I cannot. Our father is alone now,' he says. 'And there isn't enough money. I must stay in England and work for my living. I am to be clerk to Osbert Huitdeniers, the new justiciar.'

'It will be a start,' Mary says. 'Our mother's prophesies for you were assured and confident. You will do great things one day.'

'I hope so. I want to honour her trust.' Then he hesitates and eventually manages the question that has been increasingly urgent in his mind since he came home. 'Do you hear from Catherine? Is she well?'

Mary nods and looks at her brother with compassion. 'She is well, I believe. You must forget her, my dear. I know that your heart was given to her but it was not to be, not in God's plan.'

'What is God's plan and how can we know it, Mary?'

'That is the eternal question,' she replies. *'You would need someone much wiser than I to give you an answer.'*

'I'm glad Dommy's coming before Phoebe and your mum get back from France,' Kate said. 'She's doesn't really want him here.'

They were on the way to the railway station at Newton Abbot in Janice's old clapped-out Ford. 'Why's that? She's known him all his life I thought. Wasn't his mother her friend?'

Kate nodded. 'It's because he intends to become a priest – the Roman Catholic variety, as you know. I'm pretty sure that's the only reason.'

'A big reason,' Janice said.

Kate sat in silence for much of the journey. Her delight in the prospect of three days with Dominic was considerably marred by the general consensus of opinion that this friendship wouldn't do, couldn't last.

The journey seemed to take for ever but at last Janice pulled up in the station forecourt and found a parking place. 'I'll wait here for you,' she said. 'You'll want to meet lover boy on your own.'

Kate gave her a withering look. 'Thanks, and don't call him that.' She jumped down from the vehicle and grinned at her cousin. 'Wish me luck,' she said.

'The train from London Paddington will arrive shortly at platform . . .' Kate's pulse raced and her colour flared. And then it was here, crowds pouring out and amongst them Dominic. She ran towards him. He dropped his bag, opened his arms for her and crushed her tightly to him.

'Kate,' he whispered. 'Oh Katy I've missed you so much!'

Five

'The car's over there.' Kate released Dominic's hand guiltily as they left the station building. 'The disreputable old Ford,' she said, nodding in the direction of the battered vehicle. 'Janice drove me.'

'Your cousin?'

'Sort of. Phoebe's sister's daughter. What does that make her exactly?'

'Search me.'

They walked self-consciously to the car, Kate aware that Janice was watching them, probably weighing Dominic up. First impressions were crucial.

'Janice, this is Dominic,' Kate said. 'Dominic, meet Janice, my sort-of cousin.'

'Hi there.' He dropped his rucksack on to the ground and grinned at her. 'Thanks for coming to fetch me.'

Janice sat firmly in the driver's seat, hands clenched on the steering wheel. 'No problem,' she said. 'Nice to meet you at last. We've heard a lot about you. Can't think why you haven't come to stay before.'

'Me neither,' Dominic said.

'He always went gallivanting off to that place of his in the sun every summer while Phee insisted she and I just came to Devon,' Kate contributed. 'I was jealous.'

'Place in the sun?' Janice sounded impressed.

'Italy. Dad's sold it now.'

'Pity,' Janice said. 'Do you mind if we do some shopping before we go home? Need to stock up on grub with two guys to feed. Dad likes his meat.'

'Janice and I are doing all the cooking,' Kate explained. 'Aunt Talitha and Phee are in France.'

57

'Don't go to any trouble for me.' Dominic stowed his rucksack in the boot which Kate had opened for him. 'I'm vegetarian. Bread and cheese suits me fine.'

Janice eyed him appreciatively. 'You didn't achieve all that muscle and vigour on just bread and cheese.'

'A few potatoes and carrots as well I suppose.'

'Right. We'll make sure we get a good supply of those. Let's get going then.' Janice started the engine. 'I expect you two love birds want to sit in the back. It's a bit doggy, but I did make an effort to brush some of the hairs out before we left.'

Kate glared at her. 'Dominic can sit in the front with you,' she said firmly. 'He'll be able to see more of the view!'

'Righto. Whatever you like. Not much view between here and Sainsbury's though.' Janice leaned over and opened the front passenger door and eventually, with a grinding of gears, she drove out of the car park and into the traffic.

'We're not sleeping at Litford, the old house,' Kate explained when they later pulled round to the back of High Mead. 'This is my aunt and uncle's place. They own both of them. Litford is five minutes away. I'd be scared out of my wits to be there on my own while Phoebe's in France.'

Dominic grinned. 'Ghosts?'

'Probably. Presences anyway.'

'What's the difference?'

'Not a lot. Presences sounds less sensational, more Phee.'

'You've got my brother's room,' Janice told Dominic. 'He's away. You'll have to excuse the mess.'

'No problem.' Dominic retrieved his rucksack and followed the girls into the house.

Kate, a trifle self-consciously, said, 'I'll show you up.' She remembered her cousin's words when they were making the bed. 'You can shack up with him if you like,' Janice had said. Kate had replied indignantly that of course she would do no such thing. 'It would put him off completely,' she had added a trifle ambiguously. Janice had laughed and reminded her that she thought seduction was on the cards. 'Yes, but not so blatantly,' Kate had replied.

Now, recalling this conversation, she felt a flush rising from her neck until it seemed to envelop her completely. 'Will this be all right for you, Dommy?' she asked nervously. 'We tried to clear up the room a bit and stack away some of the rubbish.'

He dumped his things on the floor and looked at her. 'Great. Luxury in fact.' He went to the little casement window and stared out at the vista of moor and rocky outcrop. 'A nice change from London, and from college too for that matter.'

'We'll have some walks. There are wonderful places to discover.'

'I promised Father O'Reilly that I'd visit Buckfast Abbey while I'm in Devon. He asked me to take some photographs for him. He spent some time there apparently when he was a student. Would that be OK with you?'

Kate nodded but her heart crashed to her feet, as it was often apt to do whenever she was reminded of vocation and religion and Dominic's predilection for both. 'It's not far,' she said. 'Yes, we'll go there. I shall light a candle for . . .' She paused. What was dearest to her heart? She wanted to say *for you, Dommy*. 'For my grandmother,' she said. 'For Phee.'

1143

'Do you think the barons will swear fealty to a woman then?'
Thomas asks doubtfully.

Clement Beriset, his new friend and fellow clerk, shakes his head. 'The Empress Matilda is the old king's rightful heir to be sure, but Stephen has a good hold upon the crown.'

Thomas frowns and thinks of the anarchy and lawlessness that has filled the land ever since the death of Henry. 'Stephen isn't firm enough to be a king of England. I suppose we are an insubordinate race. We need strong rule. Do you suppose Matilda could do any better?'

Clement laughs. 'I've heard that she's tough and capable like her father. If she combines tact and goodwill with strength and competence she just might be able to sway the barons in her favour.'

'I believe she lacks all charm,' Thomas says. 'From what I hear she wouldn't be to my taste at all.'

Clement glances at his friend in surprise. 'I had come to suppose that you are not interested in women.'

'What gives you that idea?'

'You never want to come wenching.' They are striding *through the meadows that border the river in this leafy part of London. It is high summer and there is little birdsong to be heard, only the swish and plop of water from a mill wheel and the voices of peasants tending their strips of land. 'Am I right, Thomas?' Clement persists. 'Have you an aversion to women?'*

'I've no stomach for wenching if that's what you mean, but no, I've no aversion to women. My mother was very dear to me, as are my sisters.' Unspoken he adds, 'And one other.' *He hears the words unwillingly in his head and knows that they have come without his consenting. His lips are set in a firm hard line.*

'Mother and sisters are not quite what I meant,' Clement says. There is a trace of wariness in his voice.

His meaning penetrates Thomas's melancholy and he is at once amused. He and Clement have not known each other for long. It is only a few weeks since Clement joined him in the household of Osbert Huitdeniers, the justiciar. Thomas notices, with further amusement, that Clement has increased the distance between them slightly as they walk. He laughs. 'Don't worry, Clement,' he says. 'I am not of that persuasion. You are quite safe. In an excess of zeal and piety I took a vow of celibacy. Foolish perhaps but at the time I felt sure that it was the way I must go.'

'You mean to become a priest or monk?'

'My mother thought so – priest that is, not monk, heaven forbid. And now she is dead I feel I should continue on that path.'

'Do you honestly believe that you will be able to keep celibate for ever? It sounds unthinkable to me.'

Thomas shrugs. 'It's not impossible. Plenty of people do.'

They walk in silence for a time and Thomas can think of nothing but Catherine. Now that she is completely unattainable she has become, against his will, more and more beloved. She lives in his mind and in his heart, a forbidden fruit causing in him a restlessness that appears to increase rather than diminish. 'I have loved a woman,' he says, suddenly feeling the need to confide. 'She was promised to another, a man older and wealthier than I.'

Clement glances sideways at him and Thomas can feel his interest but also his slight impatience. As a clerk, celibacy is not strictly required and there are plenty of girls only too willing to satisfy both heart and body. Why then this stubborn adherence to a boyish vow, this refusal to consider a slighter love?

Clement plucks a dandelion and blows the seeds into the hot, still air. 'There are others,' he says mimicking Thomas's thoughts. 'Plenty who would be only too willing to comfort a handsome brute like you.'

'I compromised my vow once,' Thomas says. 'I can't forgive myself. I've told no one before and by all the saints I have no idea why I'm telling this to you, Clement.'

'Maybe I have a talent for the confessional. Perhaps it is I who should become a priest.'

Thomas says nothing but again remembers clearly, as though it had been but yesterday, the time when he set aside his mother's visions for him, offended his God, and worst of all, betrayed the girl he still loves. Catherine had given herself willingly to him, hardly knowing at first what she did, and he had taken advantage of her innocence and her love. He cannot put this memory out of his mind however much he tries and neither can he stomach the idea of going with any other woman.

'Forget her, Thomas,' Clement says. 'There are maids in plenty in the taverns of London. Come with me tonight and enjoy yourself.' His voice is persuasive.

Thomas shakes his head. 'You go,' he replies. 'I shall walk by the river and read.'

Clement shrugs his shoulders in total incomprehension. 'As you will then,' he says. 'And be sure to stay awake to let me in when I am sated and surely drunk.'

That first night in Devon Dominic lay in the narrow bed and looked through the small window at the stars in the clear summer sky. He knew that he had been foolish to come here, impossibly foolish to believe that he could spend time with Kate and remain unscathed. He wondered, as he frequently did, just when their childhood friendship had changed. At what stage during the past months, years perhaps, should he have recognized the signs and taken steps to lessen the bonds that had become ever deeper.

He had imagined that he and Kate would grow naturally apart when he went to college, but he had been at seminary for two years now and still the break had not happened. He constantly told himself that they were more brother and sister; that both, lacking siblings, had turned to each other for the family they so greatly missed. But now he knew in his heart that he had deceived himself totally, and since his mother's death last year, Kate had become more dear to him, not less.

Perhaps part of him had always hoped that she would announce one day that she was interested in someone else. Yet even as the thought came to him now he clenched his fists in anger and realized that this wasn't truly what he wanted at all. So, was he fit to become a priest? Could he subdue the carnal desires that troubled him so much, and more important, could he deny Kate's love for ever?

As the troublesome thoughts chased each other through his brain, sleep refused to come. He tossed restlessly, thumping the pillows every few minutes. In his more foolish moments he had imagined that this short holiday might be a help in coming to terms with the uncomfortable facts of his vocation, a sort of testing, fighting the dragon. But ever since he had arrived here he had known that he had been deceiving himself, and to involve another in that fight was the ultimate selfishness.

'Yes, you can borrow the old jalopy,' Janice said. 'Dominic drives, I presume?'

'Of course.'

'So you're going to Buckfast then?' Janice was scrubbing potatoes under a running tap. 'It's a good place to visit and they do reasonable food.'

'Dommy wants to see the great stained glass window,' Kate said.

Janice nodded, scooped the potatoes out of the sink and piled them on to the draining board. 'It's very impressive,' she said. 'Even irreligious me was encouraged to say a little prayer and light a candle. By the way, did you know that Thomas à Becket visited Buckfast? I remember reading it in the guidebook. I'll rummage around and see if I can find it.'

'Great. I'll have to go again with Phee then, won't I, and she'll probably do one of her wobblies and go shooting back to the twelfth century.'

'Shouldn't think so,' Janice said. 'It was built in the nineteenth century. The ancient one doesn't exist any more.'

'That's no bar to Phee's time travelling escapades.'

'Does she really go back? You're not seriously saying that it's anything more than a sort of dream or vision are you?'

'I'm not sure,' Kate said. 'But she's always sensed things that no one else can. She sees auras, that sort of stuff.'

'Like in the paintings of the saints?'

'Yes, haloes. But not just around their heads. She sometimes knows about things before they happen.'

Janice shuddered. 'Second sight isn't it? What a ghastly idea. I'm glad my mum didn't inherit anything like that. *Is* it inherited?'

Kate shook her head. 'I don't know. If my dad had it he left no record of it. I think it can skip generations though.' She thought of the strange dreams she herself had been having lately. Where did the girl Catherine come from? The girl with the medieval clothes and the large dog. Was there some strange power or bizarre insight that she had perhaps fallen heir to after all? She very much hoped not.

'It would frighten me out of my life,' Janice said.

'I don't think it would. Not if you really had the gift.' Kate spoke firmly, hoping that what she said was true. 'I don't think Phee is frightened. It's just part of her. She's used to it.'

Dominic stared up at the imposing grey pile of Buckfast Abbey. 'I had no idea it would look like this,' he said. 'I knew it was new as abbeys go but somehow the picture in one's mind is always of weathered stone and great buttresses and gargoyles and things.' He took photographs from many different angles, and Kate watched him with love and with irritation.

'It isn't built in a modern style though,' she said. 'I read the guidebook last night in bed. The monks kept to the old Cistercian plan. The windows are Gothic and the arches are Anglo-Norman.'

Dominic laughed. 'My goodness, you have done your homework. Let's go inside and you can tell me a bit more.'

He strode to the entrance and Kate followed him. She felt suddenly alone and detached. This abbey, like most abbeys perhaps, was a bastion of maleness, a symbol of a male-dominated religion and its worship of a male god. Apart from Mary of course. And what of her? How did she rate as a woman, and did she have any real influence at all over the men by whom she was surrounded? Probably not, Kate irreligiously thought, and as she watched Dominic and saw his fascination with this place, her sense of isolation increased. She had dreamed again last night of the girl Catherine, and of Thomas à Becket too this time. Her grandmother's Thomas was how she thought of him now, yet in her dream he had been young and handsome and he bore a strange likeness to Dominic. She shivered at the remembered clarity of this dream, a dream that was not like ordinary dreams, and she walked more quickly and caught up with Dominic at the door.

He smiled at her, held out his hand. 'Come on, slowcoach,' he said. 'I can't wait to see if the great window is as spectacular as I've been told. And I need a couple of guidebooks to take home.'

They slipped inside and were for a time caught up in the tangible atmosphere of awe and devotion. They walked down the North Aisle and Kate stared at the altar dedicated to St Gertrude. So if you were a woman you had to be a nun or the mother of God to get any acknowledgement in this male-dominated religion, she thought dryly.

At the rings of flickering lights she stopped, groped for coins to put in the box and, like Phoebe in faraway Bayeux, she took two small slim candles. She held them in her hand for a moment and then lit each one and silently lifted the two most precious people in her life up to whatever god inhabited this place. She stood quietly and watched Dominic do the same. He had taken three and she wondered who were the recipients of his prayers. And were those prayers more precious to his God than hers were? After all he was male, and a believer, she reflected cynically. But he smiled at her again and she felt ashamed of her thoughts. He took her hand once more and together they walked without speaking up the steps to the great glass doors of the Chapel of the Blessed Sacrament. It was so modern, so vivid and so overwhelming that Kate's previous antagonisms melted away in the face of that stained glass Christ. They went into the chapel and to her great surprise she felt no embarrassment at kneeling beside Dominic and praying wordlessly for a solution to the intractable problem of her heart.

Later, in the restaurant, the heightened atmosphere of the abbey gave way to more mundane feelings. It was a bright, airy building and the array of self-service food looked tempting. 'We're eating a lot tonight,' Kate said. 'I thought we were only having a drink here.'

'Can't resist the vegetable lasagne,' Dominic said, loading his tray.

Kate laughed and her mood lightened considerably. She took a sandwich. 'So, what did you think of it?' she asked when they were seated.

'I suppose you mean the abbey not the meal,' Dominic said, tucking into the lasagne with obvious enjoyment. 'The meal's great and the abbey is impressive.'

'Just impressive?'

'Too modern. Blame Henry VIII.'

Kate took the guidebook and leafed through it. 'Here we are,' she said. 'Henry I started it. Henry II confirmed its charter and the eighth Henry plundered and ravaged it.' She finished the sandwich and stirred sugar into her coffee. 'And do you know who confirmed that charter in 1156? None other than our Thomas à Becket when he was Henry II's chancellor. Janice told me that he came here. She must have read it in this book. Phee will be entranced.'

'You know a lot about it,' Dominic said. He started to stack their crockery and cutlery on to the tray. 'Perhaps you ought to write this biography instead of your grandmother.'

'No fear,' Kate said. 'Too much like hard work. I was

horrified when she first told me about it. I thought some modern dickhead like the last one she wrote about might have been easier and more lucrative, but the charismatic Thomas is growing on me.'

'Then I'm glad he's dead,' Dominic said.

Kate looked at him quizzically. 'Let's walk on the moor on the way home, shall we?' she suggested. 'The weather's lovely and our boots are in the car.'

Phoebe and Talitha arrived back in Devon from France a couple of days later. Kate rushed out of the kitchen when she heard the car. 'Lovely to have you back,' she beamed. She threw her arms around Phoebe and kissed her. 'We've missed you a lot.'

'Ha ha,' Talitha said as she climbed out of the car. 'Missed my cooking more like.'

'That too,' Kate admitted. 'Dominic arrived just after you left as a matter of fact, so we've had two guys to cook for. He's round the back trying to fix Janice's old jalopy. It's given up the ghost again.'

Phoebe had forgotten all about Dominic. 'Of course,' she managed. 'He was always good with engines.' She saw her granddaughter's flushed happy face and immediately all the old worries returned.

They retrieved various pieces of luggage and went inside. 'There's post for you, Nonna,' Kate said. 'Letters from Hugo I think, judging by the postmark and handwriting. I don't know why you both still use snail mail. You should go for email now that you've got your new computer. You don't even text do you? Amazing.'

'You know I do email,' Phoebe said, 'but Hugo is still in the Middle Ages as far as all that is concerned.' She glanced at herself in the mirror on the kitchen wall, tried to fluff up her hair and frowned at her reflection. 'Any tea? I could down a whole pot. Pass Hugo's letters then.'

Kate retrieved them from the dresser and handed them to her grandmother.

Phoebe opened the latest one first. It was short, just one page. 'Still missing you, dearest Phee,' she read. 'I propose coming down on Friday if that's all right with you. I've found some interesting stuff about Thomas.'

The other one was longer, telling her of the time he had spent in the British Library on her behalf and listing some of the facts he had discovered.

'He's coming on Friday,' Phoebe announced.

'Brilliant,' Kate said. 'Dominic will still be here I hope. We'll have a party.'

Six

*C*atherine's baby is born at Michaelmas when the leaves
are beginning to redden on the trees and the wind
*sometimes blows cold off the moor. She holds the little scrap
in her arms and although she knows that this tiny mewling
thing is the source of all her troubles, still she loves him,
wishes him to be larger, healthier. But every time she holds
him to her breast he turns his head away and refuses to feed.
Each day he weakens and before the waning of the moon his
limbs are cold and his crying ceases. Catherine holds him for
a long time.*

*'God has seen fit to punish me, Eluned,' she says through
her tears. 'This child would have come between his father and
the destiny God has planned.'*

*Eluned is ignorant of the child's begetting and she has asked
no questions. She was ordered to keep silent about her young
charge and she has obeyed her instructions faithfully.*

*She looks at the small swaddled bundle in Catherine's arms
and she remembers the births of her own children. She has
been much blessed for they are all sturdy and have not ailed.
Now she is full of compassion for the girl she has come to
love, but she cannot help feeling that this little death is for
the best.*

*'It's not a punishment,' she says. 'The ways of God are
sometimes hard to understand, but your little one is with
Him in heaven. Don't be sad for your babe. The world is
a harsh place.'*

*Catherine knows that she means the world is harsh for a
bastard, for anyone without the protection and name of a
rightful father, and she is consumed with anger. Her lips set
in a determined line and yet she is not quite sure with whom*

she is angry. Is it Thomas and his dreams of greatness, his vision of future glory and importance that come before all else, or is it the God who manipulates mankind for His own ends and appears to think so little of womankind?

She pushes the wraps away from the little white face and covers the cold soft skin with kisses. In the fuzz of dark hair and the baby features she imagines she can see the face of the man she loves and whom she has lost for ever.

'Take him, Eluned,' she says. 'Take him and do whatever there is to do.'

She holds up the little bundle and Eluned crosses herself and gently takes the baby in her arms. She too bends and kisses the small face, and then she carries him quickly downstairs so that she can prepare him for his burial. She washes him carefully and dresses him in the fine christening gown that Catherine has been stitching laboriously for so many weeks. She had brought the delicate cloth with her and Eluned had often marvelled at its softness. She had sometimes reflected that the material alone would have cost enough to feed her family for many days, and at first she had been resentful. But now when she sees the babe washed and beautiful, her grudging ceases and she weeps a little.

Catherine calls to her that she wishes the last rites to be performed in her room and Eluned carries the child upstairs again and lays him in the cradle her husband had fashioned long ago for her own babes. Catherine shall not see the small coffin that is waiting below.

The room is poorly lit by a smouldering tallow dip and the window is shuttered for warmth. Eluned lights a candle, which she can hardly spare, but she is determined that the babe shall have all the luxury she can manage to speed him on his journey to heaven, where he will surely go once a priest's blessing has been given. It has been difficult to find a priest, for the church is far off and the track over the moor is rough and sometimes impassable. And a babe without a father's name is of little importance to the holy clerics anyway. But Eluned's husband has found a travelling friar who will come and recite the words for a small reward.

Catherine smiles when she hears this. 'It is better so,' she says. 'My father does not wish anything to be known of my baby's birth. A travelling friar will be all that we need.' There has been no baptism, for no one could be called in time, but the old man reassures them that he will add special prayers for the child that will overcome the Almighty's reluctance to look kindly on an unbaptized bastard.

Eluned sighs. All these profound thoughts are too much for her. Silently she sets the candle on the table beside the cradle. Catherine sits up in bed and her face is pale, but she is composed now and the tears are controlled. She listens to the voice of the friar as he drones on. He is speaking in Latin and she is the only one in the room who can understand any of it. She has not heard Latin spoken for a long time. The melodious sounds cause her concentration to wane and soon her thoughts drift away from this cold impoverished room with its sadness and its suffering and she is back in London at her lessons with Mary, or talking to Thomas in her parents' spacious house. The world had seemed to lie at her feet then.

The child is not to be buried in the churchyard. 'No name and no Christian grave,' Catherine says thoughtfully. 'And if he had lived you would have brought him up as yours, Eluned? Is that what my father arranged?'

Eluned nods. Catherine has only recently been told of the plans that were made for her child. 'So I should have lost him either way?'

'I would have been a good mother to him,' Eluned says. 'I would have loved him as my own.'

'I know that,' Catherine says. 'You have been more to me than my own mother.' This is the fifth day of her lying in and she has been allowed to get out of bed for an hour. She opens the wooden shutter on the bedroom window and looks out at the hill rising wild and remote to the tor above the house. She shivers and pulls her woollen wrap more closely around her shoulders. 'He shall be buried beyond the garden wall here,' she says. 'I know just the place.'

'I shall ask the men to prepare the ground,' Eluned says. 'You must tell me exactly where you want it done.'

'Between the young oak and the rowan tree,' Catherine

70

directs. 'Next to the stone barn where the ground rises so that the place shall be protected from the winter wind.'

So Catherine's son is buried in the place she has chosen. But as soon as she is pronounced well enough to go outside she stands and looks at the small mound of earth and feels a great rebellion surge within her. She runs to the pile of wood that is stored ready for kindling and chooses two sticks. She unties her girdle and with it binds them as carefully as she can into a cross which she pushes into the yielding earth. Then she hurries back to the house. 'I have some money left, Eluned,' she says. 'I want a stone engraved to mark the place.'

'That would not be your father's wish.'

'He will never know.'

Eluned is doubtful. 'And what shall be written there?' she asks as kindly as she can manage. Privately she thinks that a babe without a name hardly merits a costly stone.

'I want it recorded that he is the son of Catherine, and that he was born in this year of our Lord 1143, and died aged four days.'

And so it is done. A stonemason is summoned and the stone worked as Catherine decrees. 'Engrave the words in Latin,' she directs. 'My baby shall be remembered with dignity: Tom, Catherinae filius, hoc anno domini MCXLIII natus, quarto die obiit.*'*

Eluned stares at her in awe. To be able to read and write is an accomplishment only for priests and the very wealthy, and certainly not for a girl. 'How came you to know the Latin tongue?' she asks. 'And to write it too?'

Catherine again remembers Mary and their early studies together. 'I learnt with a friend,' she replies sadly. 'She is gone to be a nun.' She pauses for a moment and looks thoughtfully at the open door and the rising hills. 'Perhaps it would have been better if I had done the same.'

'Rubbish,' Eluned says briskly. 'You are young and healthy and your father will soon find a husband worthy of you. You will have many more babes, strong, healthy ones, mark my words.'

Catherine turns away and shrugs her shoulders. It has been her greatest sorrow that she was forced to tell Thomas an

71

untruth, to tell him that she was already promised in marriage. There had to be a reason for her hasty departure from London. No one was to know of her shame. Talk of a wealthy husband in the far south-west had been the pretence her parents had devised and commanded. Now she is sure that these lies will soon be turned into reality. Perhaps it will be a kind of relief. 'I have no doubt that my father will do as you say.' There is a coldness in her voice which makes Eluned shiver for her.

When the headstone is finished and delivered to the farm-house, Catherine stares at it for a long time. She places her hands over the surface and traces the words engraved into the granite. 'Will it last for many years?' she asks.

'Aye, Lady. A very long time indeed. It is small as you said, but the best and hardest granite I could find and the words are deep and well-chiselled.' The young stonemason looks at her and smiles in sympathy for she is so sad. He cannot help wondering how a gentlewoman, which she obviously is, comes to be living in such a place as this.

'Then have the wooden cross removed and put this in its place,' Catherine says. 'And my baby will be remembered for ever.' Her voice holds authority, an authority she has not shown since she came to Devon.

The months pass slowly for Catherine. She is soon com-pletely restored to health although not to happiness. Eventually instructions come from her father that she is to go to the priory at Bovey Tracey where she will continue her edu-cation until plans for a suitable marriage can be arranged. The betrothal is likely to be in Devon, he writes, for he has some connections, and she cannot return to London for it is thought by all their friends that she is already married.

She knows that her parents do not want her home. She has disgraced them, and the farther away she can be settled, the better they will be pleased – and of course Thomas is still in London. He was never mentioned as the cause of her troubles but she knows that her parents have their suspicions. They are neighbours and friends of Gilbert Becket, Thomas's father. They have been informed of the death of her baby and she can imagine that they have given thanks for such a convenient answer to the problem she posed.

For herself she hopes for little except that the man her father chooses for her will at least be reasonably young, and above all, kind.

When the day of her departure arrives she throws her arms around Eluned and hugs her. 'I shall never forget your kindness to me,' she says. 'Come and see me sometimes. It's not too far, only ten miles or so.'

'And how should I travel so far?' Eluned says. 'But don't fret. Perhaps the good Lord will send me the means one day.'

Catherine's escort is the young clerk to the Lord of the Manor of Parke. She is to ride pillion behind him the ten miles to the priory. He has a large powerful stallion and she looks at the beast with some awe. It is the kind of mount that Thomas always told her he wished to ride. There is another man also who will accompany them, obviously a servant. It is still not safe to travel the roads of England without an armed escort.

'Calder will watch for us,' she says. The great dog is beside her, looking up, looking worried. He need have no fear. She will go nowhere without him.

Catherine kisses Eluned fondly again before she is helped on to the back of the great horse. 'Keep the grave tended for me,' she whispers tearfully.

'I shall go every day,' Eluned says. 'And I shall find the tenderest and most beautiful heather for him this very morrow.'

As they move off, the dog loping as close as he dares to the powerful hooves, Catherine waves until the Litford farmstead with its loving security is out of sight. Eluned has been a mother to her during the worst months of her life. She determines to return as often as she can for the thought of a permanent separation is not to be borne, and also her baby lies here in the cold earth. She will want to lay flowers on the tiny mound on the sad anniversary of his birth. She prays earnestly that God and her father will provide her with a kind and gentle husband who will allow her do so.

*   *   *

73

With Phoebe and Talitha back from France and Dominic soon to return to London, Kate knew that she would be required to move back into Litford for the rest of the holiday.

'I shall miss you in the kitchen,' Janice said, grinning.

'I'm not a thousand miles away, just five minutes down the lane! I thought you'd be glad to get out of the kitchen yourself.'

'I am I suppose. Back to Mum's cooking.'

The two girls were sitting in the kitchen drinking coffee. 'Where's Dominic?' Janice said. 'He hasn't had breakfast yet.'

'Gone out.' Kate's voice was suddenly desolate. 'He gets up at some impossible hour and goes to the top of the tor. Probably to pray or something.' She cupped her mug in her hands and stared down at the creamy swirl on the top. 'We haven't resolved anything yet. He's as determined as ever to go on with his vocation.'

'What are you going to do then?'

'Seduce him like you recommended.'

This unexpected answer caused Janice to look at her cousin in amazement. 'I didn't think you'd actually try it!'

'Why not? There's no other way is there? It's today or never!'

Janice took another gulp of coffee. 'Well, good on you. I've never known you so determined and calculating.'

'I have to be if I'm to rival God. We're going for a long walk later, taking a picnic. There are wonderful little river valleys and secluded hidden places on the moor. I'm trusting Dartmoor magic and my own personal allure to make a miracle happen.'

Janice was suddenly serious. 'Religious fervour is the strongest of all the passions,' she said. 'It won't be easy.'

'Stronger than sex?'

'Perhaps. Think of suicide bombers. Can you imagine how anyone could march into a crowded shop or bus stop and blow themselves to bits? But they do, and all in the name of religion. No one would do that for love or romance.'

'It's more complicated than just religion, and they're promised lots of sex in the next life, apparently.'

74

'Fat chance, I say. I still think religion has a stronger pull than sex.'

Kate finished her coffee and carried her mug to the sink. 'I shouldn't bet on it,' she said.

Dominic returned an hour later. He sat down on the wooden bench at the kitchen door and unlaced his boots. 'What an amazing place this is,' he said.

'You've been out a long time,' Kate said, a trifle coolly. 'Coffee? I'm making sandwiches for our picnic. Remember?'

'Sorry.' Dominic padded through in his socks. 'I'd forgotten about the picnic. Not coffee, thanks. A cold drink would be great.' He washed his hands at the sink. 'I'm a bit muddy.' He looked guiltily at the brown marks he was leaving on the towel.

'I can see that. Did you fall down?'

'No. I thought I'd have another look at Litford on the way back.'

Kate looked at him curiously. 'Whatever for?'

'I wanted to examine the old boundary wall again. There's something I want you to see.'

'Oh? What?'

'A peculiar piece of stone. I think there are words engraved on it. They're barely decipherable but with some expert help we should be able to make some sense of them. I think it's Latin. It might interest Phoebe.'

Kate was hardly listening. She tore a piece of foil from the roll and wrapped the sandwiches she was making. Her thoughts were all on the day ahead, and on what she had planned, and her heart thumped when she looked at Dominic sitting with easy grace at the kitchen table. She smiled at him, went to the refrigerator and filled a glass with orange and passion fruit juice and set it before him. 'That OK?'

'Fine.' He drained the glass and poured a bowl of muesli from the packet on the table.

'I'll look at your stone this evening,' Kate said without much interest.

An hour later they were swinging along a grassy track hand in hand, bracken waist tall on either side, and then suddenly they came upon a clearer place where the gorse and heather were blooming together, yellow and purple in perfect harmony.

Dominic stopped and stared at the rolling hills crowned here and there with strange outcrops of rock. 'Why haven't I discovered Dartmoor before?' he said. 'I had no idea it was so savage, so untamed.'

'Because you always went to your parents' house in Italy,' Kate said reasonably.

He laughed. 'So I did, and all the time this magical, mystical place was here waiting for me!'

'Let's have a coffee break,' Kate said. 'I brought a flask.' She took his hand and pulled him towards a fallen sprawl of rocks. 'It's an old quarry or tin working.'

The sun was bright, larks were warbling high in the sky, and ancient oak trees, bent and gnarled by years of fierce winds from the west, were struggling for life between the granite blocks discarded in another, busier age. But in contrast two rowan trees stood resplendent and beautiful, their branches festooned with bright-red berries.

Dominic unfastened his rucksack and dropped it on the grass between the trees. Kate could feel him looking at her, knew with surprise that he wanted her as much as she wanted him. She could almost feel his conflicting emotions, his inexplicable devotion to his God that kept him from gathering her into his arms and pulling her to the ground. What kind of God could create these all-powerful appetites in His creatures and then forbid the fulfilment of them? she wondered angrily. But was it God, or was it the Church she was fighting? Whichever it was made little difference, she thought cynically. Both were equally powerful.

She sat down on the grass, opened her rucksack, took out the flask and stared disconsolately at it. Why in heaven's name had she not brought a bottle of wine instead?

Then suddenly Dominic took the flask from her hands and pushed it away so that it rolled down the slope and lodged itself in a clump of gorse. He threw off his anorak and pulled her into his arms, and Kate gave herself to his fiery and inexpert love-making. She made no attempt to stop him, rather the reverse, and responded with all the built-up passion of the past frustrating months and weeks. It was both uncomfortable and painful at first and she was aware all the time of a sharp stone in the small of her back, made more agonising by his weight pressing on to her body. But when it was all over, when they lay quietly in each other's arms, she knew that she had won. Had won part of the battle anyway. Yet perhaps there had been no battle, unless it had been with Dominic's God. To fight with God and win was indeed quite awesome. Hadn't Jacob done it? It was a battle particularly fitting to this enchanted place.

Suddenly she jumped to her feet, rearranged her clothes, retrieved the flask and poured coffee into two mugs. Dominic lay quite still, hands clasped behind his head, and watched her. Over them the rowan trees made a kind of arch, a witch's dome.

Phoebe collected Hugo from the railway station and took him immediately to Litford rather than to her sister's home.

'What do you think of the modernization?'

'Sensitively done,' Hugo said. 'But I still wouldn't want to live here all the time. Think of the winter!' He stood at the tiny kitchen window and peered out. 'How old did you say it was?'

'Talitha says the name was recorded in the Domesday Book.'

'That's around 1086.'

Phoebe looked at him in surprise. 'I thought you weren't interested in history.'

He grinned at her. 'You'd be amazed at the things I've found in the British Library. It's quite some place. I wish I'd discovered all its wonders before. While you've been gallivanting in France I've been doing a lot of work on your behalf.'

'So you said in your letter. I was very touched.'

'I enjoyed it. It's a long time since I studied anything other than finance and other boring economic rubbish. I hope some of my research will be of use to you.'

'I'm sure it will be. We'll have a working session tomorrow,' Phoebe said. 'Meanwhile come and have a breath of country air outside. It's only really the ruins that date back to Domesday. The house itself isn't so old, more like fifteenth century.'

Hugo stared at the wall surrounding the small enclosure behind the house and at the tumble of lichen-covered stones. 'Pity stones can't talk,' he said. He ran his hand over the rough granite and then paused. One particular piece of stone stood out from the others. 'Look at this. It's different from the rest of the wall, it's smoother and shaped.' He fumbled for his glasses and perched them on his nose. 'It looks as though someone else has recently been looking at it too.'

Phoebe came over to him and stared at the stone. She brushed its surface gently with her fingers. 'The moss and lichen have been partly cleaned from it,' she said. 'There seem to be marks cut into it.'

'Could it be Roman?' Hugo asked. 'They were great ones for engraving the details of their lives on to stones.'

'Not here. At least, I shouldn't think so. It's like a headstone from a grave, the kind of thing you see in very old cemeteries.

Hugo examined it more carefully, traced the indentations with his fingers. 'Definitely letters I should say. I suppose folk around here used any stones they could find for their building projects, and as most of them couldn't read, the marks wouldn't have meant anything.'

'It's from a baby's grave. See how small it is.' Phoebe surprised herself with her sudden certainty. 'And the words are in Latin. This is a terrible place, Hugo. I feel cold suddenly.' Tears sprang to her eyes.

Hugo looked at her with concern. 'Come on now, old girl. We can't possibly know for certain anything about it. It's very old, medieval probably. No need to start getting upset.' He straightened up and took her arm. 'We need some coffee.'

In the Litford kitchen Phoebe searched for tissues and wiped her eyes. 'Silly me,' she said. She found biscuits and some tinned milk. 'Sit down, Hugo dear and I'll make us a cuppa. Then you must unpack your things.'

Hugo, watching her, carefully made no further comment about the stone and the words they thought they had discovered on it. 'Where are we staying tonight? Here or at your sister's?'

78

'Here of course. Kate has been sleeping over at High Mead because she said she would be scared to be at Litford on her own with the ghosts!'

'Ghosts?'

'None reported but it feels a bit creepy sometimes.' She smiled at Hugo and set mugs and teapot on the kitchen table. Then suddenly and quite unexpectedly she saw in her mind the pathetic little stone they had just discovered, but clean and newly chiselled. She stood quite still, cold and frightened. *'Tom, Catherinae filius, hoc anno domini MCXLIII natus, quarto die obiit.'* The words came from nowhere into her head and she whispered them in a soft, clear voice that was not hers at all, in Latin and then more clearly in her own voice. 'Tom, son of Catherine, born in this year of our Lord 1143, died aged four days.'

Hugo stood up, caught her in his arms, soothed her and tried to mitigate his own fears. He made no enquiries, asked for no explanation, but kissed her gently, reassured her with his comforting strength, and as suddenly as the strangeness of the moment had come, so it dispersed. Normality returned and Phoebe responded to his cheerful support with relief. It was almost as though the moments of otherness had not happened. They drank their tea and Phoebe said nothing about those past moments. Instead, and again, quite unexpectedly, she felt that the one thing she wanted was to go to bed with Hugo. She knew that she needed him as she never had before. His solid, earthy presence would be her anchor and her rock.

She caught his hand, led him up to her little bedroom, and the unhappiness of the past that she had felt surrounding that tiny headstone was lost in the joy of their coupling. Twelfth-century despair gave way to twenty-first-century happiness. The world was whole and complete, the sadness of the baby's grave diminished. She sat up in bed and looked at Hugo with love and gratitude. 'Thank you,' was all she managed before he took her in his arms again and silenced her with his lips and his body.

An hour later Phoebe and Hugo walked over to High Mead. Talitha, warned by the barking of her dogs, was waiting for them at the back door. 'Nice to see you again, Hugo,' she said. 'Good journey?' She looked from one to the other and grinned. Phoebe's eyes were sparkling. There was a glow about her that Talitha had not seen for a very long time. Good for them, Talitha thought with, to her surprise, a trace of envy.

'Come and have a cup of tea,' she said. 'I've just made some scones and there's Devonshire cream to tempt both of you. Or perhaps a gin and tonic might be more appropriate?'

'Thanks, Tally. The tea just now. The gin can come later.' They went inside and sat at the kitchen table and feasted on Talitha's cooking. The contentment of the past hour remained with Phoebe but she felt a strange sense of unreality as well. The small stone and her uncanny knowledge of its inscription had unnerved her considerably. Then one of the dogs howled, an unusual, piteous call like the cry of a wolf.

Talitha looked up, concerned, and went to the back door to call them in.

'Calder,' Phoebe murmured.

Catherine is in despair. Her father's will has been made known to her. She is to leave the convent which has given her sanctuary and where she has been moderately happy. She is to marry the minor knight Rainald de Beck. She knows little of him.

'When you are my wife,' de Beck says, 'When you come to me at my house you may not have that dog.' He looks at the animal with distaste. He knows that Calder has never liked him, always growling in his presence.

Catherine stares at him in horror. 'Calder has been my friend and companion for the past five years or more. I cannot live without him.'

'I shall be your constant companion,' de Beck says. 'You will be with me to do my bidding and to serve my every whim and desire. There is no place for a great unfriendly beast like that in my household.'

'Then I cannot marry you.' Catherine pulls herself to her full height, small though she is compared to the large bulk of the man in front of her. 'Where I go, there Calder goes.'

De Beck laughs, a great sinister bellowing laugh. 'We shall

see about that, Catherine my dear. Your father and I have made
a bargain. You have no choice at all in the matter.' He turns
and strides out of the convent hall where he has been permitted
to visit her. Once outside he beckons his serving man. 'See
that the dog is captured and strung up by nightfall if it can be
managed,' he orders. 'He is probably sent outside the priory
walls at dusk. Watch for him. If you cannot catch him then I
trust your arrows to do their work.' He laughs, mounts his
great destrier and rides from the priory gate to the lodging
house from which he is to be married in two days' time.

'You'll eat with us tonight of course,' Talitha said later. 'I
don't suppose there's any food to speak of over at Litford.'

'Thanks. We'll do some shopping tomorrow,' Phoebe said.
'What about Kate and Dominic?'

'Them too,' Talitha replied ungrammatically. 'It's all arranged.
A salad and some bought quiches. Simple. Oven chips to fill
up if anyone wants them.'

Phoebe smiled. 'You're great, Tally. What would I do
without you?'

'You'd get along quite well,' Talitha said in her bossy,
organising voice. 'Just like you do all the time in London.
And now you can wash up these tea things and then go
and sort Litford out. I expect Hugo needs to unpack.' She
scraped cream into a small plastic container and put it into
the refrigerator.

Phoebe swirled water into the sink and pulled on a pair of
kitchen gloves.

Seven

*R*ainald de Beck has second thoughts about the dog. 'We'll string the beast up in front of her,' he tells his serving man. 'That will add to the pleasure and let the wench know that there's nothing I won't do if she displeases me.'

Arnaud flinches. He was born on the de Beck lands, and must remain in servitude to this man for the rest of his life. In spite of years of conditioning to brutal cruelty he still retains a glimmer of sympathy for the victims his master frequently tortures and maims, but before all else he must look to the precarious safety of his wife and children. De Beck must never be openly crossed.

'Get him tonight and secure him. We'll keep the brute alive until after the marriage. It'll ensure a willing bed partner at the very least.' De Beck rubs his hands in anticipation. 'I shall think of other ways to further the torment if she is not compliant in everything.' He grins evilly at his servant. 'My grand lady Catherine will soon be grovelling at my feet.'

Catherine holds her dog in her arms that night and will not be parted from him. When he must go out after compline she insists that he be allowed only into the small walled garden at the back instead of being given freedom to roam outside at will. She leads him there herself on a rope and keeps close guard.

'How is he to be kept safe?' she says to her friend, Align, a young girl who is also a pupil and guest at the convent. The two girls have become very close during these past winter months. 'If Calder is killed by that evil man I am to wed, then I shall surely kill myself too.'

'That is a mortal sin, Catherine,' Align says fearfully.

'Then let God protect us both.' Catherine is angry. 'Surely all the prayers of this holy place can save one dog.'

'I shall pray with all my might.' Align feels that this is the only real help she can give, but will it be enough? Can the power of God possibly prevail over the evil monster Catherine is to marry? She is devoutly thankful that her own father has been more careful in the choice of a husband than has Catherine's. How could any parent possibly choose such a man as Rainald de Beck? she wonders. Align is devout and timid, but she has no fears about her own marriage in a month's time when she will wed the handsome young son of the Lord of the Manor of Bovey Tracey. William de Tracey is a gallant and jolly youth whom she has met twice and for whom she holds a fluttering devotion.

The two girls lie uneasily on their beds that night. Catherine frequently stretches her arm from beneath the deerskin rug that covers her and touches the head of her dog. Calder has placed himself at her side, as close as he can manage. It is obvious that he, too, is anxious. He senses his mistress's distress and licks her hand every time he feels the caress. Each time both are momentarily comforted.

The de Beck manor is small and insignificant compared to the de Tracey estate and lands, but their acres adjoin and as Align tosses sleepless in another chamber she wonders if perhaps there is, after all, more that she could do to help her friend than merely pray. Prayer is all right but perhaps something more substantial is needed.

The thought dismays her, but in the short time they have known each other Align has come to love and pity Catherine. Even Calder, large and fearsome though he is, has earned her respect for his constant devotion. She lies and ponders, and at last the germ of an idea begins to form in her mind. It is a wild and preposterous plan, but the more she thinks about it the more desirable it appears. It both terrifies and pleases her. She knows that she has always been considered a rather useless and nervous little thing. The saving of Calder will bring her the status and acclaim she has long craved as well as Catherine's permanent gratitude.

*　　*　　*

83

All the way back to Litford Kate frequently glanced at Dominic, scarcely believing what had happened. She had set out hoping that the long day alone with him might be the catalyst, might persuade him that he couldn't give her up to his God. She knew he loved her and guessed at the struggle he had been facing these past months. Perhaps today he would decide to put her first and give his allegiance to a less demanding creed.

That was this morning. All she had to do now was to win his mind as well as his body.

They came down the track to the old house hand in hand and suddenly Kate remembered the stone that Dominic had mentioned before they went out. She had shown scant interest then, but now, with heightened awareness, everything that interested him interested her. 'Wasn't there something you wanted to show me?' she asked. 'A special stone, I think you said.'

Dominic released her hand from his and slid the rucksack from his shoulders, dumping it on the grass. 'Yes, over here. This must have been the old boundary.'

Kate followed him and stared at the dry stone wall. It was similar to others all over the moor.

'Have a look at this,' he said. 'One of the stones looks as though it was especially shaped. There seems to be an inscription of some sort beneath the lichen. I made an effort to clean it up a bit this morning.'

Kate felt suddenly cold in spite of the warm afternoon sun. She shivered as she bent to examine the small piece of granite. She ran her fingers over the faint indentations of the letters. Then suddenly the blessed state of euphoria that had enveloped her for the past few enchanted hours slipped away.

'We need a brush and some chalk,' Dominic said.

'Chalk?'

'Yes. It's how you read old inscriptions without harming them. You brush off the surface dirt and dust gently and then rub white chalk over it. That way the marks can be more easily seen.'

'Where can we get chalk?' Her voice was tense and anxious. She had to know what the words said but she had no idea why she felt so strongly about them.

Dominic laughed. 'Search me.' He straightened up and looked at her. 'Steady on Kate. Are you all right?'

She knelt down on the grass, caring nothing for the stinging nettles at the base of the wall. She put both hands now on the stone, traced the words with her fingers as though she were reading Braille. '*Tom, Catherinae filius, hoc anno domini MCXLIII natus, quarto die obiit.*'

Dominic stared at her and his eyes widened in shock. 'Kate! Katy dear, what are you saying? No one can read those words as they are now, and you don't speak Latin.' He paused. 'Do you speak Latin? You've never mentioned it. You said something about Tom, son of Catherine, and the year 1143, I think.'

Kate was still kneeling on the ground, her hands clasped together now. She didn't look at him, but stared transfixed at the small stone set into the loose structure at the top of the wall. 'It was for a baby's grave,' she breathed. 'It marked a baby's grave somewhere near here. It's a sad, pitiful place.'

Dominic bent towards her, folded both her hands in his and she allowed herself to be pulled upright, to be held in his arms again, but this time it was very different from the passion of that afternoon. There was no desire in her body now, no longing for anything more than the comfort of his arms. She felt tears in her eyes and she buried her face in the rough fabric of his shirt, smelt the male smell of him, and began to realize what she had said, what she had done. Fear took the place of distress.

'What did I say, Dommy?' she asked. 'How did I come to say those things? I can't remember them now. I've no idea what I said, but I felt cold and intensely wretched. My hands seemed to read the words rather than my brain.'

'You spoke something that sounded like Latin, but I probably didn't hear you correctly. It's not an easy language. It was probably my imagination.'

Kate knew that he was trying to calm her fears. 'I don't know any Latin,' she murmured.

He looked into her eyes for a moment, kissed her and smiled. 'It happens to lots of people now and then,' he said soothingly. 'Words come out of our subconscious. Something clicks in from . . .' He shrugged his shoulders. 'From who knows where?'

'Tell me where all times past are?' Kate quoted. 'From another life, another place, another time. It's happening to Phoebe frequently. Dommy, am I getting like my grand-mother? I don't want to be psychic. The very idea frightens me to death.'

Dominic steered her towards the back door of the house. 'It was nothing to worry about, believe me,' he said. 'Now let's have a cup of something. Coffee would be great.'

Kate detached herself from him, shivered again, tried to regain her composure, tried to think about Dominic's love-making earlier on this wonderful day on the moor. She must hold to that and not imagine or dwell on eight hundred-year-old griefs and bogeys. They could have no power now in this brash new twenty-first century.

They let themselves into the unlocked Litford door and Kate flopped down on to the nearest chair. She felt unable to do anything. 'I don't want to stay here any longer,' she said. 'I should like to go home to London with you tomorrow. I feel weird here. There's an odd feeling that really gets to me. I want noise and people and shops and traffic.'

Thomas's London is a bleak and brutal place, for there is little peace in the land since King Henry I died. The king's only surviving child is a woman, Matilda, and England is not yet ready for a reigning queen, however suitable and however like her father, the great 'lion of justice', she might be.

Thomas frequently reflects on all of this and feels powerless to do anything to change things. He spends most of his time in the home of Osbert Huitdeniers, his easy-going employer. He longs for more demanding work and knows that the one place where he can achieve his dreams for position and influence is in the palace of Archbishop Theobald, Primate of England. In Canterbury there is peace and stability. Amidst the anarchy that persists in most of the towns and villages of England, Canterbury is a quiet sea of learning and calm authority.

He still thinks of Catherine, but tries every night to put her out of his mind. He wishes he could have news of her, but even his father can tell him little. 'Her father has made a good match for her,' he says, and with this scant information Thomas must be content.

'Why so far away?' he asked one day. 'The far south-west of England is a primitive place, I should think.' Thomas remembers with affection the busy towns of France and Italy, great centres of learning where he has studied. How Catherine would have loved those places. From the little he has heard Devon seems backward and inaccessible. 'But they tell me it is very beautiful there,' he says. 'I shall go one day and see for myself.'

Meanwhile most of his thoughts and aspirations are centred on Canterbury.

'You might as well have one more night here, Kate,' Talitha said after the evening meal at High Mead which they had all shared. 'You could return to Litford in the morning after Dominic has left.'

'I'm hoping to go back to London tomorrow with Dominic,' Kate said as she helped to clear up the chaos in the kitchen. 'I haven't told Nonna yet, but now that she's got Hugo here she won't need my company.'

'She won't be pleased.'

'Why ever not? She'll have Hugo all to herself if I'm out of the way.'

Talitha grinned and thought of her sister's state of euphoria ever since he had arrived. She stacked the last of the dishes into the dishwasher. 'You might be right,' she said.

'I'd like to be at home to get my exam results,' Kate explained later when they were sitting in the warm summer garden, their wine glasses filled again by Garth, and coffee brewing. 'I want to celebrate or be miserable on my own.'

Phoebe looked at her and knew at once that it was not her exam grades that were the reason. She shook her head. 'I don't like the idea,' she said. She fought all her instincts to say that she would cut her own holiday short. That of course was not what Kate wanted at all. 'Are you sure you'll be all right?' Her voice was full of doubts. 'I'd hoped to stay on here for another two weeks at least.'

'I'll be fine,' Kate said trying not to sound too eager. 'Dommy has the train times. Will you drive us to Newton Abbot tomorrow?'

Phoebe nodded. 'If that's really what you want.'

'Thanks, Nonna. And yes, I'll phone every night. Stop worrying. I'm a big girl now!'

Talitha grinned at both of them and made an effort to change the subject. 'You're going to look at Indio, remember,' she said to Phoebe.

'Indio?' Hugo looked at Talitha and then at Phoebe. The sisters' faces were softened now in the flickering candle lights that Garth had set on the terrace wall. 'Strange name for Devon.'

'It's an old house,' Phoebe explained. 'There was a priory there, hence the name. *In Deo* – I think it means a house for God.'

'Your Thomas à Becket might have had something to do with the place,' Talitha said. 'There's an ancient track from the house to the church. You can't see much of it now, but bits of footpath remain amongst the new houses.'

'We'll go tomorrow,' Phoebe said. 'I like Bovey. There's lots to do there.'

Align and Catherine are not allowed much time alone together but after angelus there is a period of meditation. Sometimes when the weather is good they are allowed into the garden where they are supposed to meditate quietly upon the rules of their lives and to pray for obedience and humility, qualities highly prized in a woman.

This morning Align signals to Catherine that she has some-thing to say and she walks outside as unhurriedly as she dares, down the stony path with its low and carefully clipped hedges, to the great oak tree that grows at the farthest boundary of the garden. There is a seat all around the gnarled old trunk. It sur-rounds the tree, appearing almost to hold it in place. Align sits down and takes her gospel from her pocket. It is one of her most precious possessions, painstakingly penned and embellished by monks from the abbey where her father was educated. She values it highly, second only to Floria, her little palfrey.

She opens the book and holds it against the soft material of her gown, but she sees nothing of the Latin words inside. She closes her eyes and prays for courage.

Catherine has followed her and seats herself on the other side of the bench for they must not be seen talking together at this hour.

'I have a plan,' Align whispers. 'Would you let Calder go to my William? He will keep him safe for my sake, and as your Rainald is only a minor knight he could not gainsay the Traceys.' Align hates to say this to her friend but it is true. William's family is descended from an illegitimate son of the Conqueror. They have powerful friends at court, much money and extensive lands and possessions. Rainald de Beck is an unimportant man, probably knighted for some little service he or his father had rendered in the past. His lands are small, his manor house rough and poor, and he is pledged to be under the supervision of the Lord of the Manor and cannot therefore offend any of the Traceys.

'How?' Catherine says. She carefully edges herself nearer her friend. 'There are no visits arranged.'

'I shall take him there myself.'

Catherine's eyes widen in amazement. 'Align, you cannot possibly!'

'I have it all planned,' Align says. 'Sister Martha will aid me. She loves all animals and when I tell her of the fate that awaits Calder she will do anything I ask. Floria will carry me safely.'

'But there are brigands in the forest, and at least two miles of wild country lie between here and the Tracey manor.'

'You are exaggerating, Catherine. There is a track to the church and another to Parke Manor. I shall be all right. God will protect me. Never fear.'

'What about the river?'

'It's low at this time of year, and Floria will easily cross at the ford. Who could possibly harm me with Calder for company?'

Catherine had her doubts about that. Calder is her dog and would protect her to the death, but would he do the same for frightened little Align? In fact he would probably refuse to go with her. 'Then I must come with you,' she says. 'We shall go together. I can't leave you to do this for me. It would be unpardonable.'

'If you come too it will be noticed, and Floria could not possibly carry both of us. I must go alone, Catherine.' Align smiles a little secret smile. She does not tell her friend the other reason for her flight. She longs for William. She hates every day at the convent that keeps her away from him. She is sure that once he has recovered from the shock of seeing her and has learned of the brave thing she has done he will greet her with pleasure. His mother, who has always been kind to her, will cosset her and she will ride back behind William on his great destrier. Calder will be safe and Catherine will be happy.

'But, Align dear, it won't work. Calder won't follow you. He'll find his way back here. Two miles is nothing for him. He'll return searching for me and then de Beck will surely intercept him and . . .' Catherine feels tears in her eyes, and her heart thumps in panic and dread.

'Then he will have to be tethered or shut in until he is resigned to being without you,' Align says.

Catherine looks at her friend with new understanding as she realizes that the plan is not totally single minded. Calder is a way of achieving the other things that Align craves. Is there any way this wild idea could possibly work? A sense of hopelessness fills her like an enveloping grey cloud and at the same time she is envious. What must it be like to have a bridegroom such as Align's William, someone loved and longed for? She thinks of Thomas and then of her baby son lying cold beneath the ground at Litford. Is Calder, her only comfort, to be snatched away too? 'We'll talk further this afternoon,' she whispers to Align. She closes her eyes and prays desperately for guidance.

Eight

*C*atherine is fearful. She has seen Rainald de Beck's man outside the priory's boundary wall a few times. He prowls menacingly and Calder is therefore no longer allowed any freedom at all. He can only run in the priory grounds and must be under constant supervision if Catherine is to have any peace of mind. The large dog is used to freedom and so he is restless and uses his boundless energy for various unpopular pursuits. He has dug holes in the soft well-tended earth of the walled kitchen garden. Carefully managed vegetables and herbs lie wilting in the sun. Earth and stones are scattered everywhere. Sister Bregenda, who is in charge of the gardens, is not best pleased.

'That dog must go,' she has said crossly on more than one occasion this week.

'De Beck wants to kill him,' Catherine tells her after the last costly blunder. 'He's threatened to string him up and let him hang if I don't obey him in everything.'

Sister Bregenda has never been a dog lover and she especially dislikes any creature who has the temerity to damage her precious plants, but she strongly disapproves of men even more. She met Rainald de Beck recently when she was obliged to sit with Catherine during one of his visits, and she has decided that this particular man is obviously far more objectionable than most. She is sorry for Catherine. 'So what are you going to do when you wed? It seems a pretty ominous outlook for Calder.' And for you too, she thinks grimly.

'I don't know.' Catherine is helping to tidy up the latest results of Calder's sins. She is holding a basket of tiny carrots. They are far too small for normal harvesting but must now be used for the evening's meal. Their feathery tops lie limp and dry in the sun. 'I must find a safe place for him to go,' she says, then she feels her eyes fill with tears for she suspects that nowhere will be safe from de Beck's bloodthirsty hands.

The dog has been tied by a long rope to an iron ring set in the wall nearby, for Catherine is loath to let him out of her sight. He knows they are talking about him and he thumps his tail expectantly.

Sister Bregenda is anxious to get him out of the priory for good but she would also like to thwart Rainald de Beck. 'If you need any help,' she says, 'I'll do what I can, and no doubt Sister Martha might also be prevailed upon to come to your aid.'

Catherine looks at her in surprise, but then realizes that the two nuns could be useful accomplices. Sister Bregenda carries the keys from kitchen to garden on her belt and another large unwieldy key that unlocks the door in the outside wall. This leads directly to the church path. 'Would you really help me?' she asks doubtfully.

Sister Bregenda crosses herself. 'Of course, child. If I can frustrate the evil plans of any man I'll do anything within my power.'

'Do you still want to carry out your crazy plot, Align?' Catherine asks tremulously that evening.

They are at the farthest edge of the garden. Sister Bregenda has sent them to pick the first blackberries which she has carefully cultivated and which are too prickly to fall victim to Calder's mischief.

'I think so,' Align says. 'I'm very frightened, but I don't see any other way for you if you want to save him.' Calder is with them and Align runs her hand down his back. The dog turns and licks her. He has come to trust her. Perhaps he even feels loyalty to her now. 'De Beck will be very angry. He might take it out on you.'

'I must risk that,' Catherine says. 'If Calder is safe I don't mind what happens to me, but if he is cruel to Calder then I would rather be dead. I shall come with you, Align. Perhaps de Beck won't punish me too much if he knows that I'm at the de Tracey manor. In fact if I find favour with your betrothed's *family then he'll have to be careful how he treats me. It will give me some importance in his eyes.'*

Align nods. 'I can see the truth of what you say. Then we shall go together, Catherine, and may God guard and protect us.'

The following night the two girls go to their beds fully dressed. Godwin, the stable boy, has been roped into the plot by Sister Bregenda and Sister Martha. He would never have allowed himself to be persuaded by the two girls, but the senior nuns have promised him absolution and reward if he does the things that are required of him. He is to see that Floria, the little palfrey, is saddled and ready at the midnight hour, but they will also take the sturdy pack pony. He is steady and used to being ridden and will carry Catherine, and Godwin too if that should be necessary.

The road surface now in late summer is easy for there has been no rain for a long time. They have chosen a moonlit night, for although Godwin says that he knows the route it is difficult to journey in total darkness. In spite of his youth Godwin inspires trust. He tells them that he has been brought up on the Tracey estate and he leads the way with confidence, holding the pack pony's bridle in one hand and Calder's rope in the other. The dog lopes easily along. His mistress is with him and he won't stray far from her. From time to time he looks up at her and puts his head on one side for he is not used to seeing her on horseback, but she whispers to him now and then. He can sense the tension she feels and all his senses are alert for danger.

They walk quietly for a time and then reach the river crossing. There is no bridge, but at this place the water is shallow and the two horses pick their way carefully across. Godwin has jumped up behind Catherine so that he will cross dry-shod.

On the other side he slides off and then stands quite still, his heart pounding. He has heard a sound from the trees in front of him. Calder growls suspiciously.

Rainald de Beck is returning from a night with his whore and he looks with amazement at the outline of the little group on the river bank. Then suddenly Calder leaps, the rope slipping from Godwin's grasp. But de Beck is mounted and his great warhorse is not easily frightened. Calder checks himself and stands still, waiting for a command from his mistress. Is this friend or foe?

De Beck laughs as he recognizes the dog in the moonlight and immediately realizes that this is some plot to foil his plans. 'So you bring your pesky animal to me do you, Catherine? Yes, very obliging to be sure. What crime has he committed that you wish to see him strung up immediately from that convenient branch just there?'

Although Catherine is filled with terror, Align feels a surge of power. She knows that this man has no authority over her, rather the reverse. She urges her mount forward and sits straight in the saddle. 'No crime, Rainald de Beck,' she says in ringing tones that she did not know she possessed. 'We are taking him to the home of my betrothed, William de Tracey, who wishes to buy him from Catherine.' She surprises herself mightily with the lie that falls so easily from her lips.

'Ha! The little Lady Align is it? I very much doubt if Sir William will want a troublesome beast like that. He'll soon be persuaded to sell him or give him to me. No doubt he'll even pay me for the privilege of taking him off his hands.' He dismounts easily and moves to take the rope which trails from Calder's collar, but Catherine slides from the broad back of the sturdy little pack pony and screams out in terror.

'No! You shall never have him.'

De Beck laughs and swings his riding whip so that it catches her across the face, and at that moment Calder leaps. He needs no orders when he sees his mistress hurt. He goes for the raised arm, and his furious bulk fells the man in one easy movement. De Beck falls backwards, legs flailing helplessly. Calder's powerful teeth pierce jerkin sleeve, flesh and muscle right to the bone as his victim screams and curses in agony. The dog catches at de Beck's throat and his teeth find further soft, yielding flesh. Blood spurts like a great crimson fountain and the dog, with the scent of his enemy's blood in his nostrils and all over his coat, is further maddened with rage.

De Beck thrusts at the beast with all his failing might and his feet scrabble ineffectually on the stony path but Calder, standing four-square over him, increases his grip. He knows only one thing. This man is a threat to his mistress and therefore he must fight to the death to defend her.

Arnaud, the serving man who has been journeying with de Beck is some way behind for his horse is old and feeble. He comes suddenly upon the scene. He has heard the garbled scream and now he sees, to his amazement and horror, that his master is fighting for his life. He can just make out the writhing form on the ground and the great dog at his throat. He unfastens his long hunting knife and slides from his mount.

At that moment Align's little palfrey, terrified by the noise and the smell of blood, raises her small feet into the air and neighs in panic. She brings her hooves right down on to Arnaud just as he is about to slash at the dog. He curses and falls and the blade completely misses Calder, but buries itself instead in the still-thrashing form of Rainald de Beck.

There is more blood, a great sea of blood seeping into the hard, dry earth, and the air is filled with tortured moans and screams until at last de Beck lies silent. Then a great stillness comes upon the forest. Catherine and Godwin are still standing beside the packhorse which has not moved throughout all the tumult. Calder releases his hold on the prone body beneath him, sniffs at the blood and looks to his mistress to see if he has won approval. Then he growls a warning to Arnaud who is lying face down trying to raise his head.

As the train pulled into Paddington, Kate was aware of a flatness descending upon her. The feeling of despondency had started around Taunton, and it had grown to gigantic proportions as every mile brought them closer to London. Why? This early homecoming had been her choice. She had insisted on coming back with Dominic in spite of Phoebe's, admittedly somewhat mild, protestations. Now she was beginning to regret her hasty decision. Dominic had been quiet and withdrawn this morning. Could he possibly be regretting what had happened yesterday on the moor?

She extracted her rucksack with difficulty from the assorted collection of suitcases and bags squashed into the luggage racks at the end of the carriage and waited for the train to come to a stop. Dominic was close behind and eventually they were swept along the platform with the faceless crowds, everyone intent upon their own purposes, some greeting friends, others struggling with huge recalcitrant suitcases on wheels, some battling with peevish children, and others locked in amorous embraces. Kate was quite overcome with loneliness.

She looked at Dominic. He was beside her now, his face set and remote, or so she felt it to be. 'Underground?' she asked.

He nodded. 'Quickest at this time of day.'

'Where then, your place or mine?'

He shrugged. 'Yours I should think. No food in mine and we need to eat, don't we?'

'There won't be very much edible in mine either,' Kate said. 'We could get a pizza or takeaway.'

'Right.' He smiled at her and her spirits lifted a little. Was the closeness they had known just yesterday going to reappear after all? 'There's a pizza bar close to the flat,' she said.

They crowded into the tube carriage and flopped thankfully into bottom-warmed seats just vacated. A crowd of swaggering youths erupted through the sliding doors at the last moment and Kate looked at them in dismay. Litford and the peace of Dartmoor's wild hills seemed a thousand miles away. She thought with sudden longing of its quietness, of the fictional shadowy Catherine and the mysterious little gravestone. *Tom, Catherinae filius, hoc anno domini MCXLIII natus, quarto die obiit.* The words suddenly sang in her head, a magical, soundless refrain. And there were tears in her eyes.

Phoebe's flat smelt musty and the rooms were hot and airless. Kate dumped the pizza on to the kitchen table beside the bottle of wine that Dominic had bought and threw open the windows so that London noise and fumes replaced the stale air.

'A bit of comedown after Devon,' Dominic said, sniffing and wrinkling his nose.

'We'll have a candle on the table,' Kate said. 'And an oil burner.' She didn't tell him that she would put ylang-ylang in the burner, the erotic oil that she used in her bath when she felt in need of some romantic lift. When the table was ready and Dominic had opened the wine they sat down opposite each other. Kate sniffed the air and wondered how long the odour of fried onion, which was thick on the pizza, would predominate.

Dominic obviously appreciated the onion and failed to notice the ylang-ylang! He ate enthusiastically, but suddenly stopped and grinned at Kate. 'Not up to your Aunt Talitha's standard.'

'I thought you were enjoying it.'

'I'm ravenous. I'd enjoy anything at the moment.'

'Have some more wine to wash it down.' Kate waved the bottle at him and hoped that he would drink a copious amount.'

'No more,' he said infuriatingly. 'I've things to do.'

'Like unpacking one rucksack?' Her voice was full of sarcasm and sudden anger. Dear God was he going to leave her? She couldn't believe it. She had come back early from Devon to be with him. 'You'll come back later?' It was more a statement than a question.

He shook his head, carried the plate to the sink, washed it and left it to drain. 'Not tonight, Kate. I've a lot to sort out. I'll ring you. Do you mind?'

'Mind? Of course I bloody mind! Why do you think I *really* gave up my holiday, sacrificed Litford for this dump? To stay here on my own? I thought things had changed between us, Dom. I thought yesterday meant something to you.'

He stood at the sink looking at her. 'It did mean something. A lot. I need you, Kate but . . .'

'Need, need, what the hell does that mean? That I'm just a convenient body for you to fuck now and then when you *need* a woman?' Kate glared at him. She knew her words would shock him. They profoundly shocked her, too, but at this moment she cared not one jot. 'I suppose you're going to tell me you need God more?' She flung the angry words at him. 'But He doesn't satisfy all your bloody needs does he? So you want a woman tucked away somewhere out of sight.'

Dominic's face was white and strained. He stood with his back to the sink gripping its edge as if he would fall over if he moved away. 'I'm committed, Kate, to the Church, to God if you like.'

Kate's fury overcame her. 'And what about me? What about being committed to me?' She picked up a wine glass and threw it at him. He ducked and it smashed into pieces on the draining board. Then she burst into tears and rushed out of the room into her bedroom and threw herself on to her bed.

Without a word Dominic retrieved his rucksack and let himself out of the flat. Kate, listening angrily, heard him go and heard the click of the lift. Unbelieving she jumped from the bed and went to the window overlooking the street below. Eventually he appeared and she watched him walk along the pavement in the direction of the Underground.

She went back into the kitchen. Angry tears coursed down her cheeks and she stared at the debris from the meal, at the wine bottle still half-full, and at the broken glass all over the sink and floor. She dashed the tears from her eyes, found the dustpan and brush and swept up the jagged shards. Then, sucking her cut finger, she refilled the remaining glass, downed the wine in angry gulps, filled it again and again until none remained.

She slept restlessly that night and awoke many times, always with a racing heart and a sense of despair, but always too with strange sounds resounding in her head. She heard wind in trees, owls screeching, the howling of a dog, a woman screaming and a baby crying. All else was silence. Not until she sat up and frantically groped for the light could she hear traffic and a police siren in the distance, people's voices and drunks in the street below. For the first time the unpleasant but familiar din of London was welcome and reassuring. The other sounds were surely from some nightmare, but were more frightening because they were eerie and, in some strange way, out of place and time.

Dominic's desertion seemed caught up in all of this as though they were both part of the bizarre events unfolding in Devon. Each time she awoke, desolation and fear swept over her afresh. She felt caught up in a great sea of despair, and not always her own. The words on the stone at Litford went round and round in her head and would not be banished. *Tom,*

Catherinae filius, hoc anno domini MCXLIII natus, quarto die obiit.

The next day, in Devon, Phoebe drove into Bovey Tracey to look at Indio.

'Presumably,' she had earlier told Hugo and Talitha, 'it is the site of the ancient priory, but no one is sure of anything, really, after so many centuries.'

She left her car at the end of the drive to the big house. She felt that a place with such a name and such a history should be approached on foot and with reverence. A silly idea, she told herself when she saw the old car and motorbike in front of the house and dilapidated children's toys scattered all over the circular driveway. She had persuaded Hugo to look around the town and meet her later, and unwillingly he had agreed. She felt this was one of the things she must do on her own.

The house was not as big as she had expected and no one had been able to tell her exactly how old it was, certainly not as old as Litford and High Mead. It was a grand house yet not a mansion and it looked Elizabethan with its E-shaped frontage. Phoebe stood and stared for a long time, then took some photographs.

'Can I help you?' The voice was young and slightly suspicious and Phoebe jumped.

'Oh, sorry. I should have knocked and asked permission.' She put her camera away and smiled. 'I'm interested in the history of this place,' she said. 'I'm writing a book, a biography of Thomas à Becket. I believe he came here?'

The young woman looked blank, then suddenly illumination dawned. 'Him with his name on the church?'

'That's right. He had connections here, I'm told. There was a priory here once, I believe.'

'I thought you were one of them surveyors.' She picked up a small battered tricycle and carried it to the edge of the drive. 'We're afraid of what the owner's going to do with the place, develop it and all that. We love it here. Better than Bristol for the kids. We'd be turned out.'

'You don't own it then?'

She laughed. 'Pity, but no. Wish we did. I'd be worth a packet if it got planning permission for houses.'

'I thought you wanted it to remain unspoilt.'

The girl shrugged. 'Money speaks don't it? Beauty's nothing if there's a bit of the ready to be made. We wouldn't have to worry about having nowhere to go if we had a few million to play with, would we?'

'I suppose not,' Phoebe said thoughtfully. 'Can I wander round the grounds?'

The suspicion returned. 'Sure you aren't one of them surveyors or architects?'

Phoebe shook her head. 'Absolutely not. Come with me if you like. Show me round.'

'Righto. Kids are with their dad today, thank God.'

Together they walked around the outside of the house through long uncut grass, dry now in the summer heat. Wild flowers grew unhindered and vast unpruned hedges and flowering shrubs were thick with blossom. The contented buzzing of thousands of bees filled the air, and swallows swooped and dived and then gathered on the ridge of an ancient roof. There were great trees too: oak, beech and ash.

'They had plans not so long ago to turn the place into some sort of New Age centre I believe, with weirdos living in holiday homes and things. Bit of a joke really, but it would have meant the end for us.'

Phoebe ignored this remark, hardly heard it. 'Thomas came here,' she said quietly, half to herself. And then came other thoughts and images. They floated into her head like half-remembered dreams, dim ethereal shadows moving across the periphery of her mind.

The girl peered at her anxiously. 'Are you all right? Come back to the house and I'll get you a drink. It's hot out here.'

'Thanks.' Phoebe breathed deeply of the scented afternoon air and brushed her hand across her forehead. 'I should like to sit down somewhere cool for a while. Do you mind if I stay here alone for a few minutes?'

'Sure. There's an old iron seat under that oak tree. You sit there in the shade if you prefer and I'll bring you a Coke. I keep plenty of the stuff in the fridge. Kids drink it like there's no tomorrow.' She pointed to a shady place with a canopy of thick branches. 'Won't be long.'

Phoebe walks across the grass, brushes leaves from the old seat and sinks down thankfully. She can see Thomas more clearly now, but not the vigorous young Thomas of her previous imagining. There are grey streaks in the raven-dark hair and he walks slowly beneath the trees, pondering, praying perhaps.

Phoebe closes her eyes as she usually does when she is drawn involuntarily into this vortex of the past. She can still hear the birds, the distant sound of traffic, the twenty-first century imposing itself on the twelfth, and she wonders at the disordered way in which the past comes to her. There is no consecutive arrangement of years. This older Thomas disturbs her, for where have all the bright, confident times gone, the times when he is resplendent and glorious, chancellor of England, the young king's closest friend?

Then her thoughts travel from known and well-recorded fact to the illusory Catherine. Is Catherine a fiction, a pure figment of her imagination? And if she was real was she ever here in this place? Could this be why the thoughts are coming so disturbingly now? Yes, but earlier. Once again there is the confusion of time, and Phoebe feels a sudden sadness, great fear. She hears the barking of a large dog, the neighing of a horse. She brushes her hair back from her forehead, opens her eyes and looks around at the peaceful neglected garden. 'Tell me where all times past are,' she says yet again.

The girl walked across the grass carrying two cans of Coke with large plastic straws protruding from the tops of each. 'Here you are then. Straight from the fridge.' She handed one to Phoebe and sat down beside her. 'What was that you said? Something about past times. There's a shop called that in Exeter. They sell old stuff. Copies mostly.'

Phoebe smiled. 'No, not the shop,' she said. 'It's a quote. "Tell me where all times past are."' She sucked at the straw and repressed a shudder. She had never liked Coke. 'I don't know that I've got it quite right but it seems to fit this place.'

101

'Oh, don't,' the girl said. 'Things like that really get to me, especially at night. They say there's a ghost in the house. Sometimes the dog barks at nothing. I'd move to one of those new bungalows if I won the lottery.'

Nine

'I thought you were writing a serious biography of Thomas à Becket,' Hugo complained. 'You don't really intend to put this non-existent girl whom you've dreamed up into it, do you? She's just a figment of your imagination.'

Phoebe's fingers stopped flying over her keyboard. She looked at Hugo and then rubbed her shoulder. 'Come and give me a bit of neck massage,' she said. 'All this sitting around doesn't do my joints any good.'

'You haven't answered my question.' Hugo came over to her, stood behind her chair and started to rub her back, both hands probing expertly. 'For goodness sake, Phee, tell me about this Catherine you're so hooked on. Have you any actual evidence for her existence?'

Phoebe rolled her shoulder muscles sensuously. 'You have a wonderful touch, Hugo dear. I feel better already.' She glanced at the computer screen again and stared at the words she had just composed. 'What about the little gravestone you found?' she asked. 'Isn't that some sort of proof?'

Hugo shook his head. 'Of course not. It could be from any time, or from any place for that matter. Farmers brought stones from all over the moor to build their walls and houses. They used pack ponies and sledges that would run over the ground. There's nothing at all to link this place or that stone with Thomas à Becket. You're letting your imagination run away with you.'

Phoebe's eyes wandered to the vista of sky and moor visible from the small window in front of her typing table. 'There's something you don't know.' Her voice was quiet, mysterious. 'Kate read those words, the ones on the stone.'

Hugo stopped his ministrations. 'What do you mean, *read* the words?'

'It's all so strange, Hugo. It almost frightens me. I know that it was a baby's headstone. The knowledge came to me out of nowhere. Call it imagination if you like, but I think it was more than that, and then Kate told me later that she had read those old indecipherable words. She read them aloud, and in Latin, which she has never learned and can't understand. Apparently the words and the meaning came to her as clearly as the strange knowledge came to me. I think that was partly why she went back to London. It scared her.'

Hugo leaned over and peered at the computer screen. He saw the name, *Catherine*. It seemed to stand out more clearly than all the other words and he frowned. 'If there's any truth in all of this then it scares me too, but there can't be. It's a lot of mumbo-jumbo. You and Kate are just too fanciful.' He resumed his massage of Phoebe's tight muscles. 'You said *knowledge*. What did you mean exactly?'

'I can see that stone clearly as it was on the day it was erected, with the newly turned earth bare beneath it, and a big bunch of heather resting at its foot.'

'Oh come on, Phee. It must all originate from dreams. You dream something in the night and then turn your fantasies into a sort of weird reality.'

'*Tom, Catherinae filius, hoc anno domini MCXLIII natus, quarto die obiit.*' Phoebe spoke the words quietly, fluently, with expression and meaning. They were imprinted on her brain and their message was infinitely sad.

Hugo took her hands and pulled her to her feet. He shook her gently. 'Stop it,' he said. 'Stop it, Phoebe. Do you hear me? We'd better go back to London as soon as we can. Would to God I'd never found the damn stone.'

Phoebe stared at him coldly. She could sense that his patience was running out, but there was something else in his face too. Fear! Was he afraid? 'You think I'm going mad don't you, Hugo?'

He shook his head but exasperation was not far from the surface. 'I think you should talk this over with someone more knowledgeable than I, a psychiatrist perhaps.'

'I don't need a psychiatrist. Just leave me to write the book. It almost seems to be writing itself. Let my readers be the judges. As for the stone, I think it was waiting to be found. Dominic noticed it too, remember? In fact I think he discovered it first.'

'It should go to the museum,' Hugo said, trying to be matter-of-fact. 'If it's really anything other than a bit of granite they'll tell us. That might give you something to back up all your weird theories. If not, then it's curtains for this imaginary girl. You'll have to get rid of her and concentrate only on known things.'

'Don't tell me how to write my book, Hugo,' Phoebe said. She was feeling the stirrings of anger, for self-doubt had begun to surface in her thoughts now and then. She wanted Hugo to encourage her rather than reinforce her niggling uncertainty. Perhaps, after all, the words she had written had little basis in reality. Maybe they were pure fiction. If the book she was writing had any truth, then Thomas, the renowned saint and holy man, had deserted the girl he loved, for his ambitions and his God. The similarity of this scenario with that of Kate and Dominic came to her with renewed force.

Her blood ran cold. Could it possibly be that Kate was living Catherine's life all over again? A baby's grave. Dominic a priest! Was the twenty-first century so very different from the twelfth? Reincarnation? She didn't believe in such things. But suddenly her fears for her granddaughter intensified, greatly frightening her. 'Let's cut our holiday short and go home,' she said to Hugo, her voice urgent and filled with anxiety. 'I want to get back to Kate.'

He frowned. 'Your mind jumps around like a March hare. I can't follow you. What has your book to do with Kate?'

'Everything,' she said dramatically. 'Can't you see the similarities? Thomas and Dominic? Ambition and devotion to God coming first. It's happening all over again.'

Hugo looked at her with amused affection. 'Problem solved,' he said. 'Now I know where this faction thing you're writing is coming from. Your subconscious has invented Catherine, and Thomas's supposed infatuation with her in order to come to terms with your granddaughter's possible betrayal by that handsome Dominic of hers. You're worried about Kate and so you unknowingly invent a parallel story in order to write it out. I've heard of authors doing such things.'

Phoebe shook her head in disbelief. Yet could it be so? Had she done that? Was she transposing her own fears into this story? 'I hope you're right,' she said faintly. 'Oh Hugo, I hope to God you're right.'

He smiled. Relief was written all over his face. 'Of course I'm right,' he said. 'I'm always right. Turn off that pesky machine and I'll mix you a gin and tonic.'

The marriage of Align to her beloved William is a happy and grand event. The lovely Bovey Tracey Manor House is decked out splendidly and all the people of the little town are given a generous measure of ale and bidden to enjoy the revelling. Catherine, as maid of honour is both joyful and sad alternately. She feels only pleasure for Align, but there is a great void in her heart when she thinks of her own life. True, she and Calder are safe from the threat of Rainald de Beck's bestial cruelty and for that she constantly gives thanks. But where contentment should be there is an emptiness, and as she looks at William, so young, so handsome, and at Align, radiant and beautiful in her gleaming gown, she cannot rid her mind of thoughts of Thomas, of baby Tom cold in his little grave, and of her father in London, seemingly oblivious to his daughter's well-being.

When all the ceremonies and feasting are over Align nervously bids goodbye to Catherine, for she and William are to spend their honeymoon as guests at the nearby castle of Berry Pomeroy. 'I love William, but I'm mightily nervous of the marriage bed,' she whispers.

Catherine hugs her slight body. 'He will be gentle,' she says. 'He loves you too. I can see it in his eyes. You are much blessed, Align.'

'Will you come here to live and be my companion when I return?' Align asks. 'I shall seek William's permission if you agree. I have serving maids aplenty but I need a friend.'

Sudden hope flares in Catherine's heart. She has been staying with Align during the week preceding the marriage and dreads returning to the convent alone. 'I should like that very much,' she says. 'I shall need my father's permission though.'

Align nods. 'I am sure William will write to him if I ask.'

And so it is arranged. Before the year is out Catherine is installed at the manor house. She is happier than she has been for a long time. Periodically she goes to Litford to visit Eluned, for William has given her a palfrey of her own and there are always servants ready to accompany her. She lays flowers, usually heathers, on her baby's grave, and she prays for his soul. Then she weeps a little, but the freedom to visit whenever she wishes has assuaged some of her grief, and she is increasingly able to put the past behind her. The future does not look quite so bleak.

She hears news now and then of Thomas but her concerns are mainly with Align who is very quickly with child, who frequently ails, and who constantly relies on her sturdy friendship. Catherine worries much about her friend and about her ability to bring her child to term and to deliver a healthy baby. William is looking forward to the birth of a son. He hopes it will be a son, for the Tracey line is important and he needs an heir, but he too is concerned about his frail little wife, and he also relies on Catherine for reassurance and support.

'I've got three As and two Cs,' Kate announced to Phoebe over the telephone.

'That's wonderful, darling. I'm so thrilled for you. With results like that you could get into Oxbridge, couldn't you?' Phoebe, beaming with pleasure and pride, repeated the news to Talitha. They were in the High Mead kitchen making supper.

'Possibly but I think I'll stay with Bristol,' Kate said.

'OK, but think about it. It's nice to have a choice. I shall ask Garth to find a very special bottle of something so that we can celebrate.'

'Lucky you.'

Phoebe was surprised by the despondent tone in Kate's voice. 'Aren't you and Dominic celebrating?'

'I'm on my own.' The line went dead and Phoebe, repressing an urge to ring back, held the receiver for a moment before replacing it. 'Something has happened between Kate and Dominic,' she said to Talitha. 'She's alone.'

'Good thing you're going back tomorrow then,' Talitha said. 'I suppose you think it's for the best if they split up though, don't you?'

'In the long run, yes, but she'll be pretty devastated at first.'

'She's young.' Talitha took garlic bread from the oven, found a board and set it on the table. 'There are plenty more fish in the sea, as they say. The trouble is that the young never realize it. If you're in love you can't get your head round that idea at all.'

'I hope there aren't any repercussions, that's all.'

Talitha wiped her greasy hands on a tea towel and stared at her sister. 'What do you mean by that?'

'They slept together. At least I'm pretty sure they did.'

Talitha groaned. 'What century are you in, Phee, for goodness sake? People do it all the time, or hadn't you noticed?'

'I'm probably back in the twelfth!'

'Well, you'd better return to the present,' Talitha said firmly. 'And hurry up with that salad. Everything else is ready.'

Kate, standing in the shower, watched the blood of her period swirl away down the drain. She soaped herself all over and felt the piercing jets of water cleanse her body. No baby! Relief and sorrow together struggled for supremacy. She knew that she and Dominic had been careless and stupid, call it what you would, but in that first ecstatic time they had taken no precautions. Was he worrying about it now? Probably not, but did he realize what a pregnancy could have done to his oh-so-precious calling to the priesthood?

But of course it was not to be. God or fate had decreed it. There would now be no evidence of their love. Perhaps he didn't see it that way. Maybe to him it was sin? But did lack of evidence make the act less unholy? Dear God, Kate thought, how weird this line of thinking would appear to my friends. They slept around happily, well prepared, with no thought of morals or after effects. Was she so different? Was Dominic so different?

She turned the shower off and reached for a warm fluffy towel and wrapped it around her body. Yes, she had to admit it, Dominic was different. He had vocation and mission. Any woman would always come second to that. She put on pyjamas and bathrobe and sat down to watch the video she had borrowed that afternoon. She had been waiting for Dominic to telephone all day, but the machine had remained miserably silent.

It is midsummer and uncomfortably hot as Align struggles to give birth to her child. Three midwives have been summoned but there is little they can do. The oldest and most experienced knows that the child lies awkwardly and Align is too weak to struggle much longer.

Catherine is horrified by what she sees for although she knows that birthing can be bloody and terrifying, she has never witnessed a labour such as this. She knew no pain as horrendous as Align's when Tom was born. Ashen-faced and with her clothes in disarray she holds a tisane of dried raspberry leaves and honey and offers it now and then to the screaming struggling girl on the bed. 'Drink a little, sweetest Align,' she whispers between the contractions that are tearing through the delicate body. 'It will strengthen you and make the pain more bearable.' But Align is almost too weak to heed her and sips only a little.

The hours pass in horror and anguish. The serving maid is sent constantly for fresh cloths, for water, for more of the soothing tisane, but nothing avails. And then, after three full days and two nights, a tiny scrap is thrust into the world, a little body that scarcely has any life at all in its wrinkled limbs. The midwife cuts the cord and holds the baby up at the casement window, gently slapping its buttocks. She breathes life into the puckered mouth and the baby utters its first cry, a small pitiful wail that contracts Catherine's heart for she hears in memory her own baby crying out, but more lustily than this one. If her Tom had not enough strength to endure the first hazardous days, then surely this pathetic mite cannot live?

'You have a daughter,' the midwife says gently to the exhausted girl on the bed. 'She must be named.'

Align's eyes are barely open, but she looks with a mixture of protective love and bitter disappointment at the child who is laid on her stomach. All this suffering for a girl when she so dearly wished to give William the son he craved.

There is more pain, more contractions, and the afterbirth slides from her body furthering the bloody mess beneath her on the straw mattress. Then she is gently lifted, washed, clean bedding laid on the pallet, and her baby, swaddled and warm is put into her arms.

But Align turns to Catherine. 'Take her,' she whispers. 'Look after her. Promise me that you will be a mother to her, Catherine.' Then as her precious lifeblood seeps away into the freshened bed linen, she kisses her child and whispers, 'She is to be called Joan. Arrange her baptism quickly. Promise me, Catherine.'

'The priest waits below,' Catherine says. She takes the baby, lays her in the little wooden cradle that has been elaborately prepared and then she kneels at Align's side. She takes the cold hands in hers and tears flow down her cheeks unheeded. 'I promise, Align dear heart,' she says. 'Your Joan shall be as precious to me as if she were my own flesh.'

William refuses to be consoled and he completely rejects the child who has robbed him of his wife. Her care is left to Catherine. A wet nurse is sent for, a buxom girl from the village who has just given birth to a healthy son, and there are servants in plenty to wash and clean and sew, but the child depends only on Catherine for tenderness and love, and both are given in plenty.

In spite of all the gloomy predictions she lives and thrives, and Catherine finds that her promise to Align is easy to keep. Joan is a gentle, easy baby, hardly ever crying, and when she is awake she smiles and gurgles, and all who care for her come to love her. But William never visits the solar, never allows himself to look at his little daughter.

Summer passes, the swallows fly, and eventually snow covers pasture and forest. Life is tranquil in the Tracey manor house and Catherine wants for nothing. Thick walls keep out the cold and the frequent gales and rain that come in from the west. There are huge fires in many of the rooms, fed with logs brought in from the barns where they have been drying all summer. William is frequently away and she sees little of him, but he never fails in generosity. He provides thick luxurious furs and numerous gowns to keep her warm.

Catherine's father appears to have forgotten her existence. She knows that William has sent letters asking if she may remain as companion and foster mother to his daughter, and that he has acquiesced. There has been no mention from him about another husband, or a return to the convent, and for those mercies Catherine is mightily pleased.

During the winter she is content. She rocks baby Joan's cradle, croons to her and plays with her when she is awake, only passing her reluctantly to the wet nurse when she must be fed. She begins to imagine that the child is her own. Calder, too, accepts the baby well and shows no jealousy. Sometimes, though, when the sun shines she leaves Joan with the most reliable servant and rides out on her little palfrey with the great dog bounding beside her. On the whole life is good but, to her surprise, as the hedgerows begin to show the first signs of fresh new growth and a few tiny violets appear in the most secret places, an unwanted restlessness occasionally plagues her. At those times, if the weather is clement, she rides out to Litford, takes much needed gifts of food or clothing to Eluned and lays a remembrance on Tom's little grave. She traces the engraved words with her fingers and reads them aloud. 'Tom, Catherinae filius, hoc anno domini MCXLIII natus, quarto die obiit.'

Ten

*T*homas *seldom thinks of Catherine now. There are other matters on his mind. He has come to the court of Louis of France with letters from his master, Theobald of Canterbury. He feels very honoured to have been chosen for this task, especially as his visit will coincide with that of more important guests.*

Henry, Duke of Normandy, great-grandson of William the Conqueror, has recently come with his father, Geoffrey, Count of Anjou, to the French court. They are to be entertained by Louis, but more interestingly by his beautiful and powerful queen. All men are attracted to Eleanor of Aquitaine. She is the greatest heiress in the world, for Aquitaine is hers, a province that stretches from the Loire to the mountains of the Pyrenees. She is twenty-nine and has borne Louis daughters but no sons, and still her beauty shines bright, dimming every other woman who comes within her orbit.

Thomas stands at the back of the hall for he knows that he is of little importance now that he has delivered his letters. He watches Henry avidly, for this young man, son of the Empress Matilda, will one day be king of England. He has been accepted as Stephen's heir. England badly needs a strong and able ruler and Thomas likes what he sees. But he also notes that like all men, Henry cannot take his eyes from the French queen. She stands regally wearing a long, trailing gown of some shimmering material the like of which Thomas has never seen before.

He has heard many tales of young Henry's weakness for pretty girls and it is said there have been plenty in his bed, but Eleanor is no inconsequential wench to be tumbled and discarded at will. She is the most powerful woman in all

Christendom and the most dazzling too. Yet is it rumoured that her marriage is a sham, her husband monk-like, and that divorce is a possibility. Thomas moves as close as he dares and watches with fascination the meeting between this famous queen and the powerful young heir to England's throne.

Henry is now the focus of all men's attention in the great banqueting hall, and not a few women look favourably upon him. He is well built and stocky, not handsome but impressive and with an air of audacious confidence for one so young. And it is obvious that he has eyes for only one person. Thomas watches him approach the dais and bow before the queen. He takes her hand in his own with the boldness of youth and privileged upbringing, and kisses it.

'Madame,' he says. 'I am highly honoured to greet the queen of France.'

She smiles but it is not a comfortable smile, rather a challenging one. 'And surely I am just as honoured to have the future king of England make obeisance to me.' Her voice is clear and easily heard, for a silence has fallen upon the crowded room.

Thomas has now moved even closer and he hopes he has imagined the leap of desire that seems to spring between the two of them as they look keenly into each other's eyes. A union between these two is nearly impossible, yet he has a strange feeling that their destinies are somehow intertwined and, preposterous as it seems, with his own future too.

He laughs at himself for his fanciful ideas, turns away and finds a place at one of the great tables laden with every kind of meat and fruit imaginable. After the meal Henry strides past him and the two men look at each other. Henry acknowledges him and smiles and Thomas feels a lurch of his heart. Perhaps the singular presentiment he felt earlier was not so far-fetched after all.

'We made good time,' Phoebe said looking around her flat, wondering for one rather sobering moment if she had made the right decision to cut her holiday short and come back to London. 'I wonder where Kate is?'

Hugo carried various suitcases from the lift and dumped

them in Phoebe's bedroom. 'Answering machine's blinking,' he said, returning to the kitchen.

Phoebe took the message. 'Dudley wishes to see me,' she said.

Hugo groaned. 'Your weirdo agent! What does he want?'

'He's read the chapters I sent recently and wants to see me about them. He's probably having private hysterics about the fantasy bits.'

'I hope he wants you to cut out all that fictional stuff. You told me originally that the book had to be a straightforward biography.'

At that moment Kate erupted through the front door. 'Hi, you two,' she said. 'Good journey?'

Phoebe nodded. 'So-so. How are things then?'

'Pretty dire, but I'll cope.' She obviously didn't want to talk about Dominic. She opened the refrigerator and poured her usual glass of juice. 'Message from Dudley on the answer phone.' She sat down and looked directly at Phoebe. 'You won't let him persuade you to take out all the bits about Catherine will you?'

'I might have to.'

'What about the grave?'

'Just a piece of granite that might mean anything or nothing,' Hugo said.

'*Tom, Catherinae filius, hoc anno domini MCXLIII natus, quarto die obiit.*' Kate pronounced the words dreamily and both Hugo and Phoebe stared at her, concerned. Hugo was the first to come to his senses.

'It's all in your imagination,' he said firmly. 'This Catherine, if she ever existed at all, could be anyone from any century. How can you possibly connect her with Thomas à Becket for goodness sake?'

Phoebe shrugged her shoulders. 'I have no idea. Absolutely no idea at all.'

Catherine frequently wonders how long she can continue to live at the Tracey manor house, and when William's father dies and he inherits the title and lands she knows that he must soon bring home a new bride for he needs a male heir. The thought makes her apprehensive. What is her position here? She is more than just a nurse to Joan. She is an honoured guest, but a new lady of the manor will see more into this position than there is, will surely see her as a rival and have her removed. She dreads a return to the priory yet the idea of a loveless marriage to some unknown bridegroom of her father's choosing is even more to be feared.

Joan, Align's daughter, lacks for nothing that riches can supply, but William ignores her and Catherine provides the security that the little girl needs. She forgets sometimes that this child is not flesh of her flesh, for she loves her as her own. She still feels the loss of baby Tom, and should she be forced to leave this second precious child Catherine knows that the grief and heartache will be almost too much to bear. She continues to ride frequently to Litford and confides her fears to Eluned.

'But do you not think that Sir William will ask for your hand?' Eluned says one day during the following summer. 'He cannot grieve for the Lady Align for ever and you say that you like each other well enough. No man can live for long without a woman to warm his bed and bear his children.'

'He may choose someone more nobly born than I, or an heiress with money and land.'

'Rubbish,' Eluned says. 'He has need of neither more wealth nor more land. He knows and likes you, Catherine. His child loves you and you are beautiful and clever. He'll make you his lady before the year is out. Mark my words.'

Catherine has just been to lay a nosegay of flowers and sweet smelling herbs at the foot of the small headstone just beyond the boundary wall. 'And what if he cannot bear the thought of a woman with a guilty secret in her past?'

Eluned looks at her sharply. 'Does he know?'

'Oh yes. He knows, and believes it to be the result of a violation I suffered against my will. He is quite happy that I should come here in order to see you and to honour my son's grave. He always insists that I have an escort too.'

Eluned keeps her counsel. She has her own thoughts about Catherine's babe. 'Then he is a good man and obviously cares about you and your safety,' she says. 'The fact that you have borne a son will be a good recommendation. He need not fear that he is taking a barren wife or one who breeds only daughters.'

Catherine laughs a trifle grimly. 'We are just brood mares, are we not, Eluned? Our one purpose in life is to pleasure our man and bear his children.'

'It was always so, and no doubt always will be,' Eluned says. 'So the most fortunate thing that can befall a woman is a good man.'

'Aye, you speak the truth, and William is a good man.'

'I shall pray to the Blessed Virgin every night for news of the betrothal, and now see, I have made some of your favourite honey cakes. The bees have been kind, and I have a honeycomb especially saved for you.'

They sit at the rough wooden table and enjoy the cakes Eluned has baked in the small stone oven beside the hearth, along with the mead which Catherine has brought. But Eluned cannot leave the subject that is close to her heart. 'Does William ever look at you, Catherine? Look at you in a special way?'

Catherine laughs. 'Well yes. I do detect a certain lustfulness in his glances now and then. His behaviour is always seemly, however, and he never makes any unchaste suggestion.'

'I should think not.' Eluned is indignant. 'You must be sure to keep your virtue safe if you wish to become his lady wife.'

'My virtue? Didn't I lose that to Tom's father?'

Eluned rises and kisses the top of Catherine's head fondly. 'I don't wish to know anything about that,' she says. 'You are kind and beautiful and a loving mother to his Joan. What is past is past. You must value yourself more highly.'

Catherine frequently thinks about Eluned's words and tries to heed her advice. She always dresses carefully, makes sure that she is demure and pleasing at all times, especially whenever William is at home, and yet she is not servile. 'Value yourself,' Eluned had said, and so it is that towards the end of the following year William does indeed ask for her hand in marriage. Her father gives his permission willingly along with generous gifts to bride and groom, and Catherine

116

feels that at last she has redeemed herself in the eyes of her family.

William is not worried about the details of Catherine's previous life. He believes that she was raped and therefore was the innocent victim. As Eluned has said, he is more concerned to have a healthy and fecund wife than anything else. He remembers Align's terrible death and he does not want another tragedy in the birthing chamber.

Catherine knows this, and she is content. There is no great passionate love between herself and William, but she is quite happy that it should be so. They are fond enough, and he gives her those things which she most desires, protection and security and the hope of another child. She also has the constant companionship of little Joan, who calls her mother.

The only sadness during the early months of her marriage is the death of Calder, but he has sired many puppies in his younger days, and when one day William brings her a little bundle of energy and love, places it in her arms and tells her that the puppy is a grandson of her old faithful dog, she is more delighted than she can say.

'William is so kind and thoughtful to me,' she tells Eluned when the puppy is old enough to run beside her all the way to Litford. 'See, I have another Calder for company.' She looks fondly at the puppy who is now fast asleep in the shade of the old house wall.

'You are indeed fortunate in the man God has chosen for you,' Eluned says piously. 'Are you quickening yet?'

Catherine smiles. 'Yes, Eluned. I have not seen my courses for these two months now. When I tell my husband I think he will forbid me to ride out to see you again until the child is born.'

Eluned nods. 'And very right too. You must carefully guard the babe in your womb, Catherine. Never fear that Tom's grave will be neglected. I shall tend it faithfully for you.'

'Until I come again with my new little son to show you,' Catherine says.

At Michaelmas there is great rejoicing in the Tracey manor house for Catherine gives birth to William's longed-for heir.

117

The baby is christened William too and will be known as Will. The birth is easy and Catherine is thrilled that she has given her husband the child he so badly wants. She has proved her worth. During the following peaceful years another son is born, then two daughters, and Catherine frequently feels that her happiness is complete. There is nothing else she could possibly desire. She still thinks of her little Tom from time to time, but the pain of his death has passed. She continues to visit Eluned and lays flowers on the little grave, but she is at ease with herself.

England is at ease, too, for there is a new and powerful king. William returns from each visit to London buoyant and usually full of good news. 'I've much to tell you,' he says after one of his frequent journeys. He clumps into the hall in a flurry of serving men and girls all rushing to do his bidding.

She looks at him and smiles. She has no wish to visit London, her childhood home, but she has heard of the brilliant and beautiful Queen Eleanor who, after divorcing the staid and boring King Louis of France, has married Henry of England, many years her junior. It is said that the two are well matched, both full of energy, both lusty and passionate.

'The new king continues to rule well,' William says. 'He is young and tireless and seems able to keep the barons in control, something poor Stephen could never do.'

Catherine laughs, rocks her tiny daughter's cradle with her foot, and reaches down to smooth Calder's rough coat. The great dog lies with his paws resting on the hem of her gown. He follows her everywhere just as his grandsire used to do.

'Stephen was a good man but a poor king,' William says. 'Henry is very different. As well as ruling the country competently, he's likeable and people take kindly to him. Some, though, fear that he's too pleasure-loving.'

'How so?'

'He's very hearty, likes to go wenching in spite of his marriage to the delectable Eleanor. He consumes vast amounts of food and wine but never becomes fat because of the speed at which he lives. He delights in falconry and every kind of hunting. He flies into rages, but they are soon over. He is fond of junketing and merriment but he does everything so

118

thoroughly and so rapidly that he accomplishes all he must do twenty times as fast and efficiently as any lesser man.'

'He sounds to be a paragon,' Catherine says. 'And what of his queen?'

'She came to him with vast lands and great wealth, and she has already provided him with a male heir. She appears to know how to handle him, too, which is no small task.'

'You saw her this time?'

William nods. 'She was in the great hall and all eyes were upon her.'

'How did she look?' Catherine often wonders about this Eleanor, firstly queen of France and now queen of England. To be queen once must be an achievement, but twice is surely awe-inspiring indeed.

William throws back his head and laughs. Then he sits and beckons to a serving man to remove his boots. 'You women must always know how others of your sex look. She was . . . like a queen,' he says weakly. He leans towards Catherine and pulls her to him, caring nothing for the assembled servants scurrying to minister to him. 'How could I have eyes for any wench, even England's queen, when I have my Catherine waiting for me at home?'

'You flatter me, sir,' she says, but she is mightily pleased. 'And this royal couple, have they any faults at all?'

'The queen, none that I could tell.'

'And King Henry? Is he also perfect in every particular?'

'It is wise to say he is faultless of course. He cannot abide dealing with money, and all the finer points of administration bore him to distraction. He is too full of energy and restlessness for those things, but he has found the perfect solution.'

'So what does he do?' Catherine's mind is now not fully upon her husband's answer for she is thinking of the meal that is being prepared for this evening. She hopes that she has instructed the cooks well enough.

'He has a new chancellor,' William says. 'One Thomas à Becket. He was in the employ of Archbishop Theobald of Canterbury and was recommended for his efficiency. From all I hear they get on very well, and have become close friends. He's like the king in many ways, although a good

119

bit older. He's fond of the hunt, delights in falconry, is wildly energetic, and mightily enjoys all the pleasures of his office.'

Catherine's interest swiftly returns to what her husband is saying. Her heart leaps alarmingly and she stares at William. 'Did you say Thomas à Becket?'

William is surprised. 'Does the name mean something to you?'

She tries to compose herself. 'I knew him in London when we were children,' she says as calmly as she can manage. 'Our parents were acquainted. He has a sister, Mary, with whom I studied a little. There were other sisters too. He was the only son and therefore much favoured.'

William is pleased rather than suspicious. It is always useful to have influence at court. 'You must come to London with me when I next go,' he says rashly. 'The pestilence which swept the town is now quite gone.'

Catherine is alarmed. She shakes her head. 'No, William. I would rather not. The children need me, and I should much dislike the long journey.'

He smiles at her fondly. 'As you wish,' he says. 'You are a wonderful wife to me, Catherine. I should never require you to do anything you had no wish for.' He goes to the cradle and peers down at his latest daughter.

Joan, his eldest, growing up now and becoming more and more like Align, says timidly, 'I have a new little palfrey, father. Will you come and see her?'

He smiles. His first wife's young daughter holds few sad memories for him now that he has his Catherine and his fine sons. 'Later,' he says. 'I promise.'

'And does the new chancellor go wenching with the king? Is he bawdy too?' Catherine asks. The meal is now forgotten and her heart is thumping dangerously in her breast. Could Thomas have changed so much? 'From my memories of him he was very chaste and proper,' she says. 'And likely to remain so. He intended to go into the Church, I believe, and talked much of taking a vow of chastity.'

William looks at his wife with new respect. 'So you knew him well enough to talk of these things?'

'We talked now and then when he was but a boy. I wondered

120

if his early enthusiasms have followed him now that he is so grand.'

'I hear that he is still chaste,' William says. 'He loves all other pleasures, but has nothing to do with women. People talk of course, but he is not known to prefer men or boys. He appears to be celibate and it is something of a mystery to those close to him. Very odd for someone so handsome, rich and personable, but as he has the ear and close friendship of the king no one dares to question openly. He could have any woman he desires.'

'I read your manuscript three times,' Dudley said. 'I read it with ever increasing amazement. It's good, brilliantly written, Phoebe, but not at all what the publishers want. Your advance was for a serious biography of Thomas à Becket.' He pushed the pages across his vast desk towards her. 'Where did all this come from?'

Phoebe shrugged. She seemed to be doing a lot of non-committal shrugging lately. 'Catherine just sprang from nowhere,' she said. 'She came into my head and into my granddaughter's too. We both seemed to feel her presence, especially on Dartmoor. We found a little granite headstone with some words engraved in Latin. It was quite an awesome experience. I expect you think I'm mad.'

'No.' Dudley looked at her shrewdly. 'Not mad. Just the owner of a fascinating and compulsive imagination. Absolutely right for fiction.'

Phoebe wanted to say that to her it didn't feel like fiction, but she knew that she must not stretch Dudley's indulgence too far. As literary agents went he was pretty flexible, but he needed to make a living, and so for that matter did she. 'What do you think I should do then?' she asked.

'Two things. Two books!' Dudley grinned at her. 'You will have to work very hard, Phoebe dear. I want the biography to be out by Christmas. That means I need to have it very soon, with all reference to Catherine removed. Then you can enjoy yourself with the novel, a sort of fantasy.'

'Fantasy?' Phoebe gathered up the neatly processed pages. 'It doesn't feel like fantasy at all to me.'

'Right then, make it faction. That's a novel with a mixture of real historical characters and some fictional ones as well, like your Catherine. But I want the biography first. Does that sound satisfactory?'

'I think so, if I work hard.'

'God's teeth, Thomas, I swear I have never seen such splendour.' The king struts around his chancellor's great hall and looks in admiration at the trestles and boards laid out for their meal. There are even linen cloths spread upon them, and a vast throng of serving men and wenches are working quietly, carrying platters, cups and bowls.

'When I entertain my king then only the best is of use,' Thomas says. 'But come, sire, and view the stables while the victuals are prepared. I have a new mount which I wager you will wish to ride tomorrow.'

Henry laughs, a great bawdy roar, and he slaps Thomas on the back. 'Lead on then,' he says. 'If he is of better mettle than my own destrier then yes, I shall deprive you of him, and gladly.'

Watched enviously by not a few assorted courtiers as well as by lesser men, Thomas and Henry stride from the hall. The king's arm is laid about Thomas's shoulder and they walk as friends and equals.

FitzUrse, baron of the court, has been invited to this banquet with many others. He has arrived early, and is dumbfounded by what he sees. He turns to another guest who is also standing in the doorway watching the elaborate preparations. 'This Thomas à Becket lives as though he were a king, even better than a king,' he says and his voice is scathing and bitter.

'Aye, in truth I think you're right.' William de Tracey has come up from Devon, riding the many miles gladly, proud to have been summoned by the chancellor. He feels a swell of pride to think that his Catherine once knew this great man who now is second only to King Henry himself in wealth, power and importance. He wishes he had been more forceful and had insisted that she should accompany him here for this visit. What honour would have come his way if Thomas had called her to the high table! 'I hear that Becket is a good man,

*and wise,' he says to FitzUrse. 'And if he keeps the king happy,
then England will be blessed.'*

*FitzUrse looks at William scornfully. 'This Thomas is wise,
certainly, but I would lay a wager that "good" is not quite the
correct epithet.'*

'Are we an item now then?' Hugo was reading the *Sunday
Telegraph*. Its many sections lay scattered around him on
the carpet.

Phoebe glanced at him momentarily and then focused again
on her computer screen. 'Don't interrupt me, Hugo, there's
a dear. I was miles away, or rather years away, to be more
truthful.'

'You should work in your study.'

'I usually do, but it's too cramped and it's not companionable. I needed company this morning.'

'*You* are not companionable when you're tapping away at
that thing.'

'I have to finish this by the end of the month. That's the
deadline I've set myself. What did you say? Something about
an item?'

'Yes, as in living together.'

'OK then, we're an item.'

'We must move. This is your place. We need to start
afresh.'

Phoebe's attention was fully on him now. Thomas and his
London vanished from her thoughts. 'You mean move into
your house?'

'Possibly.'

'Absolutely not, nice though it is.'

'Right then.' Hugo was fired with enthusiasm. 'I'll telephone
estate agents tomorrow. Where do you want to be?'

'Make some suggestions, but not now, Hugo dear. No more
interruptions please.' Her voice was slightly desperate as she
returned her attention to her computer and thought of the
enormous task she had set herself. 'I must get this first book
finished, and wherever I live, I must have a nice big study.
Just for me!'

*　　*　　*

123

A great hall, vast and airy and strewn with sweet smelling herbs and rushes. There are platters of venison, duck and pheasant and what looks remarkably like swan. The dish is decorated by great white feathers. There are large baskets of white bread. Phoebe recoils at the idea of swan and wonders at the white bread. She had not known they ate white bread in the twelfth century. *There are flagons of wine, red and white, little round cheeses and a large wooden bowl of apples. Who is this sturdy, stocky man who swaggers in and to whom all men bow? None other than Henry II, king of England, of course. And beside him is another, very tall, dark and handsome and with an imposing presence. They are laughing bawdily together. They take their places at the centre of the top table and the hall is quiet for a moment in deference. All eyes are upon them. The hall is filling up, everyone taking a place according to rank.*

Phoebe suddenly feels cold. She shivers in spite of the warm evening air, and then she sees in her head two more men talking at the lower edge of the hall. She knows their names although how she has this knowledge she has no idea. *FitzUrse and William de Tracey.* She is not aware of Hugo and her London flat.

She opens her eyes, blinks, looks around the room in fear. She hears Hugo talking to her.

'Are you all right? Phee!'

She knows that she has once more been taken into another time, another place, and the years have been disarranged as has happened frequently before. The experience is like a vortex swallowing her up and then spewing her back in the twenty-first century.

'Yes, Hugo, I'm all right.' She gets up from her typing chair a little shakily. 'I need a drink. I've just seen Henry II and Thomas à Becket feasting together, and there were other things, dark things.'

Hugo goes to her, holds her in his arms. He doesn't really believe she's serious and tries to make light of her remark. 'Take me with you next time,' he says. 'I should like to get a look at Eleanor of Aquitaine. Now that *would* be something to boast about.'

*   *   *

'*You serve a hearty meal, Thomas. How am I to go wenching tonight?*' *The words are low and for Thomas's ears only.*

'*You will fare well enough, Sire.*'

'*And will you come with me, Tom? I know of fairer maids than you have ever bedded. I wager you will never stay at home at your prayers again.*'

'*Don't tempt me, Sire.*' *Thomas's voice, too, is low.* '*I will follow you into battle, or anywhere else you command, but in this one matter I cannot obey.*'

The king takes another cup of wine and drinks it heartily, wiping his beard with his sleeve. '*As you wish then,*' *he says.* '*And may your prayers satisfy you.*' *There is fondness and amusement in his voice.*

Eleven

'So, if you and Hugo intend to set up home together, what happens to me?' Kate was slicing an aubergine. Its flesh and glowing purple skin lay in chunks on the glass chopping board.

'You can continue to live with us, of course. My home will be your home, Kate, for as long as you want it. Surely you know that.'

'Why have you decided to shack up permanently with him?' Kate scooped the aubergine pieces into a basin and shook salt over them. 'I think your present arrangements are cool, no pressures, just having fun together. That way you get to keep your freedom.'

Phoebe sighed. 'Perhaps we want more than freedom. There's something to be said for commitment.'

'I'll never get that from Dominic.'

Phoebe looked at her, concerned. 'Want to talk?'

Kate swilled her hands in the bowl and slumped down at the kitchen table. 'He walked out on me that first night when we came home from Litford. I haven't heard from him since. I don't know what to do.' She was close to tears.

'Put him on hold,' Phoebe said as brightly as she could. 'Don't make any decisions. Just go off to university, meet lots of other guys, enjoy yourself. That might sound impossible just now, but honestly, darling, it's the best thing. He might come to his senses.' She wanted to add, *'I hope to God you find someone else.'*

'Come to his senses?' Kate said. 'You mean give up his vocation?' She shook her head. 'Did men ever sacrifice something they wanted to do very badly, their highest ideals, for a woman?'

'Sometimes they do.'

Kate burst into tears. 'I just hate God,' she said.

'We must have an alliance with France.' Henry paces about the hall of his Westminster palace and Thomas stands watching him. 'Louis has a daughter from that new wife of his, more than one in fact. Even with a second wife he can only breed daughters!' He roars with laughter, takes a bunch of grapes from the trestle table and puts the fruits into his mouth, a handful at a time.

Thomas reads his mind. In the political scheme of things royal children are pawns, little more.

'Louis has one particular daughter, three months old, and a great disappointment to him. And I have a son of three years. A perfect match, do you not think so, Thomas?'

Thomas nods thoughtfully. 'And how do you propose to sell this idea to the French king? He may appear a simpleton, but he has a multitude of astute and well-informed barons and advisors around him.'

'I've taken his wife from him and so gained sons,' Henry says with satisfaction. 'And Aquitaine as well. I propose to have more of France through this alliance, but that, my dear Thomas, is for your ears only. France must perceive this infant marriage as highly desirable.'

'And how will you go about the persuading?'

'You should have no need to ask,' Henry replies, spitting grape pips on to the floor. 'My chancellor is the only man in the kingdom who I would entrust with this . . . this slightly delicate task. You, Thomas à Becket, you will be my envoy. You will lead a mighty company to France. It will be one of pomp and splendour and wealth. We shall dazzle Louis and the French people so that they cannot refuse, so that the union of their princess with a prince of England is seen as a great honour with promise of much future gain.'

'And who is to be the lady escort to this infant princess?'

Henry guffaws noisily again. 'She will have her own retinue no doubt, but most of those must be sacked. We want no French influences to surround our future daughter-in-law, possibly

England's future queen. Choose carefully, and provide our own trusty English guardians.'

Thomas thinks long and hard that night. He has been entrusted with no easy task. Not for the first time he longs for the support and advice of a woman, for part of this charge is woman's work. Small princesses are not quite his domain. Once the alliance is agreed, and he has no doubt that this part of his task will be speedily settled, he must summon some of the barons and ask for the service of their wives.

His mind turns to those present at the banquet he recently held in the king's honour. FitzUrse he dismisses at once. Robert de Pontigney is too old and John of Canterbury too young. His wife is probably busy with her own brood. William de Tracey is perhaps the right age and likely to have a steady wife who might suit his purpose. He resolves to summon him on the morrow.

Dominic was enduring his own private Calvary yet again. He was on his knees in the empty church. 'I want you, Kate,' he whispered. 'More than anything else in the world.' In the world! There lay the conflict, the battle, the pain. The call from God was to be in the world, but not of the world, to serve and not to ask for any reward. The trite phrases slipped in and out of his head for he had been raised on a diet of Church, Liturgy, Bible and hymn book. His college, to which he must return shortly, constantly reinforced the sacrifices necessary for the life he had vowed to embrace. There was no sign of any liberalization yet of the rules by which a priest must live. Surely this must come in the future, he thought, but for now it was not so.

Now that he had discovered what it was like to love a woman physically he was torn and divided even more. Kate invaded his thoughts, his prayers, his dreams. The memory of her body, given to him so eagerly on that golden day on Dartmoor haunted every pore of him. The sin, if so it could be called, tormented and plagued him while the passion and the joy lifted him to previously unknown heights. Which was more valid? To which voice should be listen?

*　　*　　*

'You mean you are married to Catherine de Quincy?' Thomas's mind reels. Catherine, Catherine of the sparkling eyes, the ready wit, the quick brain. Catherine whom he loved, whose memory he still loves and glorifies. She has become to him, over the lonely years, a sort of religious icon to whom he pays homage. Sometimes he acknowledges that this almost amounts to idolatry, but it is his glorified image of the girl he loved a long time ago which enables him to keep his vow of chastity. It is a vow which the king is constantly telling him is not valid any more now that he has, for all practical purposes, given up the Church in order to become chancellor.

He gives de Tracey a long hard look. 'How did this come about, and when?' Privately he asks himself how it could possibly be that he had not been told of this marriage.

William is surprised at the hostile reception his news has received. He had expected that Thomas would be interested and delighted to hear news of his childhood friend, for this was how Catherine had talked of the king's chancellor.

'Catherine had an unhappy experience,' William says hesitantly. He says nothing of the supposed rape or of the baby buried at Litford, but speaks truthfully of Rainald de Beck's fortunate death. 'Her intended husband met with an accident while riding. She befriended my first wife and at her death in childbirth Catherine came to look after my baby daughter.'

Thomas towers over William for he is at least six inches taller, but to the now frightened knight he appears to be much more. 'Have you children?' Thomas asks.

'Yes, my lord. Catherine has borne me four little ones and we have my eldest also, my first wife's child.'

'Are there sons?'

William looks at Thomas and perceives a grain of envy. 'Two,' he says, and tries to keep the pride from his voice.

'Then you are much blessed.' Thomas turns away and kicks the rushes and herbs strewn over the flagstones of his hall. He walks to a narrow window built into the thickness of the wall and stares out at the courtyard beyond. What must he do now? Bid de Tracey good day, send his felicitations to Catherine, forget her existence? The icon he has made of her during all these years has suddenly become a flesh and blood woman, the mother of children, a saint changed into a wife. Of course he has always known in his head that this must have happened, but his heart and his soul have chosen not to know, not to hold this idea at all. It is many years since he enquired of her welfare from his sister, Mary. Catherine has become for him a sacred token of a life he has rejected, a memory to be worshipped and remaining always unobtainable.

Now he feels deeply ashamed. He remembers as if it were yesterday, the feel of her in his arms on that night long ago when they had lain together. He marvels even now at the way their bodies had fitted so wonderfully together, as if there was no other purpose in life but this, this sublime moment. His fists clench in anger and remorse and he forces himself to turn to this man, this miserable knight standing before him, the man who can avail himself of Catherine's love as a right and a duty. All the wealth and privileges of his position suddenly seem as straw and ashes beneath his feet.

'And is your wife well? How does she keep?' He can hardly speak the words, wanting an answer, and yet perversely not wanting to imagine her hearty and thriving and far from the saint he has made of her.

William nods. 'Aye, my lord. She does very well.'

'Then bring her to London!' It is an order, for suddenly Thomas knows that he must see her, slay the dragon of his lust and yearning. He must see the middle-aged matron that she must surely have become. Only so can the icon of his imagination be removed, only so will he have peace.

William is bewildered and confused. This man may be chancellor of England and second only to the king in power, but can he command another man's wife in this high-handed manner? 'She does not like to travel, my lord,' he says. 'And there are the children to mind.'

Thomas comes to his senses and realizes that this is no way to hold the loyalty of his knights, and he remembers the king's commission, the task that led him to ask William about his wife. 'The king has commanded me to go to France on a particularly difficult mission,' he explains to the bewildered William. 'It is not my usual sort of office, for there will be no fighting but much diplomacy – and the care of an important child. I must *assemble a great and worthy company to come with me, and most of all I need a good and reliable noblewoman to take charge of this royal infant.'*

William thinks he must be dreaming all this. He gapes at the exalted and glorious figure of the man standing before him. Why is Thomas à Becket, chancellor of England, telling him of these exalted plans?

'I am not at liberty to tell you any more,' he continues. 'But I don't feel equal to this task without the help of a woman. It pains me to say so.' He grins in a disarming manner. 'I thought of you, William. You were the first of my knights whom I considered might journey with me accompanied by your wife.'

'It's indeed a great honour,' William says. 'But if we are to prepare for such a journey I think we should know a little more of the reasons for going. Without more knowledge I shall not be able to persuade my Catherine to leave Devon.'

Thomas nods. 'So will you be sworn to secrecy, de Tracey?'

'Assuredly I will not speak of any matter you choose to disclose to me.'

'It concerns one of the French princesses,' Thomas says. 'That is all you must know.' Already he is weary of this duty the king has entrusted to him. 'No word to a soul apart from your wife, and bring Lady Catherine here before the month is out.' Then his better nature surmounts his anguish. 'I beg you to pardon me,' he says. 'I cannot order your lady wife to come here. Ask her if she will help in a most difficult task, a task for her country and her king. If she will, then much splendour and wealth shall be hers and yours too, and nothing will be spared to ensure her comfort and well-being. And of course you will accompany her. I shall need a great number of trusty knights.'

'Don't ruin your life for Dominic,' Phoebe said. 'A man with a powerful ambition will always put you last.'

'Powerful ambition?' Kate was sitting at the breakfast table toying with her muesli, eating little. 'Dommy isn't ambitious.'

'I suppose I was thinking of Becket. His ambition dominated

his early life and his devotion to God and the Church governed his later years. No easy character to live with.'

'Did you know that Saint Augustine is reputed to have had a relationship?'

'Yes, I did, and he had a son too, and was so holy that he deserted them both for his God and his vocation, or so some records say. A man with a devouring passion of any sort isn't good husband material, as I keep saying to you.'

Kate spluttered on her cereal. 'Honestly, Nonna, you're about fifty years out of date. What is "good husband material" supposed to mean?'

'Perhaps I am out of date, but what's wrong with a good husband or partner anyway? I read recently that marriage is coming back into fashion.'

'I suppose it might be,' Kate admitted. 'It's not really my scene just now though.'

'Have you heard from Dominic yet?'

Kate nodded. 'Yesterday. He asked me go to a concert tonight and then out to a meal. I wasn't sure whether to accept the invitation after two weeks of silence, but he's going back to his rotten seminary next week. I suppose it's a sort of farewell.'

Phoebe looked at her granddaughter's dismal face and sighed. She couldn't think of a thing to say that wouldn't sound patronising or elderly. 'I'll be thinking about you,' she said eventually. Then she kissed Kate gently, an affectionate gesture that meant all the things for which she had no words. She carried her coffee cup and the empty cafetière to the sink. She felt saddened and helpless, but the young had to face their losses and their demons as everyone did over the years. She went into her study and switched her computer into life. She would lose herself in a story eight centuries old and yet as new as life itself.

Kate sat at the kitchen table and stared unseeing into her empty cereal bowl. She had spent much of the past night sleepless and at times weeping beneath the duvet so that Phoebe should not hear. This final date with Dominic, for she felt in her heart that it would be so, had focused all her pent-up emotions. Since childhood she had never consciously envisaged a time when he would not be there for her and she for him. In spite of her jaunty words to Phoebe she acknowledged that it *was* an old-fashioned idea, something at which her friends would be inclined to laugh, yet perhaps not. She sometimes sensed that in spite of the abandon with which most of them jumped in and out of relationships, there was a yearning for the kind of love that outlasted the years, that remained constant for ever. Maybe the idea was out of date for the new world in which they all found themselves, an impossible fantasy for the second millennium. Yet it was the quality of love she had always thought existed between herself and Dominic.

Then her mind returned to a half-remembered dream of last night, for she had eventually slipped into an unquiet sleep during those long, miserable hours. The girl from the past had been there again. Catherine had been holding a baby. Kate closed her eyes and tried to recreate that dream. The details would not come but instead the words on the little Devon gravestone rang in her head again. *Tom, Catherinae filius, hoc anno domini MCXLIII natus, quarto die obiit*, and then again in a strange voice and language which nevertheless Kate could understand, *Find another life, another love. Loving a man with a devouring passion for his God is always a difficult cross to bear.*

She pushed her cereal bowl away. The words and the intense conviction with which they came to her now were awesome, a message not to be ignored. Were all the things that had just been going through her mind about Dominic and her love for him totally misplaced?

Kate carried her bowl to the sink and automatically cleared the table of the remains of breakfast. Was a future with Dominic just pure fantasy then? Or was this warning from the past merely a made-up dream, a nightmare coming from the machinations of her own mind? Could her own heartbreak materialize into an imagined girl and a fictitious message? Tonight she would know for sure.

Twelve

'*An escort to a princess? You cannot have heard correctly, William.*' Catherine has just welcomed her husband home from London and they are walking in the garden, enjoying the last of the evening sunshine.

William takes his wife's hand and holds it close in his own for here they are out of sight of the house. The trees and gently rolling hills of Devon are all around them and he glories in the peaceful setting of his lovely home. Left to himself he would have preferred to remain here rather than face another journey to London so soon and then to France, but he cannot possibly ignore the great honour that has been bestowed on his family.

'The chancellor remembers you, Catherine, and he wishes for a discreet and gentle noblewoman to accompany him to France. He thought you would be very suitable, and I am to journey with you, of course.'

Catherine hears the pride in his voice and looks at him with affection, but she can still hardly believe this news he has just given her. It will change her life completely.

They have now come into her walled herb garden and she releases her hand from his for a moment and picks a sprig of rosemary. She crushes it and holds it to her face. The scent reminds her of her parents' home and the times she and Thomas played together in the garden there. She closes her eyes for a second and can see the young boy, taller now and stronger than she, running along the stony path between the plants, climbing the great oak tree that stood at the end of the wall, daring her to follow. Thomas!

'So you saw him, the great chancellor,' she says. 'And you spoke together?'

'Of course. He was surprised to learn that you are my wife.'

'How did you come to tell him this, husband?' Catherine's heart is beating tremulously and she wonders what passed between them.

'He enquired of my family and wished to know the name of my wife's parents too. The matter in which he requires our help is slightly . . . shall we say . . . delicate.'

'You intrigue and amaze me, William. What did you tell him of my past?'

'Merely that your intended husband met with a riding accident, that you were a good friend to my first wife, that you cared for her motherless daughter, and that we are now wed. He asked for nothing more.'

Catherine looks at William fondly and smiles, her anxiety diminishing a little. He is a good man. He will never tell of the little grave at Litford, and indeed there is no reason why he should. It is of no importance to him. 'And what of the king?' she asks.

'He and Becket are very close.'

Catherine marvels again at the great good fortune that has befallen her childhood friend. She blushes and is glad that she and William are walking side by side and that he cannot see her face. It is true that when they were children Thomas was her frequent companion, but William cannot know that he became much more than that, her lover, the father of her son, the man who still holds part of her heart. How can she possibly spend weeks in his company and not betray her feelings, her secret, the existence of the little body lying for so long now in the cold earth at Litford. Tom, Catherinae filius, hoc anno domini MCXLIII natus, quarto die obiit.

'I cannot do it, William,' she says. 'I cannot possibly leave the children and embark on this strange journey. To France you say? There are surely many other ladies at court who would be better suited than I.'

'So I thought, my dear. But when he realized that he knew you from the past he was even more adamant that he wished you to undertake this task. It was for the king, for England, he said, not for him personally. It is a matter of state and

135

very important. I believe it has to do with an alliance with France.'

Then suddenly Catherine begins to understand. She has heard that the French king can breed only daughters, that Henry has sons. 'How old did you say this child is?'

'Very small. Just a few weeks or months I gather.'

'And she is to be brought to England to marry Henry's son, who is probably also very young.'

William had not been told the details, for Becket had stressed that all was highly secret, but now that Catherine, with her quicker brain, has put these facts together he begins also to see. 'Yes, I suppose it is as you say. I think the young prince is but three years old.'

'And of course royal children are merely pawns.'

'They will have the best of everything,' William says. 'You need have no fear for their welfare. They are the hope and pride of England and France.'

'Fine words, husband,' Catherine says. 'But a baby needs a mother.'

'And the chancellor has decreed that you shall be that mother for the time of the journey. It is a great honour that he does us, my Catherine. Please say that you will agree.'

Catherine sees that he is anxious to comply with this daunting task and she smiles a little. 'Alone I couldn't do it,' she says, 'But if you can assure me that you will accompany me, then I will come.'

'Of course. We shall undertake this together. I will never leave your side.'

Catherine guesses that this will not be totally true, but nevertheless William's presence in the company will surely keep her heart safe from that long-ago passion. She has realized for some time that her love for her husband has grown with each passing year. He now has the greater part of her heart. Only a small part remains reserved for Thomas.

That night Catherine sleeps restlessly. The girl in the strange clothes has not come to her for a long time, many years in fact. But now she sees her clearly in her dream once more. She is weeping and there is a man in what looks like a priest's robe, but he is not tonsured. He has the face and build of Thomas and the girl is singularly herself. She calls out in her sleep, 'Kate!'

She experiences the sadness of this girl's heart as if it were her own, and she senses the cause of this grief too. 'Do not surrender yourself to this man.' The words are wrung from her in her strange nightmare. 'Find another life, another love. Loving a man with a devouring passion for his God is always a difficult cross to bear.'

Beside her William stirs. 'What ails you?' he whispers anxiously. 'Hush, dearest. You will wake the servants and the children.'

Catherine sits up and rubs her eyes. The words she has spoken are strange to her ears. She can remember the content of them but not the actual form. She knows that she has not spoken in her usual Norman French, nor in the Anglo-Saxon that she uses for the servants. Not Latin either. 'Did you hear what I said, William?' she asks, fearful now.

'Just nonsense, my dear,' he says to her. He takes her in his arms, strokes her willing body, makes love to her, and she is calmed. To her relief the girl with the strange blue chausses on her legs – the garb of peasants, certainly not of noblemen and never of ladies – has vanished, but when she awakes the next morning she remembers and wonders. How can she understand this girl's anguish? How can she feel it so deeply as if it were her own? And why is she so sure that this strange creature has substance and reality and is not merely a figment of some strange dream world, or worse, a fiend or devil sent to disturb and terrify?

Kate sat glumly through Mozart's clarinet concerto. The opening allegro failed to lift her spirits, tears poured silently down her cheeks during the adagio, and even the jolly notes of the rondo brought no cheer. Every now and then she stole a glance at Dominic. He appeared to be totally engrossed. Eventually she closed her eyes and gradually the music seemed to fade. She shivered in spite of the heat of the concert hall and was aware of other things, a strange haunting scent, herbs and wood smoke. Her hands, clutching a tissue, were resting on her lap, but now she felt a strange fabric beneath her fingers. A skirt? She had not been wearing a skirt. She hears a voice inside her head as strongly as if she or someone close to her had spoken the words aloud. *Do not surrender yourself to this man. Find another life, another love. Loving a man with a devouring passion for his God is always a difficult cross to bear.* The same message again! She had heard it in her dream last night and then at breakfast, powerful and impassioned. She opened her eyes, stared at the orchestra, at the row of heads in front of her, and at Dominic close beside. No one was looking round in annoyance. No one was telling her to hush. Everything had been inside her head. She clutched at the material of her jeans and felt the belt at her waist with its key ring from which swung the key to the flat. Relief flooded over her, yet she still felt frightened at the strange sensations of a moment ago. '*Catherine*,' she whispered involuntarily.

Suddenly she was surrounded by applause. Dominic looked at her at last. 'That was brilliant,' he said. 'Enjoy it?'

She nodded and clapped as enthusiastically as she was able. He peered at the programme and passed it to her. Some Tchaikovsky and then after the interval the Elgar cello concerto. Of course she had known that this was the major work of the evening. Dominic was a great fan of the tragic Jacqueline du Pré. He had all her recordings. And now there was another budding young cellist to be appraised, only fifteen years old and already a major soloist. Kate wondered how was she to sit through the whole of this sadly emotive piece of music without crying her eyes out? Get mildly drunk was probably the answer.

After the Tchaikovsky they pushed their way to the bar and without asking Dominic bought her a whisky. 'Cheer up,' he said. 'It's not the end of the world.'

'What isn't the end of the world?' Kate felt that tonight was very definitely the end of *her* world.

'Our separating for a bit,' he said.

'For a bit?' she replied scathingly. 'Don't you mean for ever?'

He sighed and downed his beer rapidly. 'You'll go to

138

Bristol, Kate, and forget me. You'll find someone else. People at universities do.'

'My God, Dominic. You don't understand anything do you? You think you can cast me off like a bit of unwanted garbage in your life just because your fucking God must have every bit of you.'

Dominic blanched and looked around to see who might have heard. One or two of the nearest couples were staring with interest in their direction. He took her glass from her, set it down on the bar, grabbed her arm and pulled her through the crush of bodies and out to the vestibule. She went willingly, not wishing to stay a minute longer.

'I don't want anyone else, Dominic.' She stumbled down the staircase after him. 'I'm in love with you. With you!' She shouted the last words just as they reached the now closed ticket office.

He released her arm and turned to face her. 'Hell, Kate, don't you know that I've got the hots for you as well, now and all the time? That I'm fighting the biggest battle of my life?' His arms suddenly went round her and he crushed her body to his. His lips found hers and he kissed her savagely. Then he pulled away, forced his hands down to his sides. 'You make it bloody impossible.'

She stared at him in disbelief. 'I what? I don't believe I'm hearing this. *I* make it impossible for *you?* For you to what? Walk away to your miserable seminary and forget all about me? Well a good bloody thing. The more wretched you are the more I shall cheer. What are you trying to say to me, Dominic?' She threw the words angrily at him. 'I can tell you just what you're saying. You're trying to tell me that you want some old man in the sky instead, a noble giving of yourself to a sublime purpose, a fucking celibate life?' The irony of her words failed to signify, and she cared not one jot that her language was deeply offensive to him. He probably thought it blasphemous. 'It's been the same down the centuries,' she went on. 'Women are the evil ones, the cause of man's temptation. I thought we were living in a new, enlightened age but it seems your Church is stuck in a time warp, still in the Middle Ages.' She gritted her teeth and slapped him hard across the face. 'I'm going, Dominic. You can listen to your blessed Elgar without me. It's all you'll have for the rest of your life.'

She rushed out of the foyer, hailed a taxi and sank into its welcome anonymous depths. *Tom, Catherinae filius, hoc anno domini MCXLIII natus, quarto die obiit.* The words came out of nowhere and went round and round in her head. Then came those other words that she had heard earlier tonight in the midst of . . . of what? The Mozart? She had no idea. They came to her again in the same voice, in a strange language, yet one that she could understand. *Do not surrender yourself to this man. Find another life, another love. Loving a man with a devouring passion for his God is always a difficult cross to bear.* The message was strong and more purposeful than it had been in the concert hall. She closed her eyes and gave herself up to its power.

'Here we are then, love.' The taxi driver slid open the glass partition. 'Traffic's not too bad tonight.'

She passed a ten pound note through to him. 'Thanks,' she said.

She groped her way to the front door of the apartments, walked up all the stairs instead of taking the lift and eventually let herself into the flat. She crept into the kitchen and put the kettle on to boil. It sprang to life with a buzz and a rumble and Phoebe put her head around the door. 'Hi, you're back early.'

'I walked out during the interval.'

Phoebe came further into the room. 'Shall I go away?'

'No, stay. He's made up his mind. I knew he had, of course.'

'But you hoped to change him. It never works! Men are too single-minded.'

The kettle turned itself off and was suddenly silent. Kate, working on autopilot, deposited mugs on the table and put a spoonful of coffee into each. 'How is he to remain celibate all his life? Can anyone do that?'

Phoebe sighed. 'We've had this conversation before and the answer is that I don't really know. I think women can sometimes remain chaste. They often have no choice. Think of all the spinsters after the First World War. I've always thought that it's easier for us. A man has a driving need to populate the earth, to pass on his genes. It's nature.'

'That's pretty gross. Is that all it is?' Kate slopped water into the mugs, found milk and added it.

'Of course not, darling. There's love. You'll find it eventually.'

'I thought I had,' Kate said.

Dominic, too, was unable to face the Elgar. He stood and watched helplessly outside the concert hall as Kate's taxi sped away into the confusing lights of London's traffic. He had seriously confronted the harrowing subject of his own celibacy for many months and lately believed that he had at last come to terms with this, his own private cross. Now he knew that he had done no such thing. A continuing platonic friendship with Kate was out of the question. He had been unbelievably naive to imagine that it was possible.

He started to walk in the direction the taxi had taken but without any idea at all where he was going. He walked for two hours and every conceivable solution came and went in his mind. All the theology, all the noble ideals, all the ambition, shrank into the one ever-continuing problem: Kate, or his career and his God?

Problem? That was the understatement of his life. Dominic clenched his fists in his anorak pockets and wondered how he could possibly have been stupid enough to allow things to develop this far.

There had been lectures about celibacy at college and open discussions afterwards, young men like himself in the overpowering grip of their own strong sexual drives all trying to face the unfaceable. Noble self-sacrifice had seemed admirable then. The presence of others in the same situation gave strength. Now, alone, it just appeared to be irrational and unnecessary.

Yet he was determined. Determined to follow the course he had set, however hard the road. In the early hours of the morning he reached his small flat, and then at last, throwing himself on to his knees beside the bed, he took the little crucifix

141

that stood on his bedside table, gripped it hard until his fingers ached, bowed his head, and wept.

'We must display all the magnificence of England before the king of France,' Henry says. 'Louis must be overwhelmed by our show of wealth and splendour.'

Thomas is only too happy to obey this part of the charge. An abundance of riches and all the luxuries that the court of England can supply have come to mean much to him, replacing almost in full measure the loss of those other things that he has so painfully set aside.

'But Thomas,' Henry continues, 'there is still one matter in your behaviour that grieves me. As my chancellor you should now renounce your vows to the Church. It would be advantageous if you had a wife to accompany you on this venture. I could arrange an influential marriage. There are plenty of noble-born women from whom you could take your choice.'

'In this one particular I cannot obey you, Sire,' Thomas says.

'Then at least take women into your bed now and then. There are plenty who would oblige and it would make you more human.' The king laughs and thumps Thomas on the shoulder. 'We could go wenching together.'

'Perhaps one day,' Thomas says placatingly, for it does not do to oppose the king too often, but he knows that in this he will never comply. He has lost his Catherine so he will have no other. 'I have sent for an admirable woman to be lady-in-waiting to the infant princess,' he says.

Henry guffaws loudly. 'Who is this woman then, Tom? Is she beautiful?'

'She is the wife of William de Tracey, a worthy matron I am told.'

'You disappoint me.' The king soon loses interest and turns away. 'But perhaps she will bring serving maids to satisfy your needs.'

Thomas bows as the king leaves. He knows that Henry will forget this part of his instructions very quickly and he puts his troubled thoughts aside to concentrate on the many other important matters to be arranged. Henry has commanded that he should have two hundred knights on horseback, clerks, butlers, serving men, and more. A mighty army, and all attired in the best robes that can be found. Provisions must be obtained and carried, cooks engaged. There are carriages to be prepared, each drawn by five horses, large beasts like destriers but accustomed to pulling in a team, and there must be a man walking beside each carriage dressed in a new tunic every day. Many presents must be purchased for the French king, for the baby princess, and for her mother, the French queen. These are to be the most prestigious gifts that England can produce.

Litters and transports of various sorts have been dispatched to Devon to fetch Catherine de Tracey and her husband, their servants and their baggage, and Thomas has seen that these are the best he can procure.

When Catherine first beholds them she is quite awe-struck. 'Jesu preserve us,' she whispers to William. 'Is the chancellor so very grand then that he can send such wonders all these miles to take us to London?'

'Aye, wife, and this is nothing. He has the ear and the purse of the king. We are much honoured, although why he holds you in such high esteem I cannot imagine.'

'He and his sisters were my close companions, William. As I have told you many times, Thomas and I played together frequently. Mary was older and more studious, but Tom and I would race and climb trees. He helped me with my Latin, and I wished so much then to be a boy.' She remembers and smiles a little to herself.

William looks searchingly at her. The king's illustrious chancellor is merely Tom to her. He thinks of the splendour and power of Thomas à Becket and marvels at his good fortune.

'Perhaps he wishes to recall the uncomplicated days of his childhood and youth,' Catherine says. She hopes this is all Thomas requires.

William shakes his head in bewilderment. 'The ways of the great are quite beyond my understanding,' he says.

Catherine kisses him lightly on the cheek, and hopes that he will never have cause to doubt her love.

*   *   *

Thomas puts aside his grandest robes when he prepares to meet Catherine's entourage. He comes to her simply and with only two of his squires for company. The litter halts and William reigns in his horse, inclines his head slightly, and feels an immediate sense of inferiority when he sees again the splendour of the king's chancellor, for Thomas is splendid in spite of his efforts to appear unpretentious.

'My lord,' William says. 'I have brought my lady wife as you wished.'

Catherine trembles. She looks up at the handsome figure on the great destrier and all the love and longing that she had thought long-buried comes flooding into her heart, into her face. She inclines her head in acknowledgement, and then Thomas leaps from his mount, takes one stride to stand before her, looks deeply into her eyes, takes her free hand and kisses it gently. He quickly recovers himself. 'Lady Catherine, I am honoured and grateful that you should come, and such a long journey too.'

'It is I who am honoured, my lord,' she manages. 'To serve the king in such a matter is indeed a great privilege.'

William looks from one to the other and marvels that this confident and beautiful woman was once the sad little girl from the convent whom he rescued and then employed to care for Align's motherless baby. He feels no jealousy, merely gratitude that in the honouring of his wife, he too is honoured.

Autumn in London, grassy squares and tree-lined side roads littered with leaves, shops full of winter clothes, and Phoebe missing Kate very much.

She finished reading the letter she had just received and then passed it to Hugo. 'She seems to be enjoying her first term. Bristol is obviously a success. I don't suppose she's over Dominic yet, but I sense that the misery is dimming.'

'Of course it is. We all have to cope with life's little tragedies and losses from time to time, and she's young.' Hugo read the two pages, re-folded them and put them on the table.

'I don't think she would have called it a *little* tragedy,'

Phoebe said. 'She's known Dominic since she was a child. I should have seen it coming, this disastrous falling in love.'

'You weren't to know that he'd be so damned set on becoming a priest though.'

'It was what his mother always wanted. She was my friend, but I couldn't go along with her strict Roman Catholic beliefs, and I suppose I hoped that Dominic wouldn't follow. We had endless discussions, but she was as stubborn as he is.'

'Stop worrying,' Hugo said. 'Kate's sensible and attractive. She'll soon find someone else.'

'I hope you're right.' Phoebe sat down in front of her computer and stared at the empty screen. She had just finished the biography and the pages lay in a neat pile on her desk ready to send to Dudley. She picked them up, flicked through them despondently. This book wasn't what she had really wanted to do, and her concerns about Kate had intruded more than she cared to acknowledge. Her mind drifted to Devon, to Litford. 'Do you believe in reincarnation?' she asked Hugo suddenly.

He lowered the newspaper he had been reading. 'Now why should you ask me that just now?'

'I don't know really.' Phoebe put two elastic bands around the loose pages of the manuscript, for this was how Dudley liked to receive them. She slid them with difficulty into the padded envelope that she had bought and addressed yesterday. 'I suppose I'm relieved to be sending this off to Dudley. I can think about the next book now, the mixture of fact and fiction that Dudley said might be a good idea. *Faction*, he called it.'

'Where does reincarnation come in?'

'Catherine, Kate, Thomas, Dominic. Aren't they all mixed up somehow?'

'In your mind and your imagination, yes, and you'll write an excellent story, but how much will be true and how much pure fiction is open to question.' He shuffled the newspaper pages and attempted to look at the headlines again. 'I don't suppose it matters as long as you produce a page-turner that people will buy.'

Phoebe searched for Sellotape, sealed the envelope and regarded it with some satisfaction. 'I feel a great longing to get into the novel,' she said. 'It seems to come from somewhere inside my head, almost a sort of *driven* feeling.'

'Then my dear Phoebe, that's what you must do. We'll have a day out somewhere, a celebration meal, and then back to work. I'll be the house husband again.'

'We aren't married!'

'No, I'd not forgotten, but I can still do the washing up.'

Phoebe looked at him with affection and amusement. He was such a practical person, always concerned with the mundane and the prosaic, never keen to be involved with the paranormal or any uncharted phenomena. 'I'll go along with that,' she said. She smiled at him, then pressed the power button on the computer and watched it flicker into life. She accessed the folder she had named 'Faction' and then closed her eyes.

She sees a great multitude, all richly dressed in brilliant colours, great horses bearing knights in bright surcoats and armour that gleams in the sun. There are trumpeters in the scarlet livery of a king, wheeled wagons drawn by horses almost as large and splendid as the destriers of the knights. And now here is Thomas. Phoebe's heart misses a beat when she sees the man about whom she has just been writing. She puts her hand on the large brown envelope on her desk. He has come alive again in her mind and in her heart. The great chancellor of England is riding tall and splendid on the most richly caparisoned horse she has ever beheld, a huge black stallion. His robes shine with jewels and gold, fur-trimmed and threaded with silver. She sees the Great Seal of the king around his neck and she suddenly understands that this is the procession sent to France to take custody of the baby princess who is betrothed to the little English prince. Phoebe has been reading an account of this momentous event and she has discovered that the wife of William de Tracey was lady-in-waiting to the French princess.

Catherine? Phoebe gasps as she sees the connection. This time she has not regressed into the past, the past has come to her, into her mind and her vision as though she had a vast television screen in her head. Her Catherine, the Catherine of Litford, of the little grave! Of course Thomas would have chosen her. *Catherine is riding in a litter close to the chancellor's prancing mount, and she looks from the curtains and smiles. She is wearing a headdress which glitters in the sunlight. Thomas raises his hand to acknowledge her, but Phoebe cannot interpret the expression in his eyes.*

Kate? Catherine? One and the same? Was she going mad? Phoebe gripped her typing chair and whirled around on it to look for Hugo. She stood up, went into the kitchen and filled the kettle. 'Coffee?' she called. Hugo was the reality that kept her in the present, anchored in the blessed twenty-first century. As she stood waiting for the kettle to boil she thought about Catherine's story. True or false? She would never know, no one would ever know, it was in her heart and in her head, it filled her mind and her thoughts. She must get it into her computer and on to paper, and then perhaps she would be rid of it and Kate would be free from her doomed love for Dominic.

Thirteen

Parke Manor stood rather splendidly in its impressive setting of gardens, lawns, mature trees and surrounding hills. Phoebe and Kate, on a short Christmas visit to Devon, stared at the large house. 'When was it built?' Kate asked. 'It looks Georgian.' She felt slightly disappointed. It was, after all, the site of the home of William de Tracey. She had pictured Catherine living here in a sprawling granite-built house looking something like a larger version of Litford.

Phoebe laughed at her aggrieved tone. 'The site was probably named in Saxon times, but the present house was built around the 1820s after an older one was pulled down. There was a medieval manor house here before that. It's the headquarters of the Dartmoor National Park now.'

Kate shook her head in amazement. 'That sounds too impossibly modern. I wish the ancient one was still here.'

They had parked in the spacious visitor car park and walked down an old path that led to the gravel drive and double front door. A notice leaning against it proclaimed: CLOSED.

'It's closed for Christmas week I suppose,' Kate said, feeling even more disgruntled. 'Do you think anyone lives here?'

'Probably just a caretaker.' Phoebe gazed at the windows and at the computers clearly visible behind the uncurtained glass. 'I can't get much atmosphere for the book here, can I?'

'There are some older bits. We passed a barn that looks as though it was once a chapel,' Kate said hopefully. 'I noticed it on the path down from the car park.'

'Thomas came here whenever he had been visiting Buckfast Abbey,' Phoebe contributed. She shivered and wrapped her scarf more closely round her to keep out the winter cold. 'I think that bit of the story is attested fact. He knew de Tracey's wife and stayed at Parke.'

'Catherine! It all ties in with your story.' Kate looked away from the house to the surrounding hills. 'The new houses rather spoil the view.' She nodded towards a building site on the opposite side of the valley.

'But it's so beautiful here,' Phoebe said, half to herself. 'Apart from the house, not much has changed in eight hundred years.'

Catherine is missing her home and her children. She sometimes longs for the sturdy house set amidst its encircling hills and for her little ones safe in the care of Eluned, who has left her own home to stay in the manor house and supervise the nursemaids and serving girls. Catherine trusts Eluned above all others. Yet still she worries, and while Eluned is away from Litford the small grave on the moor will be left unattended and vulnerable. Catherine thinks often of her first baby's grave, even more than usual now that she sees Thomas frequently. The burden of the knowledge she holds distresses her. Each time he rides up to the litter in which she travels she cannot help remembering the little body in the cold earth at Litford. Thomas knows nothing of his son. Should he ever know? And if she tells him, could her husband find out the truth as well? She is very apprehensive and fearful.

William has been put in charge of arranging accommodation for the most privileged knights in Thomas's entourage. He is to ride ahead and procure the best that each small French town can provide. This removes him from Catherine's company for much of the time and she wonders, uneasily, if Thomas has designated this task to her husband in order to have time with her alone. Yet they are now five days into the journey since crossing the Channel and there has been little time for private talk. Each meeting is very public.

On the sixth day he rides alongside as usual, but now the procession is slower and the horses walk unhurriedly. Catherine pulls the curtains apart, bends her head to acknowledge him and smiles.

'Is all to your liking still, my lady?' he asks. 'Do you continue comfortable and well?'

'Yes, my lord. I am very well and enjoying the journey. I had never thought to see another land or to travel in such splendour.'

The procession halts to allow the crossing of a narrow bridge and Thomas dismounts. He flings the reins to a serving man and pulls the curtains further apart. 'May I?'

Catherine feels her heart beat wildly. 'Of course.'

He is now close beside her and she can hardly look at him. At first they talk of general, unimportant things, then suddenly he puts his hand over hers.

'Why did you leave so suddenly, Catherine, all those years ago when we were young? For an arranged marriage I was told, but I found it difficult to believe.'

She is silent, feels tears run down her cheeks and she is glad that the day is dull, the litter dim, so that he cannot see. Tom, Catherinae filius, hoc anno domini MCXLIII natus, quarto die obiit. Can she tell him now? Is this the right time? Perhaps he should visit the little grave when they return to England? Perhaps he should share her grief? But then William might discover the truth and the whole world would know.

He sees the tears in spite of the poor light for he gently strokes them away. 'You are crying my Catherine.' There is concern in his voice. 'Does something ail you?'

She cannot keep her secret any longer. It has eroded her happiness for too many long years and she longs to share the burden. 'That day we sinned, Thomas, the time we lay together. There was issue.' The words are out now, stark and grim, the truth that ruined her young life.

He is silent for what seems an endless time, but his hand grips hers more tightly so that her fingers almost feel they will break in the strength of his. 'A child?'

She nods, speechless, and tries to free her hand but it is held firm in his.

'God's wounds, Catherine! Why did you not you tell me?'

'How could I? We were not wed. It was mortal sin. I was sent away in disgrace as soon as my mother found out.'

'Does the child live?'

She takes a deep breath and surprises herself with the anger she feels. Is this all he cares about? That he might have a son? 'No, he does not live.' Her words are sharp and bitter. 'He is buried on the Devonshire moors in a poor little grave, a bastard child without a father's name or any honour.'

Thomas releases her, covers his face with his hands and weeps. Eventually he says, 'I must make penance, and I must do all in my power to recompense you, Catherine. My poor, poor child.'

She is not sure whether he refers to her or to his lost son. She is still angry and cannot, at this moment, find it in her heart to pity him at all. 'It must be a secret between us for ever,' she says. 'Between us and no other. My husband doesn't know who the father of the child is. He thinks I was taken advantage of against my will before he came to know me, and so he overlooks it. He would not be so kind if he discovered the truth.'

'It shall be our secret only, Catherine,' he says. 'I have suffered too.'

Catherine wonders what he can mean. He seems to have everything any man could desire. She looks at him coldly, but although there is still anger in her heart there is passion too. She longs for him as much as she did when she was an innocent and foolish girl.

'I loved you deeply, and when I couldn't have you I made a vow to have no other.'

She is amazed for she has heard tales of the king's lecherous and lustful ways and she knows that Thomas and Henry are said to be as close as the biblical David and Jonathan. The king always chooses Thomas above all others. Oft-times they have been seen sharing the same platter.

'And have you kept your vow?'

He looks into her eyes. 'Yes, Catherine. I have kept my vow.'

Kate and Phoebe were staying for these few days with Talitha and Garth at High Mead, for Litford was closed up for the winter. In the early morning stillness Kate walked the short distance from High Mead to the older house. She had only one thought on her mind. She wanted to stand in front of the little headstone and feel her way into Catherine's thoughts. She had read Phoebe's unfinished manuscript and saw herself in the story, saw the undeniable similarities, the love and the passion, the rejection and the heartbreak. And in both cases it was a rejection for none of the usual reasons. There was no other woman, no lack of love and caring, but before all else was this burning zeal to serve God and the Church. Perhaps there were differences though. Thomas à Becket was consumed by his own ambition. He longed for power and position, riches and adulation. How could this square with religious ideals? She had no idea. She would leave that to Phoebe. Dominic was her own, more immediate, martyr.

Dominic had written to her once during the term, one long impassioned letter. He had set out his love for her, and in deep theological terms his greater love for God and all that that meant. She had torn the letter into shreds and she had relegated him and his God to a past part of her life. Or so she hoped. Now, as she walked along the muddy track to Litford, her anger was rekindled, and unwillingly, her love.

The stone was still there. She stared at it and wondered if her feelings about it were just dreams and fantasies. Perhaps so or perhaps not. Reincarnation? Was Catherine living her life all over again now in this modern age, living through Kate? It was scary and she had tried not to think that this might be so. There was one glaring difference between Catherine's story and her own – no baby! She bent down to the supposed little gravestone and traced her hand over the words. She spoke them now quietly and in English. *Tom, son of Catherine, born in the year of our Lord 1243, died after four days.*

She straightened up and wrapped her arms around her body, looked into the cloudless sky and gave thanks to whatever deity inhabited that limitless space, thanks that she was free and unburdened. She remembered her disappointment on that day, months ago when she had realized that she was not pregnant with Dominic's baby. Reincarnation or not, the distant past was obviously not influencing the present. She was filled with gratitude that she lived in the liberated twenty-first century and not the confining twelfth. For the first time she felt great pity for her past-time counterpart, real or imagined.

And then suddenly she was filled with the words and thoughts that she had been aware of before. They came again, that familiar refrain. *Do not surrender yourself to this man. Find another life, another love. Loving a man with a devouring passion for his God is always a difficult cross to bear.* The words were in her head, in the air around her, everywhere. She put her hands over her ears, turned from that desolate and lonely place and ran back along the path to High Mead, to Phoebe and Talitha, to breakfast and normality. As she lifted the wooden latch on the kitchen door she paused for a moment. In the few minutes it had taken her to reach her aunt's house, the mysterious, the unknown had unexpectedly lost its power of bewilderment. It was just a message from one girl to another down the ages, from the past to the present. It had validity and power, but not fear. 'Message received and wonderfully understood at last, Catherine,' she said. 'Thanks a million.'

Louis is impressed, as Henry and Thomas intend. So are the French peasants through whose villages the great retinue passes. They look at Thomas as he approaches the French court and their eyes widen in amazement. He is more magnificent than anyone they have ever seen. He rides tall, sitting on his great black stallion as if he were seated on a throne. Catherine, too, cannot help gazing in admiration and awe. She pulls back the curtains of her litter as often as she dares. He rides bareheaded and she notices that his hair is dark and glossy still, his face full of pride in the job he is doing. He wears a cloak of great beauty threaded through with silver. It lies all around him, billowing over the brilliant black of his mount's coat like a great shimmering cloud. His gauntlets are encrusted with jewels that sparkle and glitter in the sunlight, and when he rides close, Catherine once again glimpses the Great Seal of the king of England around his neck.

This is the boy she played with, the man she loved and to whom she once gave her body so willingly and with so much hope and joy. She looks at him and marvels, and then her heart bleeds for the tiny child, flesh of his flesh, who lies unacknowledged in the cold earth at Litford. The contrast is almost too great to be borne. What a future might have been his with this great Thomas à Becket as father and protector?

Soon however there will be another babe to hold and to love. The little Princess Marguerite is to be given into the care of Thomas, for this is why they have come with such pomp and pageantry. Or so she believes. This precious child in whom so many hopes are bound must be raised in the kingdom of her betrothed, young Prince Henry.

'Then why,' she asks Thomas a few days later, 'is the Princess to remain in France?' She wonders for one traitorous moment why Thomas has seen fit to bring her on this long journey from England if she is only needed for such a little time. Assuredly she cannot remain here. She thinks of her own children and longs for them.

'It's all statesmanship and diplomacy,' Thomas explains. 'Louis has insisted that the Princess should not cross the Channel so she is to go to one of our castles in Normandy.'

When the day comes for the baby's departure from the French court, her father himself rides with her. He is sad, and will see her safely to her new home where she will grow up and learn to become a queen. Catherine finds solace in this. She meets him and sees a gentle and melancholy figure. He has no sons but he obviously cares deeply for this little daughter. He has resisted all King Henry's stipulations and Thomas's persuasive tongue, that she should be taken to England. He has also insisted that the baby should have her own retinue, nursemaids and staff.

'So I have nothing more to do,' Catherine tells William. 'Nor you, husband, for our mission is surely accomplished.'

William nods and is glad. He has noticed the renewed and increasing friendship between the chancellor and Catherine. Sometimes he has been angry and disturbed yet he can say nothing for it would not do to gainsay the second most powerful man in England. 'Aye, wife,' he says. 'We can soon return to Devon, and the sooner the better for me.'

Catherine smiles at him fondly. Thomas is very splendid and still fills her heart and her body with longing and impure thoughts, but William is her dear husband in whom she has found true love and security. 'The sooner the better for me also,' she says. 'I long for the children and Calder, and our lovely home, William.' She kisses him and another yearning then stirs unexpectedly in her breast. She feels deprived of the care of the little princess for whose sake she came to France, and now she longs for a baby again, perhaps a third son for William. She blushes and looks at him and wishes deeply for the privacy of their sturdy Devon home.

It has been some years since she conceived. Their children are fast growing, and the eldest boy, Will, has become something of a problem to her lately. She hopes he has not been difficult for Eluned in her absence. But yes, she decides, she would definitely like another little one to fill her empty arms.

Phoebe and Kate stayed at High Mead for five days, but after that one visit to Litford, Kate refused to visit the house again or to look at the little gravestone. 'It's too gloomy,' she said. She stared out of the window at the mist and drizzle clouding the moor. 'It's spooky, too, with the house closed up.'

Phoebe looked up from the book she had been reading. 'You shouldn't have gone over there alone.'

Kate shrugged. 'I won't any more. I don't wish to be psychic. I prefer the down-to-earth and ordinary. Thinking about your Catherine and Thomas à Becket and all that makes me think of Dominic and I want to forget him. No one fights with God and wins.'

'Bang on,' Talitha said coming in from the kitchen and hearing the end of the conversation. 'Who is fighting with God? Wasn't it Esau?'

'Wrong brother,' Kate said. 'It was Jacob.'

'But he won.' Phoebe laughed a little, tried to make her tone light and inconsequential.

'Bully for him then,' Talitha said. 'What do you want to fight God for?'

'I used to think I might challenge Him for Dommy.'

Talitha shook her head. 'Not a good idea, love.'

'That's just what I've decided. It was Catherine's message to me over at Litford and in a concert hall in London as well.'

Talitha raised her eyes to the ceiling. 'Heaven preserve me from you two. I won't dare go over to Litford if you persist in putting these ideas in my head. I might bump into Catherine, and that would be awkward since I have to get the place ready for summer guests in a few weeks' time.'

'Not very likely,' Phoebe said comfortingly. 'Presences only select those who believe in them.'

'She's at Parke now anyway,' Kate said. 'Parke, where we went the other day. That's where Phee has got up to in her book. I don't think she'll bother you, Aunt Tally.'

'Parke?' Talitha said, grinning. 'I hope she gets on all right with all those computers then.'

'God's breath, wife, your Thomas over-reaches himself.' William throws the reins of his horse to a servant and kisses Catherine briefly as she waits for him at the door of their Devon home. The journey to France and back remains only a lingering memory. Much has happened since then and William has just returned from one of his frequent visits to London.

Catherine's alarm shows clearly in her face. 'William, what is it? Why are you so angry? I have longed for your homecoming. And he is not my *Thomas, never has been.'*

William looks at her and the usual smile is missing. 'You know of course that to add to his other attributes, he is a competent fighter? He takes up arms as easily as he sups his wine.'

Catherine has long known that Thomas likes the challenge of both tourney and battlefield and has acquitted himself well in France on many occasions. 'What now then?' she says, her heart in turmoil again just when she had hoped to have a peaceful and contented time at home with William and the children.

'The king is about to press some ancient rights that have long been disregarded. He intends to force the Count of Toulouse to do him homage because Toulouse is subordinate to the Duchy of Aquitaine.'

Catherine thinks of the beautiful Eleanor. 'And of course he has Aquitaine from his queen.'

William nods. 'The king gained much from that marriage. A lovely wife, all her lands in France, and a good quiverful of sons as well. Not content with all that, he must have more and Becket aids and abets him in everything. He is even milking the Church for funds to pay for this outrageous escapade. I thought he was a holy man, tonsured and likely to go into the Church.' He snorts in disgust.

Catherine lays her hand on her husband's arm. 'I also thought so, my dear.' She is dismayed. The Thomas she knew, the devout young man who was willing to give up everything for his vocation seems to have vanished, changed beyond all recognition. And if this is so, where is the value in the sacrifice she made? She turns to William. He is her comfort and her future now, as he has been during the past many years. 'Come inside, husband,' she says placatingly. 'At least it is nothing to do with us. Surely you will not be called upon to fight?'

The hall is warm and welcoming, herbs strewed liberally on the freshly laid rushes so that as they walk upon them the fragrance of rosemary and meadowsweet are released into the air.

William shakes his head. 'No, I think not. I have no wish for more bloodshed. Why Henry cannot choose peaceful means to achieve his ends I have no idea. Thomas should be persuading the king in that direction but apparently he does nothing of the kind.'

'I thought the betrothal of the two royal children was meant to bring peace, and to satisfy Henry's ambitions,' Catherine says.

William laughs bitterly. 'You don't know him at all, Catherine. This young king is vigorous and hearty in more ways than one, and his chancellor encourages him mightily in spite of his age!' He adds the last words sarcastically. He guesses that Thomas is over forty. 'He is too old to take part in such ruthless feuding.'

Catherine kneels before her husband's chair, draws off his tall leather boots and gives them to a serving man to clean. 'Take a measure of wine, husband,' she says solicitously. 'Then later when you have refreshed yourself we shall eat. We have a haunch of venison today and there is partridge too if you should so wish.'

At last William relaxes and smiles down at her. He takes

her hand and pulls her to her feet. 'And apples with honey to follow?' he questions lightly.

Catherine nods and also feels suddenly more cheerful and slightly amused. It is a family joke. William has a sweet tooth and honey is not always to be found. 'That too,' she says. 'The apples have kept well this year, and we still have some honeycombs in store.'

William kisses her gently. He always reserves his more exuberant embraces for the privacy of their chamber where no servants can pry. 'You rule your household well, my Catherine,' he says. 'No man could wish for better.'

Catherine feels her heart overflowing with happiness. Her husband is home again and she has been able to give him comfort and contentment. He loves and appreciates her and his compliment gives her joyous confidence. Tonight perhaps she will conceive the baby she longs for so desperately now. She will strew their bed with the sweetest herbs her still room can supply and she will pray again to the good Lord for another son.

Fourteen

Kate, well into her second term at Bristol, walked with a friend on the Durdham Downs. 'Do you believe in reincarnation?' she asked suddenly.

Sarah Brownstone looked at her with amusement. 'Why are you asking me that just now?'

'Various reasons.'

'I suppose it depends what you come back as.' Sarah's tone was flippant. 'An ant or a beetle wouldn't be very attractive options.'

'I keep dreaming about this girl from the past.'

'That's just because we're doing history.'

'Could be. She's called Catherine and she says things.'

'You're having me on of course.'

Kate's voice changed. The original flippancy disappeared. 'I'm not making it up. I keep seeing her, hearing her.'

Sarah looked at her with concern. 'Sounds dire. What does she say?'

'The words are always the same. She tells me to give up on Dominic and find someone else. *Another life, another love*, or something like that. She stresses that loving a man who has a devouring passion for his ambition or his God, or whatever, is a difficult cross to bear.'

'It doesn't need someone from the past to tell you that. I've been saying more or less the same ever since you confessed to me about your saintly lover boy!'

Kate shrugged. 'I suppose you have.'

'Why does this girl, this apparition, tell you all this?'

Kate frowned. How could she say that the Catherine of her imagination had been in love with Thomas à Becket? It

159

sounded too ridiculous for words. 'She loved a priest and it all went wrong for her,' she said.

Sarah grinned. 'Oh well, there you are then. That sort of story is as old as the hills. It happens all the time, even on the telly. It's just your subconscious taking over, giving you some good advice. What precise time in history does this Catherine come from?'

'The twelfth century.'

'My god, Kate, you do choose them, don't you? The twelfth century! She wouldn't even speak like we do. Remember what Chaucer sounds like when he's read in Old English?'

'She speaks Norman French and Latin as well as Anglo-Saxon.'

'And which does she use to talk with you?' Sarah's tone was mocking now.

'That's the odd thing. I don't know. I understand clearly what she's on about without really hearing the words.'

'I give up,' Sarah said. 'Don't tell anyone else, will you, or you'll be sent to a shrink.'

'Only you,' Kate said. 'And my grandmother of course. She has the same sort of experiences. This girl features in a novel she's writing.'

Sarah raised her eyes to the sky. 'What a pair you are. The book'll be a best-seller for sure if it's dictated from the twelfth century and all about spooks and spirits.'

'It's not like that at all.'

'Put my name down for a signed copy, first edition.'

'OK.' Kate zipped up her anorak to her chin. 'Jolly cold for March!'

'Don't change the subject,' Sarah commanded. 'And are you going to take this advice from the past?'

'I already have,' Kate said. 'At least, I'm trying hard.'

'Great. This place is littered with nice, uncomplicated, acceptable guys.'

They swung briskly along the path and Kate felt liberated. Confessing to a friend had helped. She had almost succeeded in putting Dominic out of her life now. Had Catherine found happiness and freedom too in her long-ago and so different life? Yes, Kate felt strangely sure that she had.

160

'*Tom, Catherinae filius, hoc anno domini MCXLIII natus, quarto die obiit.*'

'What did you say?'

'Just some Latin words we found on a baby's grave,' Kate said. 'Catherine's baby, actually.'

'Now I know you're crazy. Where did you find this grave?'

'In Devon, Dartmoor.'

'Aren't you frightened by all that stuff?'

Kate considered for a moment. 'No, I can't say that I am. Catherine seems to be just a girl like us. I feel sorry for her.'

'If you really believe in all this possession and reincarnation you ought to get on television, or write a magazine article. The media is keen on all that.'

Kate grinned. 'There's an idea. No one would believe me though. Do you believe me, Sarah?'

'I'm not sure,' Sarah said. 'You sound convincing. Perhaps I might believe you if you really act on this message from the past and forget all about Dominic.'

'I'm doing just that,' Kate said.

Thomas struts about in triumph. He has just unhorsed a French knight, one Engelram of Trie, in single combat. At forty-one he is considered by many to be too old for such junketing. Yet he laughs at his critics for he is fit and hardy and has no concern for his years.

This was a formal joust with spurred horse and lance, and Engelram has a formidable reputation, but Thomas is the victor and the knight's charger is his trophy. There have been other triumphs in France during the last year too. The news of these exploits reaches London, where William de Tracey hears of them and frowns.

As soon as he returns to Devon he hastens to tell Catherine for he knows she will not be pleased either. 'He put himself at the head of the army and stormed three castles,' he says. 'They were said to be strongly fortified and impregnable.'

Catherine can well imagine Thomas dressed in hauberk and helmet, seated on his great black horse, leading his troops into bloody battle. It is not a picture with which she is comfortable, particularly as the battles appear to her to be unnecessary and a violation of the peace that was now supposed to reign between France and England.

'He then crossed the Garonne in pursuit of the enemy,' William continues truculently. 'He confirmed the whole province to be in allegiance to King Henry and consequently he is in great favour and mightily honoured.'

Catherine can see that her husband is jealous of the great chancellor who can now, in the eyes of the king, do no wrong and on whom the sun shines so brilliantly. 'And what of his other life?' she asks. 'His reputed allegiance to the church?'

William smirks. 'There he falls, Catherine. I heard tell that the Archbishop Theobald, who loves him like a son, and who helped him rise to the position he now has, is displeased and disappointed. Thomas is not the affectionate and dutiful disciple that Theobald longs for. He chose him above all others, gave him a place in his palace at Canterbury as you know, and yet now that he is old and failing, Thomas neglects him pitiably. I hear that the archbishop repeatedly requests that Thomas should come to him in Canterbury.'

'And will he not go?' Catherine is shocked.

'He obeys the king and not his old mentor. Thomas à Becket has a hard heart, Catherine. The old man is dying and apparently has pleaded in the strongest possible language for Thomas to come.'

Suddenly Catherine feels numb and spiritless. She shivers and thinks of the Thomas she knew, her idol, the man she loved before all others. So idols have feet of clay. She remembers the story in the great Latin Bible that she used to read with Mary sometimes. Idols with clay feet come crashing down and should never be worshipped. It is a powerful image. 'Let us forget him, husband,' she says. 'He must not impinge on our happiness and that of our children. Will is anxious that you should ride out with him later, and Joan wishes to talk to you about her request to study at the convent.'

William smiles. 'Aye, wife. I have much to thank the good Lord for, and must not forget that although Becket has riches in plenty and the ear of the king, he forgoes the love of a family. No one knows why this should be so. In truth I often wonder why he seems to figure so largely in our lives.'

'He shall not do so any more, William,' Catherine says. 'We shall put the chancellor and his pesky ways right out of our thoughts.' Then suddenly, flashing across the periphery of her mind, she sees the strange girl with the short straight hair and the ugly leg coverings. 'Kate, Kate!' *she says in her head,* 'Find another life, another love. Loving a man with a devouring passion for his God is always a difficult cross to bear.'

She looks at William in alarm for she thinks she has spoken the words aloud, but he makes no sign that he has heard. Only her dog turns his head and stares, then he looks beyond her and growls gently, and she sees the hair along the ridge of his back standing up a little. She puts her hand reassuringly on his head. The older Calder, this one's grandsire, was never disturbed in this way. 'There's nothing to be worried about,' she says to him. 'It's just me.' He stands up and shakes himself, then turns around a few times before settling again on the flagstones before the fire. But occasionally he lifts his great head and stares at her uneasily.

'Fancy a trip to Falaise?' Phoebe said.

'Fine. When?' Hugo was leafing through a batch of papers from the estate agent. He put them down and looked at Phoebe enquiringly.

'As soon as it can be arranged. I'm getting to the bit in the story where Henry and Thomas have their first major disagreement, and it was at Falaise, in the castle there. Can I leave it to you to sort out? We could drive down.'

'The house-hunting will have to wait then,' he said. 'Yes, you're on. I'll see about booking a crossing and get some maps.'

'The castle is still there,' Phoebe said, 'so I should be able to get some atmosphere. I had to do the biography without going to see it. I managed by just looking it up in guidebooks.'

'By all the saints, Thomas,' the king says impatiently, 'I cannot spare you now.' Thomas looks at him with some disquiet. 'But Archbishop Theobald is near to death, sire,' he says. 'I have just now received another letter in which he pleads with me to go to Canterbury with all speed.'

The eyes of the king become less friendly. His temper

163

smoulders and Thomas knows that the great friendship that is between them hangs only by a thread. Henry rules absolutely and all who would please him do well not to question or thwart his will. Yet Thomas loves the old archbishop, his one-time mentor and guide. He loves him as a father in God and he owes him great allegiance. Now he is drawn between two masters, one old and ailing and of waning importance, and the other the king himself, the most powerful monarch in all Christendom. To whom should he bow?

There is no choice. The needs and orders of the king must take precedence. So Thomas sends a message back to Canterbury. He cannot make the journey from France to England at this time. Perhaps he will come later in the year.

When news of the death of Theobald, Archbishop of Canterbury, eventually reaches France, Thomas is smitten with grief and remorse. He greatly fears that he will be punished by God for his tardiness, and indeed illness overtakes him that winter. He is not patient with the wasting of his flesh, the weakness that fills his bones. Restlessly he turns more frequently to his prayers and wonders if forgiveness for his neglect of God's archbishop will ever be granted. But with the turning of the year he begins to mend, and when in the spring a summons comes from Henry to attend him in Falaise, he is cheered. He is charged to bring the little prince with him, for Thomas is the guardian of Henry's son.

It is March when they make the journey. Sometimes the boy's chatter brightens him, but occasionally it reminds him of all he has lost in choosing to remain celibate. And in his darker moments he thinks of the son he has never seen, the little body now dust and ashes in the Devonshire earth, a child who was flesh of his flesh, his and Catherine's. But as he sees the greening of the countryside, the birds nesting, and swallows returning from whatever secret place they inhabit during the winter days, his thoughts begin to mend. The king has called for him, the future looks promising again, and the little prince riding so ably beside him, is amiable and intelligent.

'Why does my father choose to keep his court at Falaise?' the child asks.

'It is one of his favourite castles,' Thomas explains. 'Your great-great-grandfather was born there.' He carefully does not add that it is rumoured that Duke Robert, nicknamed Robert the Devil, had taken a washerwoman to bed and that the son of this misalliance was the famous William.

'William the Conqueror of England,' the young Henry says. 'And one day I shall be king of England as he was, as my father is now.'

Thomas looks at him and smiles. Life is hazardous for children, and royal children are no exception. 'You must learn well and fit yourself for such a great task,' he says.

Falaise is very beautiful in spring, and Henry himself comes down to meet his chancellor and his young son. He greets the child boisterously and then sends him away to the women for he has important matters to discuss with Thomas.

'They tell me that you have become religious again,' he says. His eyes search Thomas's face and he frowns.

'I have always been religious, my Lord. Am I not archdeacon as well as chancellor?'

Henry nods good-naturedly now and grins at him. 'But we have enjoyed much sport together have we not, Thomas?' He thumps him playfully on the shoulder. 'Here in Falaise there is much to pleasure us.'

Thomas waits, knowing that the king has more on his mind than mere junketing.

'The Church bothers me, Thomas,' he says eventually. 'I need its absolution and its counsel but I wish to be more in charge. We must talk further of these matters.'

Thomas inclines his head and hopes that he will not come into any conflict with his king. Already he has angered the Church by demanding taxes to finance Henry's wars.

'But for now,' Henry says, 'the sun shines and I have two new falcons to show you.'

His moods are as capricious as an untried horse, but he is king. Together they go out into the sunshine, and for the moment, for Thomas, life is good. But he knows that this is only as long as Henry has his way in all things.

*　　*　　*

Phoebe stared at the thick stone walls of the great keep and tried to recall all the things she had read about this castle and the calamitous meeting between Thomas and the king. Hugo stood beside her, guidebook in hand. They had driven down two days ago and the French countryside in spring had charmed them both. Now they had come to Falaise and Phoebe was thrilled to be here, in this place that held so many secrets.

'It's only the keep and chapel that were here in Thomas's time,' Hugo said, guidebook open at the right page.

'Don't spoil it,' Phoebe said. 'I was just getting the atmosphere.'

Hugo laughed. 'And William the Conqueror was born here in 1027.'

'Perhaps that was why Henry was so attached to this place.' Phoebe took out her camera and concentrated on taking some photographs that had no modern signs or notices too prominently placed. 'If it hadn't been for his grandfather he might never have been king of England, of course.'

'And history would have been quite different,' Hugo added. 'Your Thomas would have died obscurely as just some boring cleric.'

'Thomas would never have been boring.' Phoebe was suddenly overwhelmed with a profound feeling of closeness to Thomas. She caught Hugo's arm, needing confirmation that she was still here in the present, still in control, that her writing was not again taking over her mind and her thoughts. 'I really do love you, Hugo,' she said suddenly.

He grinned at her. 'Well, that's nice to know seeing we are about to buy a house together. What brought on that nice little confession at this particular moment?'

'Just that I think you're a decent guy with no overwhelming passions. I was thinking of Thomas!'

'My only passion is for you, Phoebe dear,' he said flippantly and she knew with great pleasure that there was much truth behind the light-hearted words.

Spring passes into summer at the great castle and Thomas's health and good spirits continue to improve. As the king has said, there are many diversions to be had. Little serious talk or weighty matters engage the thoughts of either himself or Henry during those carefree weeks.

Then one day the king is not as carefree as usual. Thomas, looking forward to a day's hawking, stares at him and his heart races a little. He well knows the sudden rages and tempers that this monarch is heir to.

Henry strides over to the small aperture in the thickness of the wall and peers down at the courtyard below and at the pleasant countryside beyond. 'I have decided that my son is to have a ceremony, a great council at Winchester. He is to be proclaimed my heir, and all my lords, both temporal and spiritual, shall declare fealty to him.' He paces the hall, eagerness written in every line of his powerful body. 'My son shall not suffer as I suffered as a boy. His place shall be secure and safe, and I wish you to procure a golden chaplet made especially. It is to have the appearance of a crown so that there is no doubt in the minds of any of my barons that this is my will and command. All will kneel before him to pledge fealty, and when he is older there will be yet another ceremony, a great coronation, Thomas. This is to be the forerunner.'

Henry pauses and stares long and hard at his chancellor. Then he adds, 'Thomas, I charge you with this task, both the gathering of the barons to do him homage, and all the arrangements that will be necessary. There is to be much regalia and ceremony. Nothing is to be spared.'

Thomas takes a deep breath as he thinks about the enormity of the task which the king outlines. This is more the work of an archbishop than a chancellor, and there is at present no Archbishop of Canterbury. Since the death of Theobald no other has been named. He bows his head in shame as he remembers his one time father-in-God and how he failed him during his last illness.

Henry appears to read his thoughts. They have been close for a long time and it has often been so. 'I have sent word already to Canterbury,' the king says. 'The election of the next archbishop is to take place forthwith, and you are to be that man, Thomas. You will be my archbishop. You will be Primate of England. I will have no other.'

Thomas is dismayed and horrified. 'My Lord,' he says. 'I have not the stomach for this honour. My tastes are worldly, my interests more with the State than the Church.'

'I need a friend, my own man, as head of the Church,' Henry says. 'The Church will come to heel and do my wishes with you at the helm, Thomas. We shall bend it to our will.'

Thomas shakes his head. 'Please, my Lord, do not force this upon me. I am your friend in truth and your interests are always my first concern, but as the head of the Church I may not be so single-minded.'

For a dangerous moment Henry is silent, but then he throws his head back and laughs. 'Nay, Thomas, we shall always be close. You are my trusted vassal and through you the Church, too, will be my loyal servant.'

Fifteen

'*Can a man change from wolf to shepherd?' William says to Catherine when the news of Thomas's enthronement reaches Devonshire. 'Becket must now serve two masters.'*

Catherine pauses for a moment before answering. Then she nods slowly. 'I think he could do that if he wished to. But why do you call him wolf? He has not been any kind of predator.'

William laughs cynically. 'He has long been preying on the Church, or rather on their funds, for Henry's many causes, and now he is to be head of that same Church, dedicated to caring for its affairs and its people.'

Catherine thinks of the Thomas she knew. He had been full of high ideals, dedicated to service as well as to his own advancement. The self-seeking side of his nature had taken precedence during these recent opulent years as chancellor. Was that perhaps a false image, a role taken purely for the pleasing of the king? Maybe the God-fearing cleric is the truer picture. 'He always wished to serve God. He was ambitious for advancement in the Church rather than in a secular role,' she says.

'And now he has reached the very top.' William's voice is scornful. 'Yet he will keep his riches. He will still be very grand. As archbishop he will need to keep a splendid household.'

Catherine looks at her husband sadly for she realizes that, far from placating his jealousy of Thomas, this latest news is merely making him more envious. 'Why do you dislike him so?' she asks. 'He has done you no wrong, William.' Then with a small intake of breath she realizes what she has said. Has Thomas indeed done him no wrong?

But William smiles at last, walks across the solar and kisses her. *'No true reason, my Catherine. Perhaps merely that he has part of your life in his past that I never knew.'*

Catherine responds to him, but her heart is fearful. What does he mean? Has he any suspicions about the occupant of the little grave at Litford? He has accepted the fact of the child's birth and death but has never asked for more information. *'That is your past, Catherine,'* he once told her. *'It is a shameful and dreadful particular in which I truly believe you were gravely wronged, but I wish to know nothing about it. For the sake of our marriage and our children it does not exist.'*

Catherine has always been grateful for William's careful disregard of her past, yet she often wonders if he will ever discover the truth. It is a terrifying thought. She shivers and turns her mind to other, more pleasant things. *'I hear there is to be a joust at Pomeroy in a few weeks' time,'* she says lightly. *'Shall we attend, husband, and take the children?'*

'I have already arranged it,' William tells her with a ring of triumph in his voice. *'And I am to ride.'*

She feels a momentary flash of fear but manages to conceal it. *'Then you must practise well,'* she says.

'Do you doubt my strength and skill?'

She flushes. *'Of course not. You have always been outstanding on the jousting field. We shall watch you with pride. I shall prepare your surcoat and armour myself.'*

William nods. *'Perhaps I shall be as illustrious for a few short hours as your great Becket,'* he says. *'I am told that he excels on the jousting field as in everything else.'*

Fear again grips Catherine's heart. *'He is not* my *Becket, as I have frequently told you,'* she says bleakly. *'You are mine, William. You and you alone. Always believe that.'*

'Surely I do believe it. You have been a wonderful wife to me, Catherine. I can fault you in nothing.'

She smiles at him. *'Nor I you,'* she says. Her peace and serenity is restored, for now at least. *'Thomas's jousting days must be over,'* she adds. *'I cannot imagine that an Archbishop of Canterbury would be seen on the jousting field.'*

'From what I hear, that will not be to his liking.' William grins satisfactorily and Catherine knows that anything that can be said or imagined against Becket will add to her

170

husband's pleasure. The jealousy will always remain in his heart.

During the following weeks Catherine becomes sure that she is with child again. She has longed for another little one and is overjoyed. William, too, is delighted when he is told the news, and he appears to forget his jealousy of Thomas, or at least put it to the back of his mind. Another son would be a further proof of his continuing virility and vigour. If it is a girl the birth will be almost as welcome. His three daughters are much loved and very precious to him. His only concern is for Catherine. He still sometimes dreams of Align, and in his sleep occasionally hears her screams from the birthing chamber. But Catherine is strong in spite of her increasing years, and birthing has always come easily to her. He will make special prayers for her well-being during the coming months.

William is suddenly full of confidence and aplomb. As well as fathering another babe he has done well at Pomeroy, winning many events in the joust. Thomas à Becket will always be a thorn in his flesh, but as archbishop rather than chancellor he will surely be less of a threat. A man of God, they call him! William laughs scornfully to himself at the thought.

It is the morning of Thomas's consecration. He is lying full length, face down and arms outstretched on the cold stones of his sanctuary. It is midsummer 1162 and the great cathedral of Canterbury is crowded with monks and assorted dignitaries of the Church, as well as knights and barons who have been invited here to witness the miracle. For a miracle it seems to many onlookers. The worldly, power-hungry chancellor is to become harvester of souls and guardian of the Church.

The sound of the monks' plainsong soars triumphantly to the great curving roof and eddies back and forth, obliterating the shuffling and coughs of the more lowly town citizens who are crowded shoulder to shoulder in the further reaches of the building.

Amongst the privileged stands William de Tracey, and he stares at the outstretched figure before the altar. He is filled with mistrust and disdain. How can this worldling become

171

God's servant? It is impossible. Yet he wonders for a betraying moment whether it is his wife's friendship with Becket that makes him feel so. He is aware once again of the jealousy and inferiority that has always gripped his heart and his head whenever she speaks of this man for whom she so obviously has a deep affection. He thinks he has concealed it successfully, but he can never hide it from himself.

The stones beneath Thomas's face are wet with tears. He feels the love of God surrounding him, the challenge of God exciting him, and the spirit of God pervading every cell of his body. Then he is gently pulled to his feet, the kiss of peace is given to him and he receives his mitre and crozier. The bishop's ring is placed upon his finger and he is enthroned before the altar in great majesty. Finally, to the sublime tones of Te Deum, *Thomas walks, tall and magnificent, blessing his people. The seal of God is upon him. He is a changed man.*

Dominic opened the letter from Kate with some trepidation. There were women now in his college. They were right here in this bastion of male privilege and sanctification, apparently to study theology, but he knew that some of them privately wished to overthrow the Church's determination never to accept women priests. They had succeeded in the Anglican Church. Why not then, eventually, in the impregnable masculine fortress of Roman Catholicism? And if they did succeed, would not the ordinance of celibacy have to be reconsidered too?

He scanned the letter, and then sat down on the old wooden seat beside the lake, for this seminary had beautiful well-tended gardens. He read the two pages again and all hope faded from his heart. He realized then that his private hope for a miracle would never be fulfilled. The choice had been his, God and the Church, or Kate. He had chosen God, and now it was too late for any other course. There had been a vain hope in his heart that the Church would change its mind about its tortuous celibacy rules. He was fairly sure that this would come about in the future, but not for now, perhaps never for him, and certainly not soon enough for Kate.

He read the letter again and again. The new man in her life was an accountant. Accountant! He frowned in amazement and yet wondered why he was surprised. Nothing wrong with an accountant. Probably good for Kate. Anger, jealousy and resentment washed over him in waves and when the gardener came in sight pushing a wheelbarrow full of compost, his jealousy even extended to this hapless young man. He frowned at him irritably instead of giving his customary cheery nod. He wished for one faithless moment that he had gone to agricultural college instead of seminary!

He stared at the vista of garden, lake, trees, and sky for a long time, his lips moving in strange wordless prayer and then suddenly, like a shaft of sunlight through thunderclouds, came the assurance he needed, words of scripture to comfort. They flashed into his mind clear and vivid as though God Himself was speaking, words that he had read so many times that they were part of his very being.

This one thing I do, forgetting those things which are behind, and reaching forth unto those things which are before, I press toward the mark for the prize of the high calling of God in Christ Jesus. That I may know Him and the power of His resurrection.

Dominic folded Kate's letter carefully and put it in his pocket. He would keep it as a final token of his sacrifice. He walked back to the college building with a firmer step and more hope than he had felt for a long time. It was truly the end now of all his impossible and worldly dreams. Kate would be happy with someone else. And for himself? His Calvary had finally been grasped. The best of all prizes was his. The seal of God was upon him. He was a chosen one.

William de Tracey stays in Canterbury for some weeks. He is curious to know how Becket will perform his duties, how he will balance the roles of both chancellor and archbishop. He soon has his answer. Thomas has sent a message to Henry. He tells the king that he can no longer be split in his loyalties and the Great Seal of England is returned. It is reported that Thomas has become religious to the extreme. They say that he creeps out in the darkness between matins and lauds and goes to the almonery where the poor of the town are given refuge. There he washes the grimy calloused feet of the beggars and gives them a silver shilling.

William laughs when he hears this. Is the man mad or a charlatan? What ails him? He still has the affection and the ear of the king, but for how much longer? This strange behaviour will not endear him to the pleasure-loving Henry.

What will Catherine make of such performances? William decides he must go home to Devon and acquaint her of the strange conduct of her one-time friend. Was he merely a friend? Perhaps not. Grains of suspicion frequently trouble him when he thinks of the way her eyes light up when she speaks of Thomas à Becket.

William rides to Devon a week later with satisfaction in his heart. He remembers the once splendid chancellor who asked for his wife's company to France a few years ago. How great and invincible he had seemed then. And now? He would wait and see. There are rumours already of the king's displeasure with his new archbishop.

'What do you mean, you want a room set aside in our house for the archbishop?' William is aghast at Catherine's suggestion. She has not received his accounts of Thomas's behaviour with the distaste he had reckoned upon.

'I have had word, husband, that Thomas is to visit Buckfast Abbey and the priory where I lodged in the time of my greatest need. He would like to come here to pray with our family and to give us spiritual guidance and his blessing.'

'Pray? In God's name, Catherine!' William snorts. 'This is too much. I suffered his company on that mission to France but I cannot stomach his presence in my home.'

Catherine bows her head. 'Very well, William. But it is a great favour that he pays us. Not many households such as ours will be so honoured. He is the Primate of all England and the king's friend.'

'Aye, and I wonder for how long?' William sees his wife's downcast look and feels her disappointment. 'Already he offends Henry mightily in many things.'

174

Catherine is surprised. No murmur of such matters had reached Devon until William arrived. 'How can that be?' she asks. 'He and Henry were much together and their minds were always in accord.'

'Not now. Not since the king forced him to become arch-bishop. Now he puts the Church before everything else and that ill suits Henry.'

'Yet we could give him lodging at least once, could we not?' Catherine's voice is pleading now. If Thomas is in any sort of trouble, she wishes to know, wishes to give comfort and support.

William tilts her face to his and kisses her. He relents. Perhaps there might be some advantage in having Thomas here. He also remembers that Catherine is with child again and he wishes to please her. 'Very well, wife,' he says. 'Prepare a room. It can be called the priest's room. He can say mass for us and for the coming child. He will give us absolution and present us favourably to his God. We shall see that the chapel is especially embellished for his visit.'

If Catherine wonders at her husband's sudden change of heart, she keeps her counsel. Thomas will be here, in her home. Her heart lifts and she smiles at William in gratitude and love.

Phoebe had just received another letter from Kate. There was a new man in her life! She read the page over again, hardly believing such a wonderful piece of news. An accountant! Surely there would be no problems there. She hoped that Kate had found herself an acceptable guy at last, one with his feet firmly on the ground, not in some place eight hundred years back in time, like herself, or up in the clouds like Dominic.

The second page of the letter, however, intrigued Phoebe greatly. This new man, Jason, practised in Bristol, but his home was in Canterbury and Kate was going there with him soon. Canterbury! *Thomas is archbishop. He is chancellor no longer. He is in his cathedral in Canterbury. He is at variance with the king in many things.* Phoebe realized that she was thinking in the present tense and she mentally shook herself. *Tell me where all times past are.* Kate had quoted those words to her again when she last visited Bristol. Where were they then, all those past centuries, those millions of people who had lived out their little lives and died, mostly unknown? *Catherine? Are you here with me in the writing of my book? Are you spirit, or ghost, or myself, or Kate? Thomas? Is there a secret to your life which I am about to reveal to a critical world? Or is it all dreams and fiction?* And now Kate is going to Canterbury. Why did it have to be Canterbury?

Phoebe finished her breakfast and poured coffee. The biography of Thomas à Becket had dominated her life for a long time, and she had spent some weary days on the proofs. It was with the publisher at the moment. The fictional novel that she was working on now was nearly finished. During the writing of both, the past had sometimes become almost more real than the present. She would be glad to turn her mind to other things. The next book must definitely be of the twenty-first century. She smiled to herself as she remembered the surprise on the face of the electrician when he looked at the cheque she had written for him yesterday. She had dated it 1162 and then, covered in confusion had mumbled something about living in the past when she was writing a novel. He had grinned, only half believing, and she had promised him a signed copy of the book when it was printed. The event had shaken her rather, but had amused Hugo greatly. He had pointed out, with some glee, that they didn't have chequebooks in 1162. Well, probably not anyway!

Sixteen

*T*here *is great rejoicing for Catherine has given birth to
a healthy son. She has laboured long and hard, and for
many hours William has paced the hall and the solar, his face
pale and his mind suffused with fear. But now it is all over and
Catherine lies exhausted but triumphant, her child in her arms.
Her hair is damp with perspiration but it curls around her face
and on to the pillows. William is full of love for her, but he
resolves that this child shall be their last. He couldn't bear to
lose her now. If the wretched Becket can remain celibate, then
so can he.*

*Joan, now almost eighteen, is ministering to her, and Eluned
has been brought over from Litford to help.*

*'I should like the child to be called Simon,' Catherine
says. She holds him out to William, and he takes him gingerly.*

'A splendid name,' he says. 'Simon it shall be.'

*The child appears to look up at his father, then his eyes
close and he sleeps. Below the dogs are barking, for Will and
Oliver, William and Catherine's two eldest sons, have come
clattering into the yard.*

*'He will he a good babe,' Eluned says. 'See how peacefully
he sleeps.' She goes to the small aperture in the thickness of
the wall and looks out disapprovingly at the boys.*

*William gives his tiny son into the care of his daughter. 'I
shall go and bid them come quietly and see their new brother,'
he says proudly.*

*Winter passes into spring and still Thomas has not come on his
proposed visit. The new room, the priest's room as it is called,
has been long prepared for him and the chapel refurbished.*

Catherine wonders if he has forgotten the request he made so many months ago.

Baby Simon grows healthily, seldom cries, and gives no trouble, but Catherine is worried. Although his eyes are beautiful with no sign of disorder she suspects that all is not well. He doesn't follow her hand when she waves it in front of him and only sucks eagerly at the breast of the wet-nurse when he is guided to the nipple.

'I fear he is blind,' Catherine confides one day to Eluned who is frequently brought over to help with the baby. Tears come readily to her eyes, for to be born blind is a misfortune difficult to bear.

Eluned has already guessed, but so far not dared to mention her fears. 'Perhaps he will see more clearly as he grows,' she says, but she knows quite well that this is a forlorn hope. 'He is the easiest little one I have ever looked after, contented all the time.'

'All we can do is pray for a deliverance,' Catherine says. She doesn't add that she has prayed daily for her little son's healing and has placed a lighted candle in the chapel every day. She has said nothing to William of her fears.

Believing all is well, William travels that year to France to serve the king. It is a great honour. And that same year Catherine receives the longed-for message from the archbishop's office. Thomas is coming at last! He wishes to travel to the south-west to visit his abbeys in the region. Could he make a pastoral visit to the Tracey household within the next month?

'Father will be sorry to miss him,' Joan says innocently. William's eldest daughter, Align's child, knows nothing of the deep friendship between Catherine and Thomas, or of her father's feelings of antipathy towards the archbishop. Catherine has merely told her of their childhood companionship.

Catherine smiles fondly but does not correct the misconception. 'It's a pity that he's in France,' she replies. She hides her uneasiness for she doesn't wish the children to know that she is anxious about this visit being made during her husband's absence. Assuredly, William has given his permission, albeit reluctantly, and he even oversaw the refurbishment of the chapel and private room himself. Yet Catherine knows that she would prefer William to be present when Thomas comes, however difficult the meeting of the two men might have been.

'What will the archbishop do while he is here, Mother?' Joan asks.

'He will rest and recuperate, for he works long and hard, and he will give you his blessing,' Catherine says to her stepdaughter. 'You can tell him about your wish to enter a convent. His sister, Mary, who was my best friend when we were girls, is a nun at Barking Abbey, and set to become Abbess one day certainly. Thomas will help you if he thinks it right.'

'I wouldn't want to go too far away,' Joan says. 'Barking is a long way off, I believe.'

'You shall not go anywhere that you don't wish, sweetheart,' Catherine says. 'Your father and I want your happiness above all things.'

Joan smiles gratefully and then thinks about her baby brother. She too has noticed that Simon fails to respond when she goes to him, and even when she holds a candle close to his crib he takes no notice. Only when she speaks does he turn his head in her direction. So far she hasn't dared to voice her fears. 'Perhaps the archbishop can give a special blessing to baby Simon?' she suggests.

Catherine looks at her warily. Has Joan noticed something amiss? 'I'm sure he'll do that,' she answers.

'Simon is blind isn't he, Mother?' Joan can keep her fears to herself no longer.

Catherine feels tears in her eyes. She nods. 'So you've noticed too. He'll be the responsibility of all of us as he grows. He'll need our love and care to the end of his days.'

Joan goes to her mother and puts her arms around her. She, too, weeps a little. 'I'll give up all thoughts of the convent if it's necessary,' she says. 'I'll give my life to him if need be.'

Catherine shakes her head. 'I have four other children, Joan, and will never ask such a total sacrifice from you. We shall share the burden as a family.'

*   *   *

179

Kate was thrilled to be visiting Canterbury, but dubious, too. Because of Phoebe's book, because of Thomas, because of Catherine, it was special, a place of imagination rather than fact.

Jason was totally secular, nothing remotely spiritual ever troubled him. He was highly amused at many of the things Kate had told him about Phoebe's book, and some of the strange experiences they claimed had happened to them. 'OK,' he said as they negotiated a busy junction on the outskirts of the town. 'We'll go to the cathedral straight after lunch and you can enlighten me about all the things I don't know.'

Kate held Jason's hand very tightly as they walked through the precincts, and once inside the ancient building itself she looked around with awe, trying to imagine it as Thomas might have seen it eight hundred years ago.

'Yes, I suppose it is rather fabulous,' Jason said. 'I've grown up with the place so I suppose I've taken it for granted. I used to be a choirboy here.'

Kate looked at him in surprise. 'I didn't know that.'

'Boy soprano. Not brilliant, but passable, and it all disappeared in a croaky shambles one never-to-be-forgotten day.'

'How awful!'

Jason grinned. 'For the parents, yes. They loved the angelic little vision I presented every Sunday. But me, I was over the moon. No more choir practice, no more prissy outfits, no more pretending to be good.'

Kate walked slowly, thinking about the man beside her, about his reaction to this place, comparing him to Dominic, remembering Buckfast Abbey and Dommy's response to the sanctity and the splendour. 'So you came here every week and it meant nothing?'

'Not a lot.' He squeezed her hand. 'Hey, what is it with you? All that past-times stuff again?'

Tears slid into her eyes. 'This is a sad place,' she said. They had walked through the nave and down the worn steps to the Martyrdom Transept. She stood very still and shivered at the coldness all around.

'The Altar of Sword's Point,' Jason said. 'Odd name really. Becket was murdered right here. There was a splendid tomb for a few hundred years, but Henry VIII vandalized all that.'

Find another life, another love. Loving a man with a devouring passion for his God is always a difficult cross to bear. Kate heard the voice clearly in her head, and she looked at Jason and smiled. Then she reached up and kissed him on the cheek. '*I'm doing just what you say, Catherine,*' she whispered in her head.

Jason wrapped his arms around her in response to the kiss and hugged her tightly. 'Not quite the right place for this kind of thing,' he said, ignoring the glare of an approaching verger.

'Oh, yes it is,' Kate said. 'It is absolutely the right place.'

'So you have another son,' Thomas says when Catherine shows Simon to him.

The child sleeps peacefully. He is beautiful, with long lashes and soft rosy cheeks. He opens his eyes when he hears the deep voice of the stranger bending over his cradle, but he fails to focus his gaze at all.

'Perhaps you will give the babe your blessing.'

Thomas nods and it is arranged that they shall carry him into the chapel on the morrow and there will be a special service of thanksgiving. Catherine's heart thuds alarmingly in her chest. 'Could you pray for his healing?' she whispers.

'Healing? He appears very healthy to me.' Thomas looks more closely at the child and puts his finger into the little fist.

'I fear he is blind, Thomas. He makes no response to any movement or light, yet when we touch him or speak he smiles and reacts quite normally as you can see.'

Thomas is shocked. He knows that to be blind is one of the most dreadful afflictions to be visited on anyone, whatever their rank or station. He has seen blind beggars in plenty on the streets of Canterbury. 'Our Lord healed the blind,' he says, 'but I haven't His purity or His power.'

'But you can pray,' Catherine says.

Thomas bows his head. 'Yes, I can pray.'

*   *   *

181

That afternoon, after the service of thanksgiving and blessing, they try to put aside all worrying thoughts of baby Simon and ride on the moor together. Catherine is determined that she will not be alone with Thomas, however, and has persuaded three of her children to accompany them. William shall not have anything with which to reproach her when he returns from France. The two older boys are ahead and Joan is trailing behind on her small palfrey.

They talk of many things, but Catherine cannot understand Thomas's many disagreements with Henry, his one time greatest friend. 'Why do you oppose the king so frequently?' she asks him a little timidly.

'My loyalty is to the Church now,' Thomas replies. 'I spent many years pleasing Henry in everything. He forced me to become archbishop against my will, and therefore I must now serve God first.'

Catherine glances at him and realizes that he is not the Thomas she knew and loved. He has changed. There is sometimes the old sparkle in his eyes but mostly he is dour and solemn. 'But surely, Thomas,' she persists, 'this falling out with Henry over the priest who raped and murdered is a doubtful matter. As a woman I have to side with the king on this. Rape is a terrible crime and he should be tried severely by the courts.'

'He is a priest, Catherine,' Thomas says. 'He can only be tried by the Church.'

Catherine sighs. She can't understand Thomas's stand against the king on such a thing. But she says no more. She knows that there are other, more weighty matters which come between him and Henry, things of which she has no understanding. Her own family and the joys and tribulations that surround her are more important. She will not worry about Thomas and his strange concerns any longer.

It is May now and the countryside is beautiful. There is bright new growth all along the hedgerows, and the trees are showing green at last. There are wild flowers in all the sheltered places and the tall spikes of foxgloves are just opening their bell-like blooms. She experiences a pang of grief that Simon will never know the beauty of all of this. She has

182

heard the cuckoo this morning, however, and at least that is one thing that might one day bring a little joy to her son. It has certainly cheered her.

The way they take leads them to Litford, and Eluned comes to greet them. She must remain at home now for her husband is troubled with many ailments. When she sees who is with Catherine she is quite overawed. The presence of God's own archbishop here outside her humble homestead causes all common sense and caution to depart from her.

'My Lord,' she gabbles. 'Will you give blessing to the little grave beyond the wall? The babe is buried in unconsecrated ground.'

Thomas is surprised that she should speak so, for he knows full well what babe lies cold beneath the small mound. He dismounts and strides over to the grave, crosses himself and recites prayers in Latin. Catherine also slides to the ground and comes to stand beside him. She is mightily afraid, for three of her children are present and Joan is about to dismount and will ask questions. What can Eluned have been thinking to speak so? And why in heaven's name did they come this way today?

The two boys have galloped on but Will has glanced back. She hopes that he has not noticed anything amiss. Joan comes quietly, holding her pony's bridle. She peers at the stone and reads the deeply engraved words. Tom, Catherinae filius, hoc anno domini MCXLIII natus, quarto die obiit.

She turns and looks at Catherine, sees the paleness of her face, the fear in her eyes, and then she looks at the great archbishop and at the pain so obvious in his face too. The mystery of her mother's occasional sadness, and sometimes reddened cheeks when she speaks of Thomas à Becket, and many other little details that she has observed and wondered about, now cause her to wonder afresh and to marvel. She knows about her mother's supposed rape and the birth of a dead baby buried here at Litford. Catherine has confided in her alone of all the children. She looks again at the little grave, reads the words once more, and glances in awe at the two adults standing there. Tom, Thomas! Could what she thinks possibly be true? Was it then not rape at all? She prays silently, crosses herself and then she goes to her mother, kisses her gently, remounts and rides after her brothers.

Eluned is mortified at what she has done. She has always wondered about the identity of this babe whose grave she tends so carefully almost every day. Now she looks into the face of the great archbishop as he stands there and she marvels at what she sees. She suddenly begins to understand an amazing truth. Tom, Thomas! Could what she thinks truly be so? Quite overwhelmed, she runs into the house and weeps.

Catherine follows her. 'Never fear, Eluned,' she says. 'Joan is a good girl, and what she may have understood today will never pass her lips.'

'I too, Madam, will keep your secret to my dying day,' Eluned whispers. 'And the little grave will be my constant charge.'

It is Will, the eldest son, who presents the most serious threat. He returns alone later that day to Litford. Out-riding the others he has gone further, ridden hard, and just before dusk he throws the reigns of his horse over a granite post beside the farmhouse, knocks on the door, and ask for a drink. Eluned comes running and looks fearfully at Catherine's eldest son. This child has always been the difficult one. There is something dark about him. She mutters a prayer to the good Lord that he should not linger here and she gives him the best ale that her small homestead can provide.

'Who lies in the small grave yonder?' he asks. 'Is it one of your babes, Eluned? I saw my mother and the archbishop looking at it earlier today.'

She is struck speechless and can only shake her head helplessly.

He finishes his ale and strides over to look. 'It's a grand little headstone, and engraved in Latin too.' He stoops and reads the words aloud. Then he turns and stares at Eluned, looks at her long and hard. 'You knew my mother when she was very young, did you not?'

'Aye, sir. And a kind and beautiful young lady she was to be sure.'

'It says "son of Catherine". Is it then her child?'

Eluned nods weakly for she cannot tell a direct lie. 'She was wrongly done by. Sir William, your father, knows, and the matter is not spoken about.'

Will reads the words again, notes the baby's name. Tom! He asks no more questions of Eluned, remounts, turns his horse, and canters down the track that leads to his home. He can scarcely believe what he has discovered, and is amazed that his father should know and accept such a disgrace. If his mother was indeed cruelly raped, then the culprit should be severely punished, but if it was no rape . . . As he nears the house many other things begin to fall into place. Tom, Thomas, Thomas à Becket! He recalls the glow in his mother's face when she speaks of Becket. The surprising fact that the great man should deign to come to their home suddenly becomes more understandable. Dear God in heaven, that bastard child could be son to the holy archbishop, Primate of all England! He grins to himself and if his suspicions are true, he wonders how he can turn such a providential piece of information to his own advantage.

Seventeen

'Lovely to have you home again, darling,' Phoebe said. 'Even if it's only for a flying visit.'

'Have you missed me?'

'Of course, but we're both glad Bristol is proving to be a success.'

'It's mostly down to Jason.'

Phoebe looked at her granddaughter and saw the new look of contentment. So Dominic was fading from her life at last, and hopefully Jason was filling the gap. 'So how was the trip to Canterbury?'

'Fab. The cathedral is quite wonderful. You really should have gone there long ago, Nonna.'

'I know. I keep putting it off for some reason. I think I must be afraid.'

'Afraid?'

Phoebe shook her head. 'Perhaps I don't want to know that it's a modern town. And it might be some sort of catalyst. The murder and all that.'

'I felt a bit like that,' Kate said. 'Go with Hugo. He'll keep you anchored in the here and now, just like Jason did for me. You will, won't you, Hugo?'

'Will what?'

'Stop Phoebe regressing.'

'Absolutely,' Hugo said without looking up from his newspaper.

Phoebe grinned at him. 'When he's into the sports pages he doesn't register anything. I'm getting on very well with the second book by the way. I'm up to the bit where Thomas is persuaded to become archbishop.'

'How are you going to deal with the quarrels?'

186

Hugo looked from one to the other. 'Quarrels? What quarrels?'

'Oh, so you are listening! I think Kate means between King Henry and Thomas.'

Hugo went back to his paper with relief. 'Good heavens. I shall never understand you two. You slip back a few centuries as easily as having breakfast.'

Kate made herself some coffee and sat down at the kitchen table. 'How are you going to work out Catherine's story? How will it all end?'

'Wait and see,' Phoebe said. 'Most of it's in my head, but I haven't written the last chapters yet. How do you think it really ended?'

'It depends,' Kate said. 'Was she real, or was she fiction?'

'Real. I believe in her.'

'She's faded from my mind quite a bit since I met Jason. He's so pragmatic and down-to-earth that there's no room for dreams and ghosts. He can't hack anything of that sort. She seems to speak to me sometimes, though. I feel she's glad that I'm with Jason and not Dominic.'

'So she *was* real?'

'That's the billion-dollar question isn't it? But yes, I think she lived, and that she had some connection with Litford and with Thomas.'

'And that she manifests herself to us?'

Kate nodded thoughtfully. 'That too,' she said.

Will's chance to enlighten his father about his mother's indiscretions have to wait for a considerable time. William doesn't return home until two summers have passed. He is full of triumph for he has served the king well and he feels that his prestige at court is running high.

'So, what have you all been doing during my long absence?' he asks of his gathered family.

Only Simon is absent. He is playing in the garden with one of his nursemaids and a new puppy. William knows nothing yet of his son's affliction.

Joan is the first to speak. 'We've enjoyed the visits of the archbishop,' she blurts out unwisely. 'He is a great and noble man.'

William's eyes darken. 'And are those visits the most important events of the past months?'

Catherine intervenes. 'He has visited us twice, husband,' she says carefully. 'And Joan particularly enjoyed his time here for as you know, she wishes to become a nun.'

'I'm not sure I shall permit that,' William says.

Catherine speedily changes the subject for she knows that it is because of Thomas that her husband is antagonistic to Joan's wishes. The Church has become anathema to him. 'I think Will wants to show you his latest mount,' she says. 'There is just time before dark. You shall hear our other news later.' Unsuspecting, she smiles at him beguilingly and kisses his glowering face.

Together father and son leave the solar and Catherine watches them fondly. She is aware of Will's frequent bouts of surliness but she feels that it is probably just because he has missed his father. Surely now that William is home her son will grow happier and become more amenable. He needs direction and a firmer hand than hers. And there is the frightful news of their youngest child's plight to be told. She has not had the courage to tell him of this yet.

William strides back into the solar a few minutes later. 'Out!' he shouts to Joan and the little girls. 'I wish to speak to your mother alone.'

They scatter before his obvious wrath and he stands silent until they are out of earshot. Catherine watches him in terror and bewilderment. She clasps her hands together and her heart beats wildly.

'Will has informed me of your treachery,' he thunders. 'So the great archbishop was your lover, the father of the bastard in the grave at Litford.' He holds his riding whip threateningly in his hand and Catherine shrinks before this strange and terrifying manifestation of her husband.

'You knew of the child before we were wed,' she whispers. 'You said it meant little to you as long as I was a faithful and loving wife for the rest of my days.'

188

'Aye, and I believed you to have been raped, but although Becket is everything I most despise and deplore, he is no rapist, no seducer of women. Everyone knows that. His celibacy is the wonder as well as the scorn of the court, king and serf alike.'

He stands before her full of righteous anger and she is terrified. Women have been whipped to death for no more than this.

'You were and are his willing accomplice and you have made my house your whore-home.'

'No, William.' Catherine feels all colour leave her face and she leans on the table behind her for support. 'No, husband. It is not as you say. Yes, he was the father of my first babe, but that was the one and only time I sinned. We were little more than children. We scarcely knew what we did.'

'You were rightly punished by the death of your bastard child, and now we are all punished for your further foul sins, by my last son's affliction.' He grips his riding whip more firmly in both hands, flexing it menacingly.

Catherine stares at him like a rabbit before a stoat. So Will has told him of Simon's blindness too. The accusation is terrifying. Could the child's misfortune possibly be a punishment for . . . for what? She knows that she has done no wrong, that she has been a faithful and loving wife to William throughout all the years of their marriage. Yet a worm of doubt curls around her heart. Tears flood her eyes and she brushes them desperately away. 'That is a cruel thing to say, William,' she murmurs. 'The archbishop's visits here have been blameless. The children have been with me every time and he has given us all spiritual guidance and blessing.'

'You expect me to believe such sanctimonious rubbish? This is the end, Catherine. I should beat you and cast you from my house, but instead, for the sake of our children, it is I who shall leave. Guard them well. I shall send to enquire of their welfare from time to time. Do all in your power for Simon and see that he wants for nothing.' He turns from her, ignoring her outstretched arms, and strides out to the stables.

She hears his wrathful orders to his groom to fetch and saddle a fresh beast, hears the clatter of hooves on the courtyard cobbles, and knows that he has gone from her

189

life, perhaps for ever. She also acknowledges that she has escaped lightly, yet her heart is broken, for she loves him. Thomas is once more the cause of her wretchedness.

'The biography will be published by Christmas,' Phoebe told Hugo triumphantly. She held Dudley's latest letter in her hand and waved it about over the breakfast table. 'He says that the publishers have made a special effort and there is to be a launch in Canterbury in December to coincide with the memorial service they have each year on the anniversary of Thomas's martyrdom.'

'Congratulations,' Hugo said. 'You won't be able to put off the Canterbury trip any longer. I'm looking forward to it already.'

'They might even do Eliot's play, *Murder in the Cathedral.* I couldn't face all that without you beside me, Hugo.'

'I'll stick to you like a shadow,' Hugo said with a grin. 'You can't go shooting off to the twelfth century at this important juncture in your life, can you!'

She shook her head. 'I'll hold on to you tightly. What do you mean, "important juncture"?'

'Becoming a famous author, of course!'

'Not famous yet.'

'You will be, especially when the fantasy version of the Becket story comes out.'

'It might be the wrong kind of fame! Thomas à Becket was a highly prestigious saint and a powerful character in English history. Perhaps one shouldn't fictionalize the lives of people like that.'

'It's constantly being done,' Hugo told her comfortingly. 'And it was more than eight hundred years ago. No family left to complain.'

'Only the Church,' Phoebe said. 'Only the Church left to excommunicate me!'

'You aren't a member.'

Phoebe smiled and put some more bread in the toaster. 'That's true. I'm not. So I'll finish the book then.'

'And marry me?'

'That too, perhaps.'

*   *   *

190

Catherine's brother has paid one of his infrequent visits to the Tracey home and he has told his sister all the latest news of court, of king and archbishop. They are walking in the garden while Eluned and the girls prepare the evening meal. Eluned, recently widowed, has come to live with Catherine to help in the house and with the care of Simon.

'How can two men, who were once so inseparable, now quarrel over every conceivable matter?' Catherine says to her brother.

Edward shakes his head. 'It's one of the great mysteries,' he says. 'Thomas is a changed man. He opposes everything the king does or asks for.'

Catherine has often wondered if Thomas's grief over their baby son, and his long-ago love for her, has caused him the deep regrets that are turning now to bitterness. But surely not. He made his own choices. They were never forced upon him.

'I loved him, you know, Edward,' she says.

He turns to look at her closely. 'I've long thought so. And did he return that love, sister?'

'At first he did. But his ambition overcame him, and now, if it is as you say, it seems that the desire for riches and splendour has turned to devotion to God!'

'He is still very splendid, although there are rumours that beneath the gold and silver of his robes he wears a filthy hair shirt in some mistaken idea of penance.'

'Mistaken? Do you judge God's archbishop?' Her voice has lost its seriousness.

Edward laughed. 'Certainly. I have no reverence for someone who causes so much strife.'

'We had a child,' Catherine says suddenly.

The secret disgrace of her youth has been well kept, and Edward stops in his tracks. 'A child! God's wounds, Catherine! Does he live?'

She shakes her head. 'No, Edward. He lies in a tiny grave away yonder on the moor, but it is not unmarked. I had a headstone fashioned in hardest granite and the words engraved very deeply on its surface. Tom, Catherinae filius, hoc anno domini MCXLIII natus, quarto die obiit. *Our babe will not* be easily forgotten, although I fear that the stone and its sad words have been the cause of my downfall.'

'Does Thomas know?'

'Yes, and my husband too. He was able to overlook the fact that I had been with child before we were wed for he thought I was raped against my will. When he discovered that this wasn't so, and who the father was, his fury was quite terrible. My secret was found out because of the headstone.' Catherine felt herself trembling as she remembered that day. 'I feared for my life, but instead of whipping me to death, as he believed I deserved, he left us and went to join the king. He hasn't returned home since then.'

'I've often wondered about his long absence. Dearest Catherine, you should have told me all this before. I could have helped you.'

She put her hand on her brother's arm. 'We do well enough, Edward, and I know I could call on you for help if I was in great need.'

Edward clasped his hand over hers. 'It's a sad story, sister. Do you still have any love for Thomas after all these years, and after the grief he brought you?'

Catherine looks at the sky and the lowering clouds gathering now around the hills that surround the house. 'No, I don't think I do. I pray for him frequently, but the personal love has long gone. I've loved my husband for many years and, in spite of his cruelty in leaving us for so long, he's still the one who holds my heart. And I can understand the reasons for his wrath.' Then she says aloud the words that are so often in her mind. 'Loving a man like Thomas with a devouring passion for his God is always a difficult cross to bear.'

'You speak truly,' Edward says. 'Thomas could never have brought you happiness, Catherine.'

'Loving Thomas was indeed very hard,' she says. 'But loving William isn't proving easy either.' She will not tell her brother that since she was left alone life has become increasingly difficult. Many of the things her family needs are becoming less plentiful, for William has demanded that sums of money are sent to him regularly, and he has taken with him five of the most able-bodied men from the estate.

Consequently work on the land has suffered greatly, harvests have been poor, and repairs to the house are neglected. Catherine has been lonely and often sad and she frequently wonders if the quarrel between herself and William will ever be resolved.

Edward leaves for London the following day and Catherine turns once more to Eluned for support. They are sitting in the solar that evening, for the day has turned wet and cold. Eluned is busy with her spinning, but Catherine is, as always, unwillingly sewing and mending. There is no time for elaborate embroidery now. More serviceable work has to be done.

Catherine has been much cheered by her brother's visit. She slept well last night and her dreams were happy ones. She suddenly finds herself smiling.

Eluned, seeing the smile, is surprised. 'God be praised,' she says. 'You look merry for once.'

'Do you remember the girl I kept dreaming about long ago when I was in your house, when I was great with baby Tom?'

Eluned nods. She has not forgotten. The nightmares disturbed her sleep for many weeks. 'Aye and you frequently made me vexed with your crying and your strange fancies.'

'I know I was a great nuisance to you, but the girl still visits my dreams now and then. She's a phantom friend, Eluned.'

The older woman shakes her head in disbelief and fear. There is no time or place in her life for such strange presences. When she hears of such things she crosses herself against the evil they must surely bring. She does so now and Catherine laughs.

'This Kate is no malicious spirit,' she says. 'She's just a girl needing my help, and I think I've been able to give it to her. She's heeded my message to her, and I sense that she's happy at last.'

'Then thank the good Lord,' Eluned says. 'I wish the same for you, mistress, even if I have no understanding of the things you are saying.'

'Congrats on the book,' Kate said on the telephone a few days later. 'So you'll be going to Canterbury then, at last? You'll love it. I've persuaded Jason into another visit there for the memorial service and Eliot's play.'

'We'll be there at the same time then,' Phoebe said. 'You can come and see me suffering in a bookshop doing a signing.'

'Fab,' Kate said. 'Jason will see what a famous grandmother I have!'

The king is furious, beside himself with wrath. Emissaries have arrived from the archbishop's offices in Canterbury informing him that even he, the king, is in danger of excommunication if he does not follow Thomas's guidance in all matters concerning the Church. Henry wonders why he was allowed back to Canterbury after being in exile. Since returning to his cathedral he has become even more insufferable.

'God's wounds!' Henry shouts angrily to all who can hear. 'Who does this archbishop think he is that he can command his king? Have I not pulled him out of the gutter and given him everything that he owns?' He struts around the great hall of his castle and searches in his mind for some way to punish Thomas, his one-time friend and now seemingly his enemy. And then the perfect insult occurs to him. The prince, Henry's eldest son and heir, once Thomas's ward, will be crowned as the rightful heir to the throne of England, and it will be done in York and not in Canterbury. This perfect and important snub will infuriate Thomas.

The king's stormy countenance creases to a grin and he chuckles to himself, and then he remembers the ceremony organized by Thomas years ago. Not a coronation but a show of fealty by the bishops and lords. What a bright shining star his chancellor had been then. A true friend, a trusty accomplice. And now? Since he became archbishop rather than chancellor, Thomas has changed mightily. He is gaunt and severe, a man possessed with a burning passion for what he thinks is the will of God.

So the coronation of the young prince is arranged and the Archbishop of York is commanded to perform the ceremony. He places the crown on the boy's head, the people cheer, there is a great feast, and at the end of all the celebrations, Henry returns to France well pleased with the snub he has given to Thomas. Perhaps this will bring the errant priest to his knees before him.

But he has underestimated his archbishop. Thomas is enraged. Letters of excommunication are sent to the Bishops of London and Salisbury, as well as to the Archbishop of York for their parts in the false ceremony, for Thomas declares it to have been such. He contends that only he, as Archbishop of Canterbury, has the power to crown the future kings of England.

Henry, when he hears of Thomas's reaction, laughs at first. But when the announcements of excommunication are made, and he receives news that he himself is amongst those so threatened, he falls into a towering rage. All the archbishop's lands and possessions have been plundered during his long exile, but nevertheless, he is back in Canterbury now. He is taking his place as Primate of England. Henry is so outraged that he falls into one of the most undisciplined displays of his reign. He tears his clothes, rolls around on the floor of his castle, gnashes his teeth and calls out in a frenzy the words which are to be remembered down the centuries. 'Who will deliver me from this turbulent priest?'

The king's voice reverberates around the great stone walls and William de Tracey hears and exults in these words. Hugh de Moreville, Richard de Brito and Reginald FitzUrse have also heard. They look at one another and slip furtively outside. They all have reason to hate Thomas à Becket, but perhaps William has more reason than any other. He thinks of his wife, Catherine, whom he still loves, and his lips set in a determined line. He now has permission from the king to do the thing he most wants to do.

Christmas in Canterbury and Hugo and Phoebe have come for the launch of Phoebe's book, the serious biography of Thomas à Becket. They are staying in a hotel right in the town centre next to the cathedral. Kate and Jason are also in Canterbury for a short visit to Jason's sister.

Flickering lights and tinsel decorate every shop window.

There are crowds of holidaymakers, a smattering of modern-day pilgrims, for they still come to view the martyr's shrine and to make merry. And there is Phoebe, sitting at a table in a bookshop with a pile of her books in front of her and a few buyers occasionally asking her to sign her name, and to write, *Love to Sharon*, or some such on the first page.

'How many have you sold this morning?' Hugo asks.

'Nine,' Phoebe says. 'Not bad really.'

Eighteen

Phoebe and Kate went together to the Becket memorial service, leaving Hugo and Jason in the hotel bar. The ceremony was preceded by evensong in the impressive Gothic Quire and Phoebe knelt with bowed head and prayed without words, for she was unsure how or what to pray in this awesome place. Before her was the high altar and above that the marble chair of St Augustine in which archbishops were enthroned. She thought of Thomas as she looked at it and wondered how he would have felt on the day of his enthronement. She had tried to give something of his feelings in her book, but here, in his own cathedral, she wondered how she could have presumed to do anything of the sort.

Not being a churchgoer, she nevertheless felt a great sense of awe as she followed the service. *Almighty God, by whose grace and power your holy martyr Thomas triumphed over suffering and was faithful . . . Lighten our darkness, Lord, we pray; and in your mercy defend us from all perils and dangers of this night . . . Glory be to the Father, and to the Son, and to the Holy Ghost. As it was in the beginning, is now, and ever shall be.*

In a strange state of otherness Phoebe followed the candlelit procession to the hallowed place in the north-west transept, the Martyrdom Shrine, and she was grateful for Kate's steady presence beside her. She walked as in a dream, seeing nothing of the great vaulted roof, the stained glass windows, the tombs of other archbishops. All she was aware of was the Altar of Sword's Point and the stone flooring with the name Thomas engraved upon it.

She grasped Kate's arm as the prayers for Thomas and all martyrs were intoned. *Almighty God, you have built up your*

Church through the love and devotion of your saints. We give thanks for your servant Thomas, whom we commemorate today. In the distance the organ was playing very quietly and she felt the power and sanctity of this place all about her.

Then gradually the lights faded, the cathedral became dark, and the candles were small and dim. The shuffling and coughs of those around her ceased and the solemn tones of the organ changed imperceptibly.

Plainsong, *Kyrie eleison, Christe eleison, Kyrie eleison.* Phoebe stood quite still, her eyes fixed on the stones beneath her feet and the name etched there, but gradually it faded from her sight. There was only the great pillar nearby. All else was dark and eerie in the shadows. And there was the chilling cold. Candles flickered uncertainly in the draughts that blew cruelly through every crack and cranny of the cathedral.

Monks are chanting in the choir, which is lit only by the steady glow of the altar lights as Thomas comes calmly in to vespers. Phoebe looks up and as her eyes become used to the dimness she sees him and can hardly believe her eyes.

Then her heart thuds in terror as she hears a loud crashing, angry shouts, metal on stone and a voice calling in mad fury, 'Where is Thomas Becket, traitor to the king?' She tries to leap forward, in some way protect him, for she suddenly knows which event this is she is miraculously witnessing. But history cannot be altered. She wants to escape now, to cry out, but her limbs appear to be frozen to the ground. She can neither move nor speak.

Thomas has already spoken to these knights for they came to his dwelling earlier demanding his confession of treason. He knows that he must surely die and he feels no fear. He has done what had to be done for his God and his Church. If martyrdom is to be his then he is ready, welcomes it almost. 'I am here,' he calls. 'But no traitor to the king. What do you seek from me?'

'Absolve!' one of them shouts. 'Restore to communion all those you have excommunicated. Confess your treachery.'

William de Tracey feels his heart pounding, his head throbbing and the bloodlust is upon him. He peers through the gloom and sees the man he has hated for so long, the man whose life and power and magnetism he has constantly coveted, the man in whose arms his wife has lain.

Thomas is tall and impressive as he faces his accusers. He stands taller than any of them. 'I cannot absolve those men for they have violated God's law and the law of the Church.' His voice is clear and with no trace of fear. 'I am ready to die for my Lord and for the Holy Church of God on earth.'

'Then die you shall!' one of the four knights screams. They approach the altar, swords drawn, but they had not bargained on Thomas's fight for his life. In spite of his impassioned words he will not die without defending himself. It is not in his nature, and for a moment, before his eyes pass images of past battles, all of them ending in glorious triumph. He stands against a pillar and flings FitzUrse backwards then grapples with de Tracey. But FitzUrse swings his sword through the air. It takes the bishop's cap from Thomas's head and grazes his scalp.

Then William de Tracey, holding his sword high and strongly in both hands, shouts, 'Strike, strike!' And he brings the weapon down with all the venom that has been stored in his heart for so long. The blow falls with immense power on the consecrated head of God's archbishop and slices right through the arm of the monk who is standing with Thomas.

Thomas still stands immovable, hands clasped together now, all resistance stilled. A third blow fells him to his knees, but he speaks clearly so that all can hear. 'For the name of Jesus and the protection of the Church I am ready to die.'

The words inflame the knights, and another sword is swung viciously and with such power that the top of Thomas's head is sliced right off and he falls on his face to the sacred stones, his brains spilling on to the ground.

The knights turn and rush out of the church into the great storm that now fills the sky, but inside, in the quietness, the monks creep from the shadows. One binds the severed part of the archbishop's head back into place and they carry him to a place before the High Altar. In the Martyrdom Transept *the scattered brains and blood are carefully scooped up and blood seeping from the body is also collected and saved. These are precious relics that will work wondrous miracles and they must be closely guarded.*

The memorial service came to an end. People were leaving quietly as if the twelfth-century grief for a murdered saint was a present reality, and to Phoebe it was just that. She brushed tears from her eyes and realized that she was still intensely cold in spite of the now efficient central heating and the cheerful modern lights of the cathedral.

She looked around in confusion. There was no blood now, no fear. The organ was playing quietly as Kate took her arm and together they walked out into the precincts and into the garish Christmas-decorated, but still medieval street. There were tourists and late-night shoppers, Boots the Chemist advertising three shampoo bottles for the price of two, and rock music from someone's radio. A few brave souls were sitting at tables set on the cobbles outside the pub. They were smoking and drinking, laughing and talking loudly, no one aware of what Phoebe had just witnessed, or of the history that lived again in their ancient cathedral.

'You went back, didn't you?' Kate's voice was anxious.

Phoebe nodded. 'What happened? How did you know?'

'You just stood there, white as a sheet, and you didn't join in at all.'

'I saw it, the murder. I saw *him*. He was real. So were they. I saw William de Tracey, FitzUrse, de Brito and Hugh de Moreville. I heard their voices loud with hatred, and I saw and felt the terror of the monks.'

'I'm going to get you back to Hugo as quickly as I can,' Kate said.

Hugo and Jason were sitting in the bar laughing together. They sprang up when Kate pushed open the door. 'Phoebe needs a stiff drink,' she said. 'Brandy I should think.'

Hugo helped her out of her coat. 'What happened? You look as though you've seen a ghost.'

Phoebe grinned at the apt remark and sank down in the proffered chair.

'She's just witnessed one of the most famous murders in English history,' Kate said.

Phoebe took the brandy that Jason offered her and tried to minimalize what had happened. The impact of it was gradually sliding away from her. 'All in my head,' she said as lightly as she could manage. 'I wish I didn't possess such a vivid imagination.'

'Then you couldn't be a writer could you, Nonna?' Kate, feeling shaken herself, drank her brandy thankfully.

'I got it right in the book anyway,' Phoebe said. 'It happened just as I told it.'

'Of course it did,' Hugo said comfortingly, and refrained from adding that perhaps what she had witnessed in her mind had merely been a materialization of the words she had so vividly written. He winked at Jason and, after he and Kate had left, he took Phoebe's hands in his and grinned at her. 'You *could* call it first-degree research,' he said.

The old hotel was so close to the cathedral that it almost appeared to be part of it. Phoebe slept fitfully that night. The murder she had witnessed had seemed as real as if it had happened that very day, the twenty-ninth of December, in the twenty-first century instead of the twelfth. Perhaps she had lived then in another life? And Kate? How did Kate fit into all this? Phoebe closed her eyes again. Thank God for Jason and his pragmatic approach to life. No spirits of the past troubled Jason, or Hugo for that matter.

In spite of the peace this thought generated, sleep still eluded her. She tried to remain still and not to disturb Hugo who was snoring peacefully beside her. At home, in the little mews house they had bought together, they had a spacious bedroom and large twin beds close together. 'At our age,' Phoebe had insisted, 'we can do without the constrictions of a double bed.'

But here in the hotel, Hugo had opted for a double, king-size in fact, cosy and comforting when sleep came easily after love-making, but difficult when thoughts and nightmares crowded the mind. Now in the bleak early hours Phoebe was quite sure that sleep had completely deserted her. Eventually, when she could bear it no longer, she slid carefully from between the sheets. A duvet would have been easier, she reflected.

She padded over to the window and pulled the curtain gently aside. The night was clear and cold and the silence was mysterious, almost unearthly. The ancient walls of the great cathedral glowed golden and bronze in the brightness of the modern floodlighting which had not yet been switched off.

She remained at the window for a long time until she was so cold that she longed for the warmth of Hugo's bulky frame. He was always there for her whenever she needed comfort and reassurance. She shivered and rubbed her hands together, letting the curtains fall back into place so that she could see only the pleasant modern furnishings in the dim light filtering through, and also, reassuringly, the corridor light shining from the substantial crack beneath the old door. Hugo was still snoring quietly. She slid back into bed, and in his sleep he reached out for her and held her close so that fear and phantoms disappeared, allowing her to slumber peacefully and dreamlessly at last.

The news of Thomas's death takes a long time to reach Devon. Catherine has felt a heaviness within her heart for a long time, and whether it is the natural way of women at her age, or something more sinister, she cannot tell. She longs constantly for William but there has been no word.

When the winter snows have cleared a little and the roads are passable, Edward de Quincy once again visits his sister bearing the news that he knows will devastate her. That her own husband should have been one of the murdering knights who killed Thomas is too terrible to contemplate. How she will ever come to terms with these unspeakable tidings, he cannot imagine.

Brother and sister sit together in the solar. Eluned has brought wine and victuals and has left them alone, taking Simon with her. Although he is nearly twelve years old now his blindness makes him very dependent. He does not like to be far from his mother or from Eluned.

Edward watches his sister's face. She is drinking wine and smiling at him. They have talked about his children, about general things, but he cannot keep his terrible story from her for much longer. He leans towards her, takes her cup and places it on the hearth and takes both her hands in his. 'There is bad news from Canterbury, Catherine,' he says gently.

Immediately the colour rushes from her face in spite of the fire's crackling flames. 'What news, brother? Is it Thomas?' She guesses that if he speaks of Canterbury it must be the archbishop. 'Does he ail? I know that he has frequently been sick these past years.'

'He is dead, Catherine.'

She does not remove her hands from Edward's but her fists clench in his grasp and she closes her eyes for a moment. 'Then he is at peace.' It is all she can say at first for she feels an emptiness, as if her own life had come to its purposeful end.

There is a silence in the room broken only by the spitting and crackling of the logs on the fire. Eluned has brought in a goodly pile and made a large blaze in honour of their visitor.

At last Catherine pulls her hands away from her brother. 'His many disputes with King Henry brought him much suffering,' she says. 'But how did he die, Edward? Was it the wasting sickness? Was he ill for long?'

'He did not ail at all, sister. He was killed. Murdered in his own cathedral. People reckon he is now God's holy martyr.'

Catherine stands up, puts yet another log on the fire to calm her nerves. 'Tell me.'

And then, fitfully, with many pauses, Edward speaks the words which he has been rehearsing all the way here through the dreary winter miles. He tells her the names of the knights who were apparently carrying out the command of the king, and last of all he gives her William's name. She stares at him, uncomprehending at first, and he has to tell the whole story over again, and then she utters a piercing cry, a scream that brings Eluned running, Simon too, and the youngest daughter, Amabel, not far behind.

For many days Catherine lies semi-conscious and will not accept the terrible thing that has happened. Her husband, whom she loves, has murdered her friend, her one-time lover, *the father of her precious first son, the man who held so much of her heart for so many long years.*

It is not until the primroses deck the lanes again and the swallows return that Catherine will leave her chamber, dress and return to some semblance of the life she knew. During all that time Eluned and Catherine's two daughters, Maude and Amabel, have cared for her, fed her, washed her, and attempted to bring her back to life, for it has been indeed like a living death. But at last Catherine's strength improves and at last she is riding on the moor again, Calder at her side. Always Calder, the first Calder's great-great-grandson now. In her times of deepest melancholy her dogs have always given encouragement and love. But her heart is still full of black and cheerless thoughts.

And then comes news again from London. The king has come in sorrow and deep contrition to Canterbury to pray for forgiveness at the tomb of his one-time friend. He has walked through the streets in sackcloth and has commanded that he should be scourged by the monks and prelates there. The knights who carried out the murder have repented too. She hears that William has journeyed all the way to the Holy Land that he might pray for forgiveness in Jerusalem itself.

Catherine is bewildered when she hears all this. She is even more amazed to know that in the name of the murdered archbishop miraculous healings are coming to pass in Canterbury. Pilgrims are making the dangerous journey to the site of Thomas's martyrdom. His tomb has become a sacred shrine. Holy water is dispensed, water said to contain traces of his precious blood, and the lame are walking again, the blind seeing! Catherine needs no further spur. She looks at her young son and knows that she must take him to Canterbury. The murderer's child will go to his victim for healing and for forgiveness for his father. It is a preposterous idea, but it grips her imagination and her heart and she can think of little else.

It is high summer before she feels fully recovered in body, and then she calls Eluned one day and announces her plans. She has kept them secret until now. 'I shall go to Canterbury,'

204

she says. 'If those who never knew Thomas are being healed in his name, then surely he will look kindly on my son whom he blessed as a small child.'

Eluned is mightily alarmed, for the roads are dangerous for a woman. She also looks at Simon and sees his father's likeness in the boy. 'The master's child?' she says, and at once Catherine understands what she means but dare not say. Is it right to take the son of the murderer to the murdered? She has been questioning herself over this for many long weeks. She walks to the window and looks at the rising hills where she and Thomas rode together during that last visit.

'Yes, Eluned,' she says quietly. 'Thomas would hold no grudge against a child.'

Eluned crosses herself and mutters something under her breath.

'Will you come with me?'

Eluned sinks down upon the bench before the empty hearth. 'My bones ache all the time and I am old now. I think I should be more a hindrance than a help. Nevertheless I'll try to summon the strength if you need me.'

Catherine can see her extreme weariness and feels ashamed that she has asked such an enormous sacrifice from her old servant and friend. 'I think perhaps I would prefer you to remain here after all,' she says. 'I shall be away a long time and will need to know that someone I trust is in charge.'

Eluned sighs with relief. 'Then I shall stay,' she says. 'And I will offer up prayers for your safety and for master Simon's healing every day in the archbishop's chapel.'

All is arranged as quickly as Catherine can manage, and to her great pleasure, her stepdaughter, Joan, is given leave from her priory to accompany the little group. Maude, her next daughter, will come too. Catherine is also persuaded to take three menservants rather than two, for there are dangers on the roads of England, and Canterbury lies many weary miles away from Devonshire.

By the end of July all is ready. Simon is excited although he has been told little of what is planned, and he rides his small palfrey with aplomb and self-assurance. On horseback *his blindness is not so obvious for his mount is sure-footed and intelligent. Catherine and Maude ride astride, bundling their skirts on the saddle between their legs, and only Joan sits more decorously, her nun's robes gracefully positioned to one side of the beautiful roan mare that Catherine has chosen for her. The three men are well armed and strongly mounted on three great destriers, animals that William left behind because of their immaturity, but which are now fully grown and well trained, powerful and swift. There are also two packhorses laden with clothes and food for the journey.*

Nineteen

*C*atherine has joined the throng approaching the cathedral. The horses have been left at a hostelry where they will be rested and cared for. She and Joan are walking either side of Simon, with Maude close behind. Simon is gripping his mother's hand firmly. To him the noise of the crowds is quite terrifying.

They enter the great door and are directed towards the tomb. Catherine can hardly breathe for emotion as she approaches, and when she is in touching distance she falls to her knees and her children do the same. She releases Simon's hand and reaches out to put her fingers on the cold stone. 'Thomas!'

A monk approaches her, attempts to raise her to her feet, to guide her away. She stands and looks at him. 'My son needs healing,' she says humbly. She takes a large gold coin from the bag, which is hidden in the folds of her skirt, and holds it out to him. 'The boy is blind. He has been so from his birth. Our Lord healed such a one.'

The monk nods, takes the money and secretes it away in his grimy habit. Then he leads the little group into a shadowy and quiet corner of the crypt. There he produces a piece of cloth and Catherine recoils as the stench of death and filth assails her.

'In truth,' he mumbles, 'this is cut from the under garment of the Holy martyr. He wore a hair shirt of penance. His blood has stained it. Your child will be healed if he wears it close to his body for all this summer.'

Catherine takes it in her hands and she is smitten with guilt, for this blood came from a wound made by William's sword, the weapon which she had so frequently polished. Gently she pulls Simon towards her, unbuttons his leather jerkin and fastens the cloth inside next to his fair and sweetly smelling flesh. He shrinks away and tries to stop her for although he cannot see or understand what she is doing he can smell the foul stench and feel the roughness of the cloth.

'Let be,' she orders firmly. 'This is a precious thing, Simon. It is a relic of God's Holy martyr and will bring you health and well-being.' She does not specifically say healing, for her faith is not so great as she had hoped. She produces another coin and gives it to the monk. Then she turns and walks back to the tomb. She lights a candle and prays again for a miracle. Thomas surely stands at the throne of God and intercedes for all who come to him. Wistfully she wonders if perhaps he might plead a little more strongly for the child of someone he knows and once loved.

The journey back to Devon is long and wearisome and there is no immediate sign of the miracle that Catherine hopes for. As the little party approaches Exeter her faith is beginning to falter, and then the worst that she can imagine happens. Simon's horse, frightened by a marauding pack of dogs, rears up, and the child falls heavily on his head.

For a time he lies quite still on the grass. Catherine bathes his forehead and weeps. This is the final punishment. She has been so wrong. How could she have expected Thomas to look favourably on her or on her child? William de Tracey's son is tainted with the murder.

As she bathes Simon's face she sees his eyelids flutter and he looks up at her. He puts his hands over his eyes and screams with such frightening intensity that folk come rushing from the hostelry nearby. He struggles to his feet and buries his head in her gown.

It is Joan who first understands. Prayers have been answered, the miracle has happened. When the screaming stops she realizes that her brother can see, and the revelation must be as terrifying to him as a nightmare. She closes her own eyes and tries to imagine what it is like to have lived for twelve years in darkness and then suddenly to have that darkness removed.

She tries to comfort her mother, to assure her that all

will be well, but it is not until much later that Catherine acknowledges the wonderful thing that has happened. Simon keeps his eyes firmly closed for a long time, and only when they are home again does he attempt little peeps at this brilliant and alarming world.

'This miracle is like some we read about in the Holy Scriptures, Mother,' Joan says. 'It may be some time before Simon can see as everyone else can, but it has happened! Saint Thomas has answered our prayers.'

William comes home to Devon a changed man. He has heard much of the miracles done in the name of Saint Thomas but he knows nothing of how his own family has been blessed.

He stands before Catherine and weeps for the sin he has committed. 'I know now that you were innocent. A man who was guilty of adultery could never cure the lame and the sick. I slew God's innocent archbishop and caused my loving wife years of misery.'

It is always heard to see a strong man cry, but Catherine trembles for joy at his words. She has waited many years to hear him admit her innocence.

'I have sought forgiveness,' he says. 'As you know, I've journeyed to the Holy Land and given many alms, and prayed for absolution in Jerusalem and in Rome.'

'And God has forgiven you,' Catherine says. 'As I forgive you, William.'

'How can I be sure?' He holds out his arms to her and she goes tentatively into them.

'There is a way.'

He has not yet seen his youngest son. Simon is at his lessons in the home of the tutor to whom he goes every day.

'Then show it to me, wife,' he says. 'Show me proof of my forgiveness from God if you can, for I have received no confirmation of it from any source.'

'Your son has been healed of his blindness,' she says jubilantly. 'Even now he is away learning to read and write and he makes good progress. This is surely God's sign that he forgives you.'

William stares at her in bewilderment. 'Healed! Don't trifle with me, Catherine. A child born blind is never healed.'

'We went to the shrine of the Holy martyr in Canterbury,' Catherine says, and she trembles as she speaks. 'We prayed there at Thomas's tomb for forgiveness for you, husband, and for healing for your son, and it came to pass, just as we asked.'

Before they left Canterbury for London, Phoebe persuaded Hugo to go with her for one last visit to the cathedral. They stood in the Trinity Chapel and looked at the Thomas panel in one of the stained glass windows. 'Saint Thomas,' Phoebe said. 'He looks slightly formidable there in his mitre and chasuble, don't you think, Hugo? I like to remember him as chancellor, having a good time, and not so serious.'

'He would never have achieved fame if he had not given all that up for God,' Hugo said.

'Probably not.' Phoebe glanced at the new guidebook she had just bought in the cathedral shop. 'The other panels show how he brought help and healing to those who came to his tomb.'

'Do you believe all that?'

'I think so,' Phoebe said. 'Some of it, anyway. Who are we to doubt?'

'And your book, the story of this Catherine?'

'"Find another life, another love",' Phoebe quoted. 'Did that really come from my Catherine, or is it something I dreamed up?'

'Kate took the message to heart,' Hugo said surprisingly. 'It seems to have worked for her, so perhaps this mysterious creature isn't just imagination after all.'

Phoebe looked at him and smiled. 'Canterbury is getting to you too, isn't it?' she said. 'And working miracles still.'

William and Catherine climb the stony track to the small wooden church near their Devon home. William has said mysteriously that he has some good news to announce and he wants to be here in the little churchyard to give it more import. As they approach the church door Catherine looks at him expectantly, wondering what it can be that needs to be said in this place. Why must his news be announced here?

He stops and takes her hands in his. 'I have received further word of my pardon,' he says quietly. She feels her body trembling. It was a terrible thing that he did and although she has forgiven him, she has found their relationship difficult, but she is trying hard to understand and put the past behind her.

'The Pope himself has decreed that I shall be absolved of my crime if I pay for the building of a fine new church here in Bovey. It is to be dedicated to Saint Thomas.' He hesitates for a moment and then brings her hands to his lips and kisses her fingers gently.

She can see tears in his eyes. So the messenger who arrived this morning was as important as she had guessed. She had given the man food and wine after his long journey, and he and William had been closeted in the solar for nearly an hour. But until this moment William has not told her anything of the message that has come from London. She looks at her husband and her eyes brim with tears. 'God be praised,' she says.

'It will be named the Church of Saint Peter, Saint Paul and Saint Thomas of Canterbury,' William says. 'Your Thomas will be remembered in this place for ever, Catherine. His name will have a place of honour beside two of Christ's apostles.'

Kate took Jason to Bovey Tracey during the summer holidays. 'We must visit my aunt at High Mead,' she told him. 'And I want to show you Litford.'

'What is Litford?'

'An old Devon longhouse, a kind of ancient farmhouse.'

'Is the little gravestone still there?' she asked Talitha almost as soon as they arrived. It was strange being here again. During the past months Kate had not dreamed about Catherine. The twelfth-century world had almost completely withdrawn from her life.

Talitha nodded. 'We thought it should stay where it had been found.'

'We'll go to see it,' Kate said and she shivered, and wondered after all if she should have come back here. But she felt that she was safe with Jason at her side. He would keep her anchored and sane, just as Hugo did for Phoebe.

'Can you see the letters etched on the granite?' she asked him as they stood looking down at the stone.

'Just about. What do they say?'

'*Tom, Catherinae filius, hoc anno domini MCXLIII natus, quarto die obiit.*' Kate recited the words without hesitation.

'Jolly impressive,' Jason said. 'What does it mean? My Latin's pretty rusty.'

'Tom, son of Catherine, born 1143, died at four days.'

He bent down and examined the stone more closely. 'Interesting. It ought to be in the church, or in a museum.'

Kate shook her head. 'We thought so at first, but this is where it belongs.' Then suddenly she found herself unable to say any more about it. Jason was her future, Catherine her past. She had no wish to explain.

It was only later when they went to see the church in Bovey Tracey that she felt the presence of Catherine for one last time. They parked their car on the road outside and walked up the steep path and the flight of wide granite steps between the old yew trees to the entrance. They stood looking at the ancient stone heads on the Norman arch.

'We think those might be Thomas,' Kate said. 'One as archbishop and one as chancellor of England. He's younger in that one and he has a coronet. In the other he's wearing a mitre. No one really knows who they are though. That was just Phoebe's guess. And those could be the Pope and William de Tracey.' Kate walked around the porch and stared at yet more grim stone faces on the church walls. 'I like to think that they are all there, immortalized for ever, watching us all, the characters of Phoebe's book, murderer and murdered, king and courtiers. It's an incredible story.'

Jason laughed. 'It's all beyond me. How come I fancy a historian? History was never my strong point.'

Kate looked at him and smiled, took his arm and they walked into the church, but they failed to see the figure standing in the shadows of the porch.

Catherine is smiling. The years are all disarranged but she

*feels a sense of peace, of happiness. She hopes that she will
not dream again of this girl, this Kate, with the outlandish
clothes who has just gone into Thomas's Church, for so she
always thinks of it. Catherine is happy now and she knows
that Kate too has found contentment and happiness with this
young man who is with her. How she knows, she cannot tell, but
she feels a radiance about this girl from another age, another
time. Since her William decreed that a new church should be
built here she has been at peace, and although Thomas will
always remain in a small corner of her heart, her happiness
is in her husband and her children. May it also be so for Kate.
She smiles, crosses herself, and blesses them.*

As Kate and Jason walked back to the car, Kate suddenly
stopped and threw her arms around him. 'Thanks a million,
Jason,' she said.

He had no idea why he was being thanked just then, but
he responded heartily. 'That's quite some church, and some
story,' he said when she eventually let him go. 'I shall have
to get a copy of your grandmother's book and find out more
about this Thomas à Becket of yours.'

'Not my Thomas,' Kate said. 'Nor Catherine's either. God's,
I suppose.'

Author's note

Thomas à Becket has always been a controversial figure. As chancellor and great friend of King Henry II he evoked immense jealousy. Then surprisingly, during the latter years of his life and for a considerable time after his death, he symbolized the resistance of the Church to the authority of the State. These were conflicting aspects of the same man, and the king was not alone in finding his character difficult to fathom.

During his early years he was certainly handsome and charming, a lover of luxury and wealth. He was highly intelligent and very fit and athletic, with a great enthusiasm for the joys of hunting and hawking. His ostentation and worldliness are well documented.

All these attributes endeared him to the king who was well known for his boundless energy and love of any kind of adventure, as well as the pleasures of bed and table. Both men were not averse either to a spell on the jousting field or the excitement of battle. Thomas became the king's closest friend and confidant, and for six years they were almost inseparable. The great change in him when he became archbishop was therefore all the more remarkable.

I have given some thought in this book to the early claims that he was celibate. This has often been disputed, and it is said that his first biographers proclaimed his celibacy because they were writing just after his death when many miracles of healing were being professed in his name. His canonization by the Pope not long afterwards would have made it highly undesirable to write anything prejudicial to his good name. Whether or not he was truly chaste for the whole of his life has long perplexed later biographers. Some have said that he was homosexual. The truth will probably never be known. As a student and then a clerk he was part of a society in which worldly pleasures of all kinds were the way of life. Later his name was linked with one of the mistresses of the king, and also with the wife of William de Tracey, one of his murderers.

All the modern characters in my book are fictional, and parts of the twelfth-century content is also pure fiction. I have sought to give a possible reason for Thomas's celibacy, a reason that is honouring to him. However, my ideas are total fiction. Catherine is fictional, as are her children, but the factual link of William de Tracey's wife – whose name I have not been able to discover – with Thomas à Becket is recorded. All that I have written of King Henry is based on recorded fact, and the murder of Thomas and the identity of the knights are also well chronicled.

I have endeavoured not to debunk a great hero and saint of Christendom. Thomas remains for me a very enigmatic and fascinating figure worthy of much more research and analysis.

The county of Devon has many links with Thomas à Becket. The parish church of Bovey Tracey is dedicated to Saint Peter, Saint Paul and Saint Thomas of Canterbury, and some of the new housing estates are also named in his honour. I often wonder what he would think about Becket Close and William de Tracey Park. The supposed site of the home of William de Tracey is now in the hands of the National Trust, and the Dartmoor National Park Authority uses the present house as an office. The grounds are open to the public and the whole area is a favourite place for dog walkers. I go there almost every day to enjoy the same views of the surrounding hills and woods that the de Tracey family must have loved, and I often feel the presence of my fictional Catherine!

It is said that a priest's room was set aside for Thomas in the original house and I often think of him coming here for rest and relaxation during his troubled years as archbishop. It is a truly wonderful place, and perhaps the spirits of the past still wander the lanes and riverbank. I do hope so.

Eileen Stafford
May 2003